*For David, my family
and little Lenny*

Dear Stephen,

Enjoy!!

Best wishes,

Ben

The author would like to thank the following individuals for their letters and messages of good wishes for Klarkey's War:

Tony Benn,
Clive Fairweather,
P D James,
Margot Livesey,
The Very Reverend June Osborne, Dean of Salisbury
Right Honourable Lord Tebbit CH

Special thanks to Tim Randall, for help in editing, choosing the name and having total faith.

My object all sublime
I shall achieve in time
To let the punishment fit the crime
The punishment fit the crime

William Schwenck Gilbert
(1836 - 1911)

CHAPTER ONE   KLARKEY

A bubble of perspiration escaped from Klarkey's forehead and trickled down the pronounced hairline along his right sideburn. He shook it off. As he stared at his mobile, waiting, Klarkey toyed with the empty ashtray on the small café table by the Paris Nord station. The phone rang and he slid his clammy fingers over the green button. "Yes?"

As soon as the man calling from London whispered, "Everyone's through, safe and sound", Klarkey rang off, taking a deep breath as he pushed his hands back through his thick wavy hair. Despite going through the same routine every week for months, he would still become uncontrollably nervous. But this was the last time. As he considered the uncertain months ahead, he swigged at his double espresso and reflected how he'd reached this improbable point in his life.

Francis Klarke was born thirty-five years ago, to a French mother and an English father. In spite of his four-part name, ever since he was able to speak, he always introduced himself as "Klarkey", choosing to avoid using his middle names, Umberto and Charles and the unavoidably embarrassing initials they created. His mother, Marie, insisted on naming him after French, Italian and British past Kings, believing this would bring him good luck and social standing in later life. Protestations from his father fell on deaf ears. He knew only too well the cruelties of children and adults alike, being called Simon Ian Cameron Klarke. From an early age, thanks to his playground peers, Klarkey realised his name could plague him through life and so avoided his full name at all costs. Klarkey was his chosen name, and anyone who knew him from the age of ten would call him this. For essential formalities, Francis Klarke would suffice. As far as he was concerned, his middle names were specious and unhelpful and he never used them again.

Stories of Chinese snakeheads turned Klarkey's stomach. Taking people's savings of up to $20,000; herding them into the back of trucks and hoping for their safe arrival in the UK was not how he operated. He accepted that he was a people smuggler, but he considered himself a sophisticated and caring one. When he thought about the poor Chinese people who died in a sweltering Dutch lorry years ago, he felt sick. If only they had come to him, he could have helped them in a way they could never have imagined. That tragic incident at the port of Dover had a lasting effect on him. But in those days he wasn't in this business. He used to be something of a drifter spending time between London, staying on friends' sofa-beds, or in the south of France with his mother enjoying the delights of the beach. His life was different now. Klarkey cared about his charges. He ran his people smuggling operation as a proper business. He ensured the safety and security of his clients. Above all, he wanted to help people desperate to get into England, by making their passage as safe as possible, whilst making a good living out of it for him at the same time.

Theoretically he could make much more than the average $180,000 a week after expenses he already pocketed. Greed breeds mistakes and mistakes lead to prison. It would certainly mean the end of the business. Smuggling about 40 people per week was enough for him. Each of them paid him $6000 and his weekly costs were about $60,000 in total. This produced a more than handsome profit.

The whole operation was masterminded from Klarkey's base in Rue de la Chapelle in the 18th Arrondissement.

Above three shops in a rather non-descript neighbourhood on the northern edge of central Paris was his "Grosvenor School of English", ostensibly a private school offering six-week intensive classes in English. Anyone accidentally stumbling across the premises would find a perfectly plausible language school and would be greeted by a smiling receptionist. She would then casually inform them of the fees, set at $6000 American for 6 weeks. Anyone genuinely wandering in from the street would always leave at this point, thanking the receptionist for her time, and choosing to settle for a rather cheaper language school in a much better area. Those who knew the real purpose of the school would happily part with the $6000 in used notes, or Euro equivalent. It was mostly US dollars. These were dollar bills that had travelled thousands of miles stuffed deep into layers of clothing, only to be handed over to Klarkey in the hope of a better life. Being enrolled in the Grosvenor School meant that at the end of six weeks' study, the ultimate prize was to be smuggled into England. You didn't know how, but you knew it was the most reliable way to realise your dream of becoming a Cockney, Brummie or Geordie, even if you were from Afghanistan or Turkey or China.

The Grosvenor School of English didn't advertise for pupils. It certainly didn't engage in the distribution of leaflets on the Paris streets like other language schools in every major capital city. There were no hired members of staff wandering the streets wearing embarrassing A-boards, desperate to gain the attention of potential clients. Like most thriving small businesses, Klarkey's Grosvenor School depended upon word of mouth to ensure its success. Despite the $6000 fee, the classes were always full. There was always a full complement of 240 students, replaced by a fresh batch of 40 every week without fail. Large classes of 40 would begin and end the course together. They would take every class together and would not be allowed to miss even one lesson. In the French tradition, all classes were taken exclusively in English. At any one time, there could be up to 28 different countries represented by any group of students – all of them illegal in France, smuggled across various borders. Some would come from the previously troubled clutch of Balkan countries, through Slovenia or Hungary across through the open borders of Italy and up into France; others across from Albania into Italy through the Strait of Otranto. Some would take the hashish route from Africa across into Spain, or maybe the longer route from the northern point of Tunisia into Sicily. Indians and Pakistanis, normally culturally divided, would unite as they found passage through Turkey and into Europe. So many people from different nations across the world had heard about the Grosvenor School of English and they too wanted to be legal entrants into England. Their aim in life was to move to the UK, where they firmly believed their lives would be richer and ultimately more free. They were all eager to part with $6000 for that new life, complete with a new name and a new identity. These people were proud of the title "economic migrants". They had nothing to be ashamed of, like so many generations of economic migrants before them. They were not looking for welfare or other handouts from the UK Government. All they wanted was the opportunity to start afresh and to work hard in what was perceived as Europe's most tolerant country.

On arrival in Paris, many migrants would be disoriented after a long journey or unsure what was to become of them. After handing over their fee, students would be photographed and then asked to complete a detailed questionnaire. Various linguists would assist with this process. Klarkey's carefully co-ordinated process was to put his 'students' at ease. He needed the operation to be smooth and for no one to cause any upset to the systems he had set in place. Most had learned of the School through relatives who had already made it to England. It was truly one of the

4

world's best-kept secrets. It was in everyone's interest to keep it so. For those who wanted other relatives or neighbours from their villages to come to England, the last thing to do would be to risk the very operation that could enable their family and friends to join them. Other contacts were made through the low paid porters and foreign staff of the Hôpital Lariboisière, or the Hôpital Widal in the 10th district of northern Paris. These hospitals were the starting point of Klarkey's people-moving project. It was here where the project was hatched less than a year before.

Klarkey had been visiting his mother near Montpelier in the south. He didn't yet have a permanent home and had been temporarily staying with friends in London. Water-skiing and parascending were two of his favourite pursuits, and he'd just spent an exciting two weeks in his mother's house, in her waterfront home. This wasn't a chateau or grand house, but a rustic cottage near the sea with old vines stretching back over the hill into the countryside that he could call home. He loved it there, but still felt the need to make a life for himself in London. What he would do for work in London was the question he'd been trying to answer for many years.

The two-week break was the happy, problem-free part of this trip. Getting back to London was to prove much harder. He took the new TGV fast train via Marseilles to Paris. This was without incident. Crossing the city to Paris Nord on the metro was bearable, but struggling onto the platform with luggage at Paris Nord was his downfall. An accidental trip and subsequent fall down an escalator left his ankle badly twisted. He instantly knew he'd be the butt of his friends' jokes for the next few weeks. He'd just spent two weeks water-skiing, only to end up in a plaster from falling off an escalator trying to get onto the Eurostar train to London. The only way to take his mind off the pain on the way to the hospital was to invent a cover story to tell his friends back in England. There was no way he could say he broke his ankle getting on the train. 'Bloody Paris Nord. Bloody Eurostar.' he thought as he was carried off on a stretcher by paramedics.

The short journey across the street to the Hôpital Lariboisière next to Paris Nord was to lead to the biggest change in his life. A couple of days in hospital taught him a lot. He spoke with porters, kitchen staff, doormen and cleaners. Anything and anyone to take his mind off the boredom and the pain was good as far as Klarkey was concerned. Many of the people he spoke with had similar stories. They wanted a new life; a life in England. They would choose not to claim benefits or to be a burden on the State. These were people who wanted to work. They were also people who had become unhappy with an intolerant French nation. France was a country where the far right led hate campaigns against immigrants. This was a country where the Front National had gained power in cities as large as Marseilles, and they were worried.

Klarkey had never really considered this before. There was no reason for him to have done so. From that moment he started to work out how he could help these people, and within a short time a thriving new business was created. He left hospital after four days and stayed in Paris for the next three months planning his most daring project to date, using the cash savings kept aside for his London new-start. The Grosvenor School for English was born. This was his people-smuggling business.

For six intensive weeks, the students were educated in how to act as British citizens. They were given instruction in small talk, appropriate for various locations such as shops, or the post office or at the library. They had map-reading classes, where they would study the layout of towns across England. They would engage in role-playing at

English food markets and were made to watch British television, especially soap operas and history programmes. Football was a priority subject for the men, where they learned the essential local differences between Arsenal and Tottenham Hotspur or Birmingham City and Aston Villa. Klarkey believed it was crucial they understood city rivalries and the complexities of these deeply held opinions. The women were taught the basic differences between Whites and King Edward potatoes; Kenyan beans and sugar snaps and other nuances of food culture. There was no time for political correctness, only time for study of the nuts and bolts of being British. They were taught how to use English Pounds, the political and judicial structure of the United Kingdom, and most fundamentally, how to dupe the British customs officials if they were stopped on their way into England.

In addition to renting the building that housed his School, Klarkey took possession of a large garage opposite the Paris Nord station, close to his hospital. Here he stored a piece of equipment purchased cheaply from a property developer who's company was going bankrupt, based in one of Paris's sprawling southern suburbs. This was his expanding tallascope: a rather ingenious piece of machinery usually used for workmen to reach high ceilings for painting or to make repairs. It was essentially a portable, extendable scaffold on wheels. There was a built-in hydraulic that extended its height to about three stories: almost 15 metres. Ladders would be raised into position to allow anyone climbing the tallascope easy swift access to the top. "Michelangelo could have done with this in the Cistine Chapel", he said to the developer when he tested the hydraulics for the first time. The developer shrugged and took the money.

The military style operation took place just three times per week. Each time Klarkey would oversee the plan personally and his students would take comfort, knowing that he was close by. They trusted him. They also knew he had as much, if not more to lose than they did if things went wrong. About 12-14 migrants would assemble at one of the local cafés close to the station. All of them would be wearing clothing chosen by Klarkey's staff. Men and women from all nationalities would form part of the group, but it was always just men or women on each trip, never a combination of the two, and never children. Men would wear jeans or tracksuit bottoms, with football or Polo shirts. They would carry sports bags with various sports kits inside and fake programmes indicating their participation in some kind of football tournament. The women would wear outfits from Marks and Spencer or Debenhams. Any obvious visual reference to ethnicity would be removed. Excessively hair sprayed curls, lipstick, trouser suits and sensible skirts replaced all veils, scarves or saris. Imitation Fendi or Gucci handbags would be carried with shopping bags from the Parisian department stores, Galeries Lafayette and Printemps, providing evidence of a day's shopping trip to the French capital. Along with gaining their new clothes, the day before departure meant adopting a new identity. False British Passports were provided by a master forger based in the city of Lyons, whom Klarkey had met in a bar in Cap D'Antibes during one of his drunken jaunts to the south east coast. The exchange was made on a weekly basis: a carrier bag full of 40 British Passports for $20,000. A meeting in a quiet café close to 35 Rue du Faubourg St. Honoré was supposed to be the forger's idea of a joke: it was very close to the British Embassy. Each passport was carefully chosen to reflect the student's background. Indians would be called Khan and Pakistanis were called Patel. Britain was truly multicultural and the students reflected this eclectic mix.

7pm on a typical day of departure signalled the first meeting point of the students at the Arc de Triomphe. Under the grand arch, everyone collected silently pondering where he or she hoped to be in just a few hours time. Some yearned to be in a café in north London, or in a relative's living room in a Birmingham suburb. Whatever they hoped for, the expectation would lead some of the travellers to be sick with nerves. Klarkey was used to this. When everyone had gathered he would take the group along the Champs Elysées to a restaurant for a light meal. At dinner there would be hushed excited chat about their new lives ahead in England, and their new identities would be finally digested to ensure no slip-ups on their short but precarious journey.

A metro trip to the Paris Nord station would be their final view of Paris and the mainland continent. From now on, the plan they had rehearsed many times over, would finally be put into action. Under cover of darkness, the tour group walked along the side of the station towards scaffolding covered in a France Telecom banner, and then they would quickly disappear beneath it. Within the canopy, they hastily climbed the ladders and the group of 14 would patiently wait at the top of the tallascope in line, ready for the signal.

Meanwhile, on the first floor of the waiting area of the Eurostar departure lounge, groups of Americans, children, businessmen and women and smart couples would jostle for positions on the uncomfortable benches waiting for their trains to be called. Some would be crowding in and around the Belgian chocolate store or Madame du Barry's store of French delicacies, where day-tripping tourists could spend their last remaining Euros on some foodstuff that would probably remain in their mother's pantry for years.

Close by, the blue boiler-suited cleaning staff would from time to time make the effort to clean the lavatories within the waiting areas, and when they did so, the "Nettoyant/Cleaning in progress" boards would go up in front of the doorways for just a few minutes to allow the efficient staff to mop and freshen the overused conveniences, preventing any of the waiting multitude from entering. These members of staff were always happy in their work. It was not difficult to understand why. On days like this, they would earn 10 times their normal weekly wage, just for closing the gents or ladies toilets for 5 minutes and turning a blind eye to Klarkey's operation in progress. The toilets at Paris Nord had windows onto the street, and although they were quite high up, a cleverly positioned tallascope could comfortably reach the window and deposit a dozen or so tourists into the welcoming tiled void of the toilette. Once inside, the well-rehearsed travellers would quickly position themselves in various points of the toilets, some inside the cubicles, some by the urinals or hand basins or dryers and the tallascope would be rapidly lowered and returned to the safety of its nearby garage. Now in the Eurostar inner sanctum, the visitors, like their fellow passengers, had already passed customs and were beyond passport control. They were well on their way to the UK, clutching their new identities and Eurostar return tickets, pre-purchased by the London base of Klarkey's network.

When their train was called, hundreds of passengers crowded onto the bridge, beyond which stairs descended to the train. The bridge was manned either side by staff who were supposed to check the tickets of the pushing and shoving passengers, but it was time consuming to give too much attention to everyone's papers. The staff believed that everyone had already passed through customs and the main ticket barrier, so they were only too pleased to guide the massing crowds down to the train on the platform below as quickly as possible.

Once on the train, the Klarkey group knew exactly how to pass the time – this period formed a fundamental part of their training. They knew how to smile at the British customs officers who could pass through the train. The men knew how to say "Awright mate" and the women "Hello love" to anyone official-looking should the need arise.

Occasionally one person in a group would be stopped at Waterloo and the remainder of the party would always pass by, ignoring their friend who had been stopped. The stoppee would know exactly what to say. He or she would be completely co-operative, and would make sure "I know you're only doing your job mate" was thrown into the conversation at the appropriate moment. As far as the Customs officials were concerned, these were people that spoke better English than most of the British school kids on trips to Paris. There seemed to be no problem.

The system was foolproof and had worked for several months bringing Klarkey untold wealth.

But Klarkey was no fool. He knew this operation was not going to last forever and was preparing to bring it to a swift close, taking his profit and any evidence away with him. He now planned to move to London and there was no way he was travelling there as a guest of Her Majesty. He knew how to control greed. He knew when to stop. And just as quickly as the operation had started some months before, he stopped it in its tracks, closed the school, donated the tallascope to the Opera de Paris and moved to London leaving no forwarding address for his Parisian contacts.

CHAPTER TWO   OVERCROWDING

BBC News

Reports out today state that 8 out of 10 prisons are overcrowded. A total of 82% of prison British Board of Visitors (BBOVs) said their institution had been adversely affected by spiralling prison numbers.

Whilst the Prison Reform Organisation suggests the situation is putting security and safety at risk, the Prison Service Body describes the report as excessively melodramatic.

The report is based on 200 BBOV visits and results show suicides have become more frequent than ever, with tension rising within prisons to potentially explosive levels.
Overcrowding had led to a number of assaults on officers and fellow inmates in several jails, where many prisoners had to sit on their toilets to eat meals because of the cramped confines of the cells.
The report further highlights the ever-increasing problem of drug taking in our institutions and almost all cells originally designed for one are now accommodating two or more inmates.

PORTSMOUTH, Hampshire

The new CCTV operations room, located in the bowels of the imposing Guildhall building in the City centre, was buzzing with the flickering screen images of the litter-strewn maze of shopping streets which reflected the moonlight of a damp late autumn evening.

Operator Jake MacFardle was twiddling. His toy was the joystick that swung the images from camera to camera; screen to screen. It was still early on Friday evening: not quite late enough for trouble to pour onto the streets after the pubs closed. Usually a mixed-up-mess of locals and sailors, boozed up insurance salesmen and lads from the estates. If a ship was in town, especially an American one, you could be sure of plenty of finger action on that joystick. But then it was still early. Just a few commuters were leaving Portsmouth and Southsea train station, making their way home, and the usual workaholics leaving the office late. Someone caught Jake's eye, and he knew from experience that something could be going down soon.

"Uh huh", he exhaled with his bottom lip curled over his teeth and his tongue rapidly licking the centre of his lower lip with excitement. He considered himself a schadenfreude free zone, but he couldn't help get a bit of a kick from viewing some kind of action, especially this early in the shift. Watching his world played out on the screens somehow made everything seem like a late night TV show. Here he was, safe in the bowels of the city in a concrete bunker with all the action unfolding before his very eyes. He loved it.

Camera 5 picked out a tallish woman making her way from the train station. He hadn't seen her before, but then even in his job he couldn't be expected to remember everyone. Most people having left the train were either picked up or jumped in a cab, as not many people lived close to the station. At that time of evening all the shops had closed and Commercial Road, the pedestrianised shopping precinct running north away from the station, beyond Guildhall Square, was pretty deserted. What caught Jake's eye was the group of three lads walking aimlessly towards the woman on Camera 7. He'd seen it all before, and if he could somehow stop history repeating

13

itself over and over he would. If he could one way or another warn her to take care, to keep herself moving along the road and if she could miraculously find a cab, jump into it. The problem with these situations is that he wasn't supposed to assume every group of three lads would be planning to cause trouble. Therefore he couldn't just call out the Police and get them to drive by to stop potential troublemakers. Frustrating as it was, Jake's experience led him to believe that these lads were up to no good. They would find an easy target, and take their ill-gotten gains into one of the many pubs in the surrounding area. Meantime, the Police would arrive at the scene of crime just too late to catch them and their evil faces, courtesy of Jake's video-capture, would go up in poster form around the city to try to flush them out. There was no chance of stopping the crime before it happened; only mopping up afterwards.

"What the hell's she doing now the stupid cow", Jake spat at the screen, as the tall woman bent down to fix her shoe. Maybe the strap had broken or a stone had found its way into the heel. It was all so hopeless as far as he was concerned. "Don't make yourself a target love. Don't ever make yourself a target."

By now the three lads were approaching her and Jake had one hand trained on the joystick to follow the victim, and the other ready to dial up to the Central Police number for rapid response. He'd been reprimanded before for calling the Police before an incident had taken place, but he was damned sure that he would be ready to call them just as soon as something HAD taken place. He criticised the Council's policy of not warning lads like these they were being watched. In his opinion, the Police would prefer to leave the woman and others like her to their obvious fate, only to attend to them after the event.

"Here we go"…as the adrenalin pumped through Jake's veins, his sweating fingertip hovered over the dial to connect to the direct line of the Portsmouth City Police. At the same moment, the first baseball-cap clad assailant experienced the same adrenalin rush as Jake, which began to pump through his body as he came face to face with the woman outside the entrance to Dixons. And then something happened. Something unexpected. So unexpected that Jake slipped off the front of his leatherette and chrome five-wheeler chair and banged his backside with such force that he let out a loud yelp and pulled the receiver of the phone down to the ground. Struggling to get back up, with wide eyes peeled to the screen he tapped out 151 with touch-type speed to reach the incident room in Portsmouth's busy Central Police Station.

What Jake had seen was something he had always wanted to see but thought would never happen. What he saw was someone fighting back. Not with a panicked, messy, haphazard response, but in a proper, full-on, taking-no-prisoners, no-shit reaction. The tall woman, who had just started to stand up from having adjusted her shoe, came face to face with thug number one. Quick as a flash thug number one doubled up with his hands clutching his stomach. Jake's pain seemed to disappear as he stared spellbound at the screen. He wished he had sound as well as vision at that moment, if only to hear that 'oooh' exhale of air as the lad took a thump. As Jake stumbled to his feet, knees shaking, cold sweat was running across his face, his hot armpits were stinging where his jacket and shirt gripped him so tightly and the pain from his throbbing coccyx was finally kicking in. He couldn't believe it. His over-excited pupils dilated as he stared at the screen. He simply couldn't believe what his eyes were telling him. Thug number two and three had long gone by now, and baseball one was still doubled up on the pavement. He could see a pool of what must be blood coming from him and was pretty sure that if the cameras had been colour, the pool in front of the lad would certainly have been a match for the bright red logo of Dixons next to where he lay.

But where was the woman? Frantic finger action took him to someone walking near the top of Commercial Road on Camera 9, but that person was going out of range. The height was right, but it didn't look like her. Not the same hair…but the walk was the same. Then she was gone.

"Incident Room there's been what looks like a shooting outside Dixons on Commercial Road! Yes it's all on camera mate…bugger me I'd never have believed it. Yeh…don't worry, I ain't going nowhere."

BBC News

Three Police forces have arrested 86 people in an operation to tackle street and car crime. Leicestershire Police are leading the operation with officers from Nottinghamshire and Derbyshire. Operation Midlands Collective involves about 140 officers and aims to stop criminals travelling between counties. Police in high-performance vehicles and several helicopters are being used.

Offences resulting in arrests so far have included burglary and possession of controlled drugs. Property worth £80,000 has been seized. Chief Inspector Marshall Roberts said "The offenders targeted often have little care for the safety of others on the roads and in many cases they are involved with street crimes and other serious offences.

"These arrests will put more criminals into jail and will make the public feel more safe. Criminals must be made aware that there will be nowhere for them to hide"

The operation is expected to continue until Saturday.

ABERDEEN, Scotland

Union Street is the East-West vein running through the Granite City on the northeast peninsula of Scotland. A shopping mecca from its earliest days, many stores had left this street for more fashionable locations, such as shopping centres located on the multiple branches off Union Street, like the Bon Accord or Trinity Centres. Others had simply closed down, driven out because of high rents or because the area had become less popular.

An example of this was the store entrance formerly belonging to SofaSoGood, a once trendy furniture shop that had gone out of business because of the pressures from larger more price-competitive warehouse stores in out-of-the-way industrial estates on the edge of the city.

Despite its empty shell, the store displayed a big bold bright poster supplied by the City Council, extolling the virtues of shopping in Aberdeen. Clearly it was designed with the hope of encouraging the sale of the property to another multi-national, or local start-up. They didn't really care to whom, so long as the stores in Union Street were let again.

Aberdeen is a largely successful and proud city. However on this particular night in September, the frontage of the old SofaSoGood store told a different story.

Three drunken tramps had taken the place of customers in this deserted doorway. They were assuming their nightly residency in the covered doorway of the store and settling in for the evening. Having moved around from the various streets and squares in the area, they had slept off the previous few hours near to the harbour where the prostitutes and Norwegian fisherman spent their valuable time, and made their way back up the hill to their favoured spot in Union Street, in front of SofaSoGood. Even within these dire conditions there was a sense of domain for its residents. A sense of territory. For these three miserables, their space at night was in front of this store. Anyone seeking to buy the lease on this shop would have to forcibly remove their rather too comfortable temporary tenants before smartening up the piss-soaked doorway.

Just like in any other town or city, tramps and the dispossessed would sit in doorways begging for a few pennies to make up the cost of a precious can of beer, or maybe a sandwich. These three down-and-outs were no different to any others occupying most city centres. They were faceless unfortunates to the shoppers who would normally reside in the nooks of the street just in front of their mud-ingrained sleeping bags. Shoppers would be busy going in and out of the jewellery shops and fashion stores, shopping centres and Starbucks.

Sometimes a friendly student would drop some silver into their bags, and the ashen-faced trio would stretch open their eyes to try to focus on what scraps they had been thrown. Occasionally a do-gooder housewife would pop into Marks and Spencer and give one of her sandwiches to them, saying "Hope you don't mind mayonnaise" and before they could answer would slip away down a side street to one of the car-parks before they closed for the evening to retrieve her comfy Mercedes.

A fairly well built man approached them carrying just a plain carrier bag.

"Bizzies"…one of them said to the others who were sleeping, believing their visitor to be a Policeman.

"Nae your alright. I'll give yae nae bother…Here" And at that point the man brought out three cans of beer from his bag and went on his way.

The talkative tramp quickly opened a can and the sound of the ring-pull immediately awoke the other two with a start and the beer was nearly spilt…but not quite. They'd all had far too much experience in ensuring not a drop of precious alcohol would be wasted, whatever the circumstances. If Aberdeen had experienced its first major earthquake with its epicentre under this shop doorway, STILL their priority would be to ensure not a drop of precious lager nectar would be spilled.

The three men now had an aluminium tin in each right hand and pshhh pshhh, the remaining unopened pair of cans were released in a flash.

The most lucid of the three thought to himself, 'Bloody hell the cans are even cold!' Then said, "What a pal! Cheers!"

Then an unusual series of events happened. With the third gerglug of the beer hitting the backs of their furry throats, the cans dropped to the floor and rolled down the pavement into the road. The road hissed and steamed and the trio attempted to let out a chorus of screams, but only succeeded in waving their arms in the air and stretching their fingers, in the same way that deaf people shout with their hands. And then they fell. They were already sitting down with their lower halves tucked inside their rancid bags, but now it was the turn of their torsos to flop over and crumple onto each other like dominoes.

BBC News

Police in Birmingham have raided five premises believed to be involved in the laundering of more than £10m of drugs money. The West Midlands Police force is investigating the transfer of the cash from the city to Jamaica. Officers say it represents up to 1 million crack cocaine deals and more than 60 officers were involved in the raids, codenamed Operation Forceps.

10 people were arrested and about £150,000 in cash was recovered in the raids early this morning.

Chief Inspector Greg Molyneux said,

"It is quite clear that the sale of crack cocaine on the streets of Birmingham has resulted in this substantial sum being discovered. It's part of our investigation to clamp down on drug dealers who use these methods to launder

their money. We are not only trying to stop the drugs
reaching the streets of Birmingham in the first place, but
also intend to arrest the dealers and put them into jail and
disrupt their line of finance by seizing their cash"

Drug dealing has become a big problem in some parts
of Birmingham with dealers working openly on the streets
and it is now Government policy to arrest and detain as
many of them as possible to make the streets of our cities
safer again.

SOUTH LONDON

The Scorpion nightclub had been a popular haunt in this
south London backwater since the early 1990s, and there
was no sign of it losing its pulling power. Nigel Ngote was
well aware of this and worked as a mini-cab driver outside
of the venue. He was one of a band of drivers licensed by
the club to operate from its facade. The taxi prices they had
to charge were relatively high, even for London, because
they were forced to set aside an additional three pounds for
every journey, to line the ever-deepening pockets of the
head of security. Nevertheless, at least these drivers were
guaranteed customers. They had an official badge to wear
around their necks showing they were licensed to the club
and they had regular business from the venue. Normally,
Nigel wouldn't complain about his lot.

Nigel Ngote was Nigerian, choosing to come to
England four years earlier to make his fortune. His primary
aim was to earn enough money to buy a bus back in Lagos.
All he wanted was enough money for a bus. If he had his
own bus he could start his own business. He calculated that
£6000 should be sufficient. This was hardly a fortune in
London, but represented unattainable riches back in Lagos –
at least for those people like him who worked within the
law. Achieving this would set him up for life back home
and he could get away from this horrible place. This city

was not only a horrible, cold place but also full of West Indians who hated him because he was Nigerian. It was horrible because he had to face what he considered to be 'disgusting weirdoes' in his car every night of the week. Sometimes they were ill and almost always they were out of their minds on drugs: the drugs that kids took at discos to keep themselves dancing all night. They could barely speak when they got into the car. They would be laughing and screaming and dribbling, often grinding their teeth and chewing gum after gum relentlessly. Their eyes would be wide like saucers and their eye sockets black set in anaemic faces. Even Easy-Listening FM wouldn't calm them. When he was driving on his own he would play his Evangelical tapes of Christian sermons. He tried playing these once with a customer in the car and was sworn at - he chose not to do that again. He thought the fluffy seat covers or the hanging sandalwood aroma tree might soothe them, but generally nothing would keep them still.

This night was like any other at first. A busy Friday and it was close to 6am. This was the Friday-night-free-for-all. This was a dangerous time. Licensed mini-cabs like his were parked up against the club doors where doormen would be trying to speedily usher the dazed customers into the sweet-smelling Datsuns. Double-parked and triple-parked, a frenzy of vehicles tooting and shoving, plying for the trade of 2000 club-goers seeking to get home for less than the cost of a black cab; but this was a no-go zone for official black cabs.

Nigel was about to encourage his next customers into the cab, a couple: man and woman, dressed a little smarter than the other clubbers. 'Maybe they would be less likely to throw up than the rubber-clad, demented types' he thought. However, in a flash a touting illegal cab usurped him. It was someone who was known to be trouble.

"Cab boss? Jump in" he heard the tout say. Nigel was furious. This had happened before and he was damned sure these thieves needed to be told exactly what they were. 'No way are they Nigerians', he thought, 'they must be West Indian…don't know which island, they're all the same'. He was so furious that he decided to follow the tout who had stolen his fare, although at that point he didn't know exactly what he was going to say if he came face to face with him. And he was acutely aware that by travelling away from the club he would be losing the potential of another fare. His actions weren't logical, but his heart was ruling his head at this point.

The man and woman had deliberately chosen the tout over the licensed mini-cabs outside of The Scorpion. Nigel simply didn't understand why they would do such a thing. Perhaps they were from out of London and didn't understand?

The man carried a sports bag and his partner held a small clutch bag. They climbed into the dog-hair covered back seat of the Ford Sierra and said "Camden".

"OK boss," the driver said…but he had other ideas. He was about to commit an offence that he had reaped rewards from in previous months. He was looking forward to a lucrative night ahead. On several preceding occasions he had taken unsuspecting passengers to places off the beaten track, had pulled a knife and then robbed them. Sometimes he had taken their cash cards and forced them to give him the pin number. One time he had even taken the person's house keys and stripped the property of valuables. Every time he had left his passengers destitute and tearful in an area of London they had little idea how to escape from, with no money to help them on their way.

The car headed along the south side of the River Thames, and as Nigel passed Lambeth Palace, he saw the Houses of Parliament lit up by the streetlights on the north side. The sun was coming up and there was tranquillity over London that most of the 10 million inhabitants of the wider capital never ever saw. 'Perhaps it wasn't such a good idea to follow the car after all', Nigel thought. He knew he was losing money by driving with no one travelling on the back seat. Nevertheless, a combination of anger and curiosity led him to follow the car. The illegal cab passed County Hall, towards Waterloo Bridge, but instead of taking the turn over the bridge, towards the West End and then Camden, he chose to continue along the road through south London.

The passengers were strangely quiet, and the tout was happy this was the case. Sometimes he would find them complaining about going the wrong way. More often than not, as he believed in this case, they would be so drunk or drugged that they wouldn't recognise where they were until reaching their own street – if they ever made it to their street.

Somewhere south of Blackfriars Bridge the car made a sharp turn, left then right, then left into a darkened courtyard of garages attached to a giant faceless Council estate. The driver turned to face his passengers, brandishing a large kitchen knife in his right hand, and demanded the couple hand over their wallets, keys and money and tell him where they lived or he would kill them. He spat into their faces, "Pin numbers, pin numbers!"

The male passenger said his wallet was in the bag and carefully opened the side zip. Without wasting any time, completely composed, he pulled out a handgun with a silencer attachment on its end, and shot the tout through the chest. This was a clinical and efficient professional killing. The bullet went cleanly through the driver's body and into his right kneecap. The power of the shot threw his chest against the steering wheel and the knife flew out of his hand wedging between the windscreen and the dashboard on the passenger's side. The couple looked at each other silently, the woman biting her lip for a second. The man took a deep

23

breath, squeezed the woman's hand and they both got out of the car, walking quickly out of the estate and towards the nearby Southwark tube station.

By now it was light, and Nigel had turned the headlights of his car off so as not to draw unnecessary attention to himself. He had pulled into the estate and turned the corner towards the garages. It was at this point when he saw the Sierra ahead of him. The lights were on but there was no sign of the passengers. The tout was slumped into the driver's seat. He got out and tiptoed over to the Ford. What he saw was a scene of carnage he had never experienced before. His eyes bulged, his heart missed a beat and he exhaled, "Sweet Jesus". He felt sick but managed to stop himself from throwing up.

He had hated the tout for what he had done earlier, but he believed no one deserved to be treated like this. His Christianity had taught him to love his neighbour and now he felt sorry for the man he had cursed just half an hour earlier. He was reluctant to call the Police. He could give them no valid reason for being there. Perhaps he would even be accused of a crime himself? He decided to leave. Nevertheless, he did shiver deeply when he thought of what could have happened to him if he had picked up the murderous couple.

"This God-forsaken city." Nigel said as he staggered back to his car. He was in no mood to work for the rest of the night and decided to go home to the warmth of his bed and his wife.

BBC News

A repeat of the notorious Strangeways prison riot is growing ever more likely, unless measures are taken to tackle overcrowding in Prisons, the Prison Officer's Union has warned. The Union representative's comments came as the National League for Penal Reform released findings, which suggest nearly two-thirds of prisoners are living in overcrowded conditions. The prison population currently stands at 81,000 and has already risen by 8,000 this year alone.

The riot at Strangeways Prison, Manchester in 1998, claimed the lives of two men and raged for 25 days. It caused £60m of damage to the jail, which has since been rebranded as HMP Manchester.

CHAPTER THREE   THE ETERNAL CRIMINAL

John Jamieson, like so many habituals, had spent most of his adult life in prison. He had just been captured having committed an armed robbery on a Southend branch of BritBank. Not a terribly bright chap, he was caught within 2 days of the robbery by the local CID led by Detective Chief Inspector Robert Shore. Jamieson had hidden his identity in the bank with a balaclava. The getaway car was abandoned on the London Road, just a few miles away from the scene of crime. A witness noticed two men getting into the car and then removing their balaclavas. One of them had distinctive red hair.

Robert Shore had a team of 14 men on the case and had more than 100 witness statements to take. The station Superintendent had no choice but to give him the manpower he needed. This case was too high profile not to solve quickly. Nevertheless, it was DNA that would seal the fate of the armed robbers. A single red hair on the headrest of the abandoned car was enough to direct the Police to Jamieson. Then it was just a matter of finding him.

The Police swung into action.

Shore, a slightly overweight man of about fifty, swaggered through the briefing room to discuss the strategy with his team of officers as he confidently drew a shiny metal comb through his thinning hair.

"What's happening is this. Jamieson's been seen coming out of a house in Claybridge, accompanied by a woman and driving off in the direction of the town centre.

"Now Claybridge's DCI has told me there's no sign of the other bloke, but they've got a positive ID of Jamieson. What they're asking me, is do we want him on his own without the other one. Is everyone agreed I should tell him 'Yes'? We can't after all, have an armed robber wandering around the streets."

Everyone present grunted and nodded in agreement. "Sir…Sir"

One of the men said, "I'll set up an ID parade for tomorrow shall I?"

"Perfect" Shore concurred as he left the room to make his call to Claybridge.

John Jamieson, career criminal, was a striking man at 6 foot tall, with tattooed arms and receding red hair. Accompanied by his girlfriend Lorna, they got out of his prized black Opel Manta, and headed towards the shops. In the back of his car were a few tools and a sports bag. Nothing was on his mind except buying Lorna an engagement ring at the jewellers in the Precinct. He was looking forward to surprising her.

Before he could make any move and certainly before he could explain himself to Lorna, they were surrounded by six officers.

"John Jamieson?"

"Yeh," he said, knowing what was ahead of him,

"I'm arresting you for armed robbery. You do not have to say anything but what you do say may be taken down in evidence and used against you. Do you understand?"

"What the hell's going on John?" Lorna said, genuinely shocked with flaring nostrils. She really had believed that he was going straight after the last time.

"Sorry love." John was head-pushed into the back of a waiting Police car and taken directly to the Police Station.

Robert Shore's mobile rang. "One…nil…to the Ar..se..nal…" the phone sang.

"Shore!" he answered authoritatively. "Uh huh…great." Offering a thumbs-up to his colleagues, he had instantly made it clear to everyone that Jamieson was exactly where he should be.

"Lads, he's safe in the Claybridge nick."

27

Jamieson stood calmly in front of the desk of the Custody suite. The arresting officer was by his side and the custody sergeant stood across from them both on the other side of the desk.

The arresting officer asked the questions as he had a hundred times before, as Jamieson himself had heard more than enough times in his chequered adult history.

"Have you any illnesses or injuries that we should know about?"

"No"

"Are you taking any tablets or medication for anything?"

"No"

"Do you suffer from depression or from any mental problems?"

"No"

"Have you ever tried to harm yourself?"

"No".

And so the officer continued, "You've been OK with me. Obviously you've been wearing handcuffs, and as far as I'm concerned I'm gonna put down you're no known risk. If I could ask you to sign here, just to confirm I've asked you those questions in your presence."

Jamieson signed wherever, whatever.

Then the custody sergeant spoke,

"I'm going to authorise your detention here because I believe it's necessary to secure and preserve evidence of the offences for which you've been arrested and to obtain evidence by way of questioning. Do you understand that? OK."

Jamieson signed wherever, whatever.

"We'll put you in cell number 6, down there and second on the right," he pointed with his pencil to the arresting officer.

Walk walk walk. Clang clang bang. Turn of the key.

*****

PLEASE STAND/SIT UP STRAIGHT AND LOOK
DIRECTLY AHEAD OF YOU AT ALL TIMES WHEN
THE PARADE IS TAKING PLACE.

DO NOT SPEAK OR DO ANYTHING TO DRAW
ATTENTION TO YOURSELF

THESE PROCEEDINGS ARE BEING VIDEO
RECORDED.

Jamieson gave a cursory glance towards the notice
below the two-way mirror in the identity parade room. He
knew if the Police failed to get a positive identification and
to charge him within 96 hours of bringing him into the
station, he'd be walking right back out and home to the
wife-to-be. Maybe he'd even have time to get that ring for
her. 'That should keep her moaning at bay' he thought.

"Please stand up gentlemen", said the officer overseeing
the parade to the group of men sitting on the hardwood
benches.

"The time now is 8.23pm, there are 14 persons paraded,
so do you object to any of those being paraded?"

Jamieson's solicitor whispered into his ear and pointed
across the line of casually dressed men.

"Sorry, you sir…would you mind?" Silence. "And you
please sir". And so five men were removed from the line
that seemed most dissimilar to Jamieson, leaving himself to
stand in whatever position he wanted. Jamieson stared
around the room, palms sweating, desperate to work out
how best to lose himself in such a small crowd. His lined
face led him to stand next to a grey-haired 50-something
man, and the addition of baseball caps on everyone's heads
to conceal various hair colours, gave him his best
opportunity to prevent identification. He had to cover his
carrot-top. He'd got away with it before, so why not again?

"Even though you've selected the position where you are in now, you can change for any other position," the officer droned, "are you happy where you are? Happy with who's next to you?"

"Yeh", Jamieson conceded.

Then the men stood in more silence. All with their hands behind their backs and with fixed stares ahead of them.

Jamieson knew from the muffled tone behind the glass that the witnesses were being prepared for the identification. They would see him for the first time since the armed robbery.

"Right…you've been asked here today to see if you can identify the person you saw on the 12th November last at 2.14pm, on the London Road, sat in the front passenger seat of a blue Vauxhall Astra".

The witness was softly spoken, slightly built, and in his 70s. He was the warden at St. Vitus Church on the London Road, and as an avid viewer of the BBC's Crimewatch, always hoped he'd have his 15 minutes of crime-fame, identifying a criminal or better still, talking about it on television. A line-up with no television crew would have to satisfy him. He couldn't believe what he had seen at first when Jamieson and friend had pulled up outside St Vitus's wearing balaclavas. He'd seen them pull the woollen masks off and jump out of the car and into another, parked just out of viewpoint. Fortunately he did get a good look at the redhead. He was never going to forget that face. He had also become something of a celebrity…at least in the local parish. Despite the number of worshippers falling to about 27 he was grateful to be recognised as a good citizen by his peers, rather than simply as the chap that locks and unlocks St Vitus's doors.

At first, the witness stumbled. "I'm looking for red hair" he said to kill a few seconds of time.

"Take your time sir and concentrate on each person in the line-up. You can have as long as you need" the officer said reassuringly.

The witness viewed and reviewed the line, and sure enough he kept coming back to the same man. He knew that his reputation depended on choosing the right man. He also knew he'd have a court case to attend which would bring him even more fame in the world of local church politics.

Within a few minutes Jamieson had been identified. The witness was permitted to leave, knowing that he'd accumulated enough material to keep the ladies of St Vitus happy with gossip for weeks.

Jamieson meanwhile was pissed off. He didn't get away with it and he certainly wasn't going to get Lorna's engagement ring. He might not even be able to keep Lorna. He knew that it wasn't unusual for some women to just give up on their men in prison. It wasn't exactly like being in the army, away for months at a time, with a regular salary being sent home. This kind of life was difficult. He knew only too well the stigma of going out with a criminal, along with the lack of money, and the constant fear of a dead-end future.

Jamieson was certainly heading for jail and made his way to the Police cells for the umpteenth time. He would be up in front of the magistrate to plead before long, and in the meantime he would be transferred to prison: his home from home.

The key turned in the lock behind him, as the muffled sound of the Policeman saying "Sweet Dreams" could be heard as he walked away from the Police cell, leaving Jamieson alone and dejected. He picked up his feet from the floor and tucked his arms round his knees and stared at his cheap trainers, laces removed, squeaking against the plastic covering of the thin mattress he was supposed to lie on. At this point he realised just how much he'd messed up.

No more football games in the park with his mates on a Sunday. No more drinks at the pub with a kebab on the way home. No more drinks, period. No more private moments with Lorna.

"Bloody hell I've really fucked it up this time". And then he obsessively rubbed his eyebrows upwards using his sweaty palms. Rubbing and rubbing. Rocking and rocking. His parents had given up on him years before. Now he was worried that Lorna would do the same. What destroyed him the most was that he knew there was no one else to blame but himself. He was back in prison with a wasted life. After a long deep sigh, Jamieson stretched out his legs and turned onto his side, hands gripping the plastic pillow as he quickly drifted into a slumber disturbed by images of guns and diamond rings; bunches of keys and bleached floors; faded images of his mother pointing her finger shouting "You'll never turn out to be no good."

*****

DCI Shore stood outside the station drawing hard on a Marlboro Light cigarette, ignoring the sign just outside the front door NO SMOKING WITHIN 10 FEET OF THE FRONT OF THE BUILDING.

A female officer, Julie Patterson, was also smoking in the strong low sunlight in front of the Station, "Why're you looking so miserable sir?"

"I used to smoke the red ones you know Patterson, but they're no good for you. So I've progressed onto the low-calorie ones. Don't worry about me...I'm happy as Larry", Shore said confidently brushing ash from the creases of his shirt sleeves, "It's the system that gets me down from time to time...been in the job too long I suppose."

"But Sir..."

"Don't mind me Patterson, just finish your fag and get back to work."

He flicked his cigarette butt towards the street where it pinged against the hubcap of an old banger stuck in the traffic, before falling into the gutter. That reminded him of Jamieson, as he turned on his heels, blowing the last puff of smoke back into the station. He believed the gutter was where the likes of Jamieson came from, and where they'd always end up.

His mind continued this train of thought as he made his way towards his desk. 'There are some criminals you see time and time again. Crime committed. Catch the toe rag. Send him down. He gets let out. Crime committed again. What a cycle. What a waste of everyone's time. And public money of course.'

He then thought about a speech he gave a few weeks before, to a local neighbourhood watch group in what he considered to be a decent area located a couple of miles away.

Someone had spoken out "Well we hardly ever see an officer in this area. In fact, when you come to think of the amount of money we all pay towards the Police in Council Tax and through the Government, you'd think we deserve more attention than we get."

But that was just it, he thought harder, clenching his teeth. 'A vast majority of the population don't meet, interact with, or even need to see a Police officer from one year to the next. That's counteracted by the likes of Jamieson and his cronies, who spend their whole lives inside a jail or in the company of Police officers. Maybe that's how the system really works. There isn't much middle ground. Just good people who hardly ever deal with the Police and animals who constantly deal with the Police.'

And then he was sitting back at his desk with another pile of cases to deal with and not enough staff to help.

CHAPTER FOUR   PRESS CUTTINGS

THE PORTSMOUTH NEWS
"GANG-SHOOTING IN TOWN CENTRE"

Portsmouth City Police are baffled with a crime that has left one person dead and another fighting for his life in Queen Mary Hospital.

The victim, as yet unnamed, is thought to have been part of a criminal gang that has been targeting commuters on their way home from Portsmouth & Southsea Station for the last few months.

A reliable source informs us that this bunch of hooligans, which includes the victim and the injured man, were preying on a tall woman leaving the station yesterday evening, heading north through the pedestrianised precinct. The details remain unclear from this point, but the evidence so far, suggests the woman was about to become a victim herself of an attack by the gang. This woman, however, fought back, using a gun that sources suggest was concealed in some kind of pouch attached to her leg.

A family member of another woman, recently mugged in the same area told The News,

"I'm well pleased that someone had the guts to fight back. OK, so she may have gone too far with a gun. Let's face it, I don't know anyone that would actually carry a gun, but all credit to her. She was going to be mugged and she did what she had to do. In my book that makes her a hero and it takes these bastards off the street."

An un-named member of self-styled vigilante group Peace on the Streets, told us,

"I wish I could claim responsibility for this fight back against the muggers, but I have to concede it is nothing to do with us. It just goes to show how crime has got out of hand in this area. It takes a special sort of person to respond to an attack, and the only language the criminals understand is physical force. This time, they got what they deserved, so I'm quite happy to congratulate the woman that found the courage to do this. Maybe the criminals will think twice before causing trouble on our streets again."

A spokesman for the liberal Prison Reform Society stated,

"Too many new expensive properties in this City, occupied by too many out-of-towners and not enough jobs and quality housing for those on lower incomes are clearly what has contributed to the escalation of crime in Portsmouth. No-one can excuse the activities of muggers or burglars, but we want to see greater opportunities for these disenfranchised people so that less crime takes place and so less men, and it is in most cases men, go to prison. If the reports are true, and this woman did indeed shoot her potential muggers, we are adamant there is no excuse for taking the law into your own hands, and certainly not with such an extreme response. Problems must be tackled at the root, not shooting off the branches from high up."

A Police spokesman refused to comment on whether a woman had been involved in the shooting. In fact, there was no information forthcoming as to whether the victims were in fact muggers who had attacked the person using the gun.

"We will be interviewing a man currently held under guard in Queen Mary Hospital, but at this time I can inform you that we are looking for a lone person in possession of a handgun. I cannot give any further information about this person until CCTV footage has been analysed and our witness interviewed."

EDITOR'S COMMENT:

This shooting must act as a wake-up call to all people in our fine City. For centuries Portsmouth has been the pride of England, the home of the Navy and a defensive shield for our British Islands. In recent years, the Navy's presence has declined and other modern industries have sought to take their place. Yet naval pride still swells as the historic dockyards and other museum facilities draw the crowds. Even new shopping areas and quality housing and freshly developed marinas draw in the day-trippers and day-sailors, keeping our population expanded.

But this rejuvenation hides an underlying problem. A problem not confined to this great city of ours, but one that stretches the length and breadth of the country. This is a problem that has existed forever, and it is hard to consider how a solution may be easily found. It is the problem of the division between the haves and the have-nots. And it is also the problem of increased violence in society, often fuelled by drugs and deprivation.

In Victorian times the have-nots would spend their lives pick-pocketing to make a crust - everyone knows the story of Oliver Twist and Dickensian London, or Dickensian Portsmouth for that matter. In the 21st Century, life couldn't be more different. The gulf between the haves and have-nots is probably far less than in Victorian times. In the 19th Century, there was no National Health Service, no Council Housing nor unemployment benefits. Today, however, television advertising entices us to believe we can have anything. The internet offers a high-speed solution to all our shopping needs, if you have the money, and the cult of celebrity leads many to want to be the celebrity rather than to worship them. Society today creates a culture where guns are more easily available than ever, with an underclass more confident and prepared than ever to use them.

Society's problem is that the have-nots are never destined for success. There is less of a desire to earn a living and more of an inclination to take one from others.

The City of Portsmouth must find a solution to a large hard-up population that finds itself left behind. This is an underclass that lives in poor housing, with few job prospects, wallowing in a life of crime.

Let's celebrate the great things that are happening with our Port and City centre, but let's also recognise the need to attack the cancer of deprivation, before more people become victims on our streets.

ABERDEEN EVENING EXPRESS
"ROUGH SLEEPERS MURDERED WITH KILLER BEER"

Police closed a section of Union Street this morning after the grizzly discovery of three homeless men found dead in an empty shop doorway.

Patrick Craigy, 43, manager of Le Dejeuner Café in Union Street, arrived for work as usual at 7.30am this morning. The streets were deserted except for the squawking seagulls walking brazenly down Union Street or flying overhead. Next door to Le Dejeuner is the empty shell of the former SofaSoGood store and Craigy was used to seeing the three victims asleep, snoring loudly in this doorway. Normally he would pay no attention to them. This morning was very different. Craigy told us,

"When I got to work I saw the three dossers as usual next door, but something wasn't right. I mean, they really stank man, and they're throats had, like, holes in them, and they were covered in blood. It was totally disgusting. I just felt sick and rushed to get inside the café. From there I phoned the Police and they came within about 4 minutes. After that it was mental. The Police wouldn't let me open the café to the public and they sealed off the front of SofaSoGood, Le Dejeuner, and the gift shop on the other side with that blue and white tape they use. Then they said I should put the kettle on for everyone and they interviewed me. I couldn't tell them anything more than they could see for themselves. Then they sent me home. Ambulances had already got the bodies inside when I came out of the café, and in the front of SofaSoGood Police were looking around, for evidence I suppose."

Police were staying tight-lipped about the incident, but our own enquiries suggest something sinister on the streets of Aberdeen.

The three men were all drinking beer, nothing abnormal about that you may say, but in this case the beer appears to be what has killed them. All three men had serious injuries to their throats and it seems that the men had drunk some kind of acid solution.

When The Evening Express questioned Police today about this particular point, we were informed that no further information, except a simple statement, could be released until post-mortems had taken place. These post-mortems are due to be performed this evening and will be undertaken by Aberdeen's leading pathologist, Dr Mervyn MacFarlane.

The City waits for the results from the post mortem, but in the meantime, Police have issued this statement requesting any help in finding witnesses to this heinous crime:

"A crime has taken place in Union Street that has resulted in the death of three homeless males. Anyone with any information that can assist us in our enquiries will be gratefully received at Police Headquarters in Queen Street. We cannot issue any further details of the incident until we have followed various leads open to us, but we would appeal to the public to be on their guard as we cannot say exactly what the motive of this attack was. Nor can we say whether this was an isolated incident or part of a pattern of behaviour. We would therefore guard against panic, whilst at the same time emphasising vigilance."

EVENING EXPRESS COMMENT:
What's going on in the streets of Aberdeen? Are we less safe than we were? Is there a crazed killer on the loose? Who is at risk?

All these questions will be troubling the minds of the citizens of the granite city. The deaths of three vagrants in the heart of Aberdeen may not seem like a great loss to some, but it is an affront to the freedom of everyone in Aberdeen. The death of anyone in violent circumstances is a tragedy. This particular crime appears to have been perpetrated under the noses of shoppers and partygoers in the main thoroughfare of Aberdeen.

Did the killer know his victims? Does the killer intend to kill again? Was the killer intent on killing only the homeless? Are the homeless still at risk? Are we all at risk?

The shocking deaths of these three men certainly throws up more questions than answers.

The Evening Express appeals to the public to assist the Police – the killer must be caught. Who knows who may be next?

It does seem that the victims had drunk some kind of acid from the contents of a beer can. Perhaps they knew their attacker? Or perhaps a stranger fed them the evil mix that led to their certain deaths.

In our recent double-page feature on date rape, we appealed to everyone NOT to accept drinks from strangers in bars, restaurants and nightclubs. Once again, we would re-iterate our call to be vigilant when it comes to accepting any kind of drink or even food from strangers. As children we are indoctrinated with the parental commands to never accept sweets from strangers. If only these three men had not so willingly accepted the lethal cocktail from their attacker, they would most likely have been alive today.

LONDON EVENING STANDARD
"MINICAB DRIVER GUNNED DOWN AT THE WHEEL"

As most of London slept, an unlicensed minicab driver was gunned down in cold blood last Saturday night in a South London estate. No witnesses have yet come forward and Police have started a house-to-house search on the estate for any information leading to the capture of the gunman. So far no one on the estate has come forward as a witness to the terrible cold-blooded murder.

The shooting is believed to be related to the actions of rival minicab firms operating from the same south London music venue. It is not thought to have been the result of a robbery turned sour because we understand the victim's cash remained on the body. Other theories being put forward include the violent reaction of a customer, a family feud and even the extreme actions of a love rival.

Little is known about the minicab driver, except that he was Afro-Caribbean, living in Brixton, where he has lived with his girlfriend for 6 months.

Shootings in South London are of course not unusual. The Metropolitan Police's task force dealing with black on black crime has become involved, but it is by no means clear whether this is the appropriate team to investigate. During the last ten years, there has been an escalation in tension between the Nigerian and West Indian communities across South London, which has erupted in violence on many occasions. Little has been written about these deep-seated rivalries, as most media have preferred to focus on racist violence between white and black groups. This may be relevant in some cities outside of London, but within the confines of the boroughs of south London, West Indian and Nigerian conflicts have become one of the most significant factors, which have increased crime statistics in recent times.

This incident is still yet to be proven to be part of this emerging pattern, but if it is, it will mean a worrying acceleration of what seems to be a race and turf war, played out on the streets of London.

TWO DAYS LATER

LONDON EVENING STANDARD
"MINICAB MURDER SEARCH CONTINUES"

In what now seems to be a bizarre twist of fate for one unlicensed mini-cab driver who met his death last Saturday night, news has just surfaced that a disgruntled customer may have perpetrated his murder.

Police have released information stating that a witness has come forward who confirms seeing a well dressed couple climb into the mini-cab of dead driver, Leroy Churchill, of Brixton Terrace. The witness claims to have followed the driver at about 6am last Sunday morning and is still being held at Brixton Police station for questioning. No information is yet available as to why the witness followed the dead man's vehicle.

It is unclear at this stage whether the witness, a 36-year-old Nigerian from Peckham, did in fact witness a couple entering the car of the deceased, but it is hoped that Police CCTV footage will assist in resolving this matter once and for all.

In the meantime, the West Indian and Nigerian communities are in shock at this new level of violence and community leaders are meeting in Central Hall Brixton later this week to try to find ways of bringing the two factions closer together to create greater harmony on the streets of south London.

Police spokesman Inspector Norris has told The Evening Standard:

"I can confirm this morning at 9am, a 36 year old man from the Peckham area has been brought in for questioning to assist Police with their enquiries relating to the murder of a man last Sunday morning. This witness is not being treated as a suspect but at this time all lines of enquiry are being kept open. Currently there are 8 officers working on the murder case. Whilst this is the fourth murder to take place this month in our area, we will be putting as many resources into finding the criminals who have perpetrated this crime as we do with any serious offence of this nature."

Inspector Norris would not be drawn to answer why he believed his witness is not the prime suspect in the case, but forensic experts have suggested it is likely that evidence from the High Road's CCTV monitoring system must have given credence to the witness's story.

CHAPTER FIVE   PASSAGE TO ENGLAND

When Klarkey closed the doors for the last time of the Grosvenor School of English in northern Paris, he didn't do it without serious deliberation. To bring to an end the smooth flow of a gross turnover of $240,000 per week was certainly one of the toughest decisions of his life. But Klarkey knew he could only operate for a few intensive months, and he'd planned his exit strategy from day one in order that he could provide a comfortable future for himself.

He knew that moving approximately $7.4 million into the UK was not the easiest of jobs to achieve. In his travels, Klarkey had heard of stories of businessmen walking through airports from Jersey carrying loaded suitcases full of money. This wasn't Klarkey's style. It also wasn't a risk he was prepared to take. Certainly he could have tried to take in cash to the UK in several stages. Perhaps he could have sent Matisse to do the job on a few occasions. She was after all his trusted friend and assistant. He quickly discounted sending Matisse; it would be too dangerous even for her, especially as English was her second language.

He chose to carefully formalise a plan for a sensible, systematic pattern of behaviour that would not arouse suspicion, and at the same time would keep his money safe.

There was another important factor to consider. Even in $100 bills he had given little thought as to how much space over $7 million dollars takes up. He could hardly go to the various bureau de changes in Paris and change up a Dollar fortune for British Pounds. He laughed to himself when thinking of that. "Let's just pop into American Express by the Opera Garnier and change up a few million. NOT," he said to himself.

Equally he could not open various bank accounts and transfer the funds to the UK. The Money Laundering Acts closed this kind of loophole many years ago. Since then, the banks were only too keen to talk to the authorities for fear of reprisals from The Treasury and the Bank of England. Jersey and Guernsey certainly weren't safe havens anymore. Even Liechtenstein and Switzerland were not completely safe. Austria was possibly the only place one might have been able to get away with hiding money, but even then, it was not certain. After much thought, Klarkey had resolved that European banks were not the answer, especially when any transaction over $10,000 would come under severe scrutiny. He knew there had to be another way, and he drew on knowledge from his childhood to pursue it.

When Klarkey was six years old, whilst the family lived in leafy Kingston-upon-Thames, he had been given a Stanley Gibbons stamp catalogue. He marvelled at collecting the stamps, which he picked up at various philatelic fairs and shows across the home counties. As he got into his teens, his collecting specialised away from blandly collecting everything he could get his hands on in exchange for his pocket money. He decided that postal history would be the focus for his ongoing collection. He was much more excited by the history of well-travelled envelopes or covers, and the way in which they were used, rather than just the stamps themselves. He collected "first flights", with images of aeroplanes and markings reflecting the path of the flight: Australia to Singapore, or Lima to Cape Town. Staring at these covers he would dream of travelling the world and following the path these planes first took in the early 20th century. Other times he would collect covers sent from Concentration Camps in the Second World War: From Auschwitz to Krakow or from Dachau to Munich. He couldn't understand the Polish or German scripts, but he imagined the pain these victims must have felt, locked away and brutalised by the Nazis, sending their letters of hope to friends or relatives whom they would most likely never see again. For £20 or £30 he could hold in his hands a little piece of history that still shocked the world, with the Nazi postage emblem stamped in red or purple or black on the cover, reminding him how different Europe was back then. A distant world condemned to ancient history by so many, but in his hand it was vivid. He held the evidence showing real people affected by the tragedies of a horrific past.

He had reluctantly sold his collection to a dealer just before moving to University, in order to finance his student lifestyle and the fees. A life spent between London and Paris studying wasn't going to come cheap. But he deemed the sad loss of his collection necessary - it was the trading of commodities to suit his life at that time.

The Grosvenor School of English provided him with a pile of money and a need to hide it. It was his youthful passion for postal history that provided the vehicle for carrying his funds in a non-cash format, and it also gave him contentment. This was pleasure that transported him back to his innocent childhood. Two-day trips to various parts of the world would yield philatelic fruits of museum quality.

Matisse simply didn't get it. She thought stamp collecting was for geeks. But then she also knew the value of money, and just as she could appreciate a pair of shoes worth 1000 Euros over a pair worth 50, she chose not to dismiss Klarkey's oozing enthusiasm over his latest purchases before he confined them to his floor safe.

"Matisse, look at this!"

"What now Klarkey? Another letter from Inspector Clouseau to Miss Marple?"

"Don't be facetious. Look at it. This cover has a group of 4, 10 kopec rose stamps from Finland dated 1856. Did you know that Russia owned Finland at this time? I love these. I bought it in Geneva for 70,000 Swiss Francs."

"That is just INSANE. 70,000 Swiss Francs for an envelope?

"Of course…it is exceptionally rare."

"Oh look," Matisse perked up as she flicked through some of the pieces. "This one is sent to France."

"Yes. From Port Louis in Mauritius, to Lyons. It has the 1848, 2 penny blue and is sent via Cork in Ireland. Look at the number of cancels on it. I bought it in New York for…let me see, $22,000."

"My god, it's unbelievable. So much money tied up in such little things."

"Exactly. This one's from Western Australia. I love the black swans on their stamps. One day I'd love to have a lake with black swans. It's a cover I bought in Sydney for 49,000 Australian Dollars. It dates from 1854 and there's an error on the stamps. Can you see it says P E I C E instead of pence? I was bidding fiercely against the Mint Museum that really didn't want it to leave Oz. Too bad eh?"

"Shouldn't the Australian stamps have said 'cents'?"

"They had pence and pounds like in the UK right up till about 40 odd years ago."

"Oh…you know this is like a history lesson and a geography lesson rolled into one."

"You think I make a good teacher?"

Matisse paused, tilting her head and raising an eyebrow…"Not bad" And with that he picked up a pillow and started beating her with it.

"Careful of the stamps Klarkey!"

Then realising he shouldn't fool around unless his prized collection was hidden away, Klarkey tidied his stock into a filing box, and unlocked the floorboard to conceal his precious pension.

During the months Klarkey had been operating the Grosvenor School of English, he had concurrently built up one of the finest collections of postal history in the world. He had attended auctions in New York, Paris, Geneva, Sydney and Cape Town. He'd visited all the major European exhibitions such as Stampex in London and made sure he never spent more than US$50,000 at any one visit. There were other big spenders in the Philatelic world, but the last thing he needed to do was to draw too much attention to himself.

It was this incredible collection, inconspicuous to the untrained eye, which left Paris in his smart, but slightly battered briefcase, for a new life in London.

****

Klarkey took Matisse to London. There was no question of him leaving her in Paris. She was his assistant, best friend and confidante. He had other friends in London; people he had stayed with from time to time, but he felt that he had grown distant from them with the events of the last year. He had certainly grown to be a different person. When he occasionally thought of how he would talk about his life to his old friends he stumbled. Once he shouted into a bathroom mirror, "You've been a people smuggler for Christ sake!"

He'd built himself a fortune, which meant he could have anything he wanted, and do anything he wanted to do. He wasn't the same Klarkey that stayed on friends' sofas in the winter or the beach bum that dossed with his mother in the summer.

This was an ever more confidant Klarkey. This was a Klarkey that could take over the world if he chose to. He certainly had things he wanted and needed to do.

They checked into the Kensington Mews Boutique Hotel after arriving by taxi from Heathrow. He couldn't face Eurostar after his activities of the last few months. This was a hotel that had been converted laterally from five mews houses and contained just twelve suites of one and two bedroom apartments from £550 per night. Fortunately Klarkey had noticed on the hotel's website that "US dollars will be gratefully accepted", so their 2 bedroom room rate of $8000 per week was easily paid out of the half a million in cash accompanying them. A few weeks in the hotel would be great until such time as they decided what to do and where to do it.

"I want to see EVERYTHING." Matisse gasped. I'm so excited to be in London I can't tell you.

"I want to see the palaces and I want to see the old sailing ships. I want to see Stonehenge and I want to see Princess Diana's island."

"Calm down Matisse. You'll see everything you want, I promise. First I've got some business to attend to and then we'll start relaxing."

They had a light lunch in an Italian café on the corner of the street, then Klarkey left Matisse to wander down to Kensington Palace on her own, while he made his way, briefcase in hand, to The Strand, to move his Philatelic money-making-machine into its final stage.

Klarkey's appointment with Mr Hadaway of Westminster Philatelic Auctions in The Strand had been made when he was in Paris. He had emphasised the importance of his collection at the time and he could hear Hadaway's voice trembling as Klarkey gave him some examples over the phone of what would be on offer.

When Klarkey walked into the auctioneers' front office he could see Hadaway at a rear desk. He knew his face from the auction catalogues he'd received in France. The mid-fifties expert had a magnifying glass permanently lodged into his right eye socket and his face was buried in a pool of stamps and catalogues.

"Mr Hadaway I presume. Francis Klarke here to see you."

Hadaway's eyeglass fell to the page below him and he noisily pushed his chair back along the herringbone wooden floor, to rush forward to greet Klarkey with a two-handed handshake.

"Mr Klarke, Mr Klarke. A pleasure to see you at last."

"Please, call me Klarkey."

Hadaway had no idea how Klarkey had come to build up such a collection; especially for one so young. Collectors seemed mostly to be either children or old men, with not a lot of representation in between. Perhaps he was one of the few dot-com survivors? It mattered not. Hadaway was just pleased that he had been chosen over the other auction houses to sell the collection.

"I'm looking forward to a fruitful liaison with Westminster", Klarkey said, breaking off the endless hand-shake and opening his briefcase, "You see here a range of covers from Cyprus, Mauritius, Western Australia, and New South Wales; through to USA, Sweden, Germany and France. Something of an eclectic, yet valuable group of lots. I trust you'll be pleased to sell them for me."

"Mmm..." Hadaway started to look through the pieces, rapidly replacing his eyeglass;

"An 1869 Falkland Islands with the red frank. That'll reach about £10,000.

1862 Hong Kong 96 cents on cover. I should think that should estimate at about £12,000.

New Foundland. It's the 6 pence scarlet-vermilion from 1857! On cover. My goodness. I would say at least £20,000 for that.

"This is unbelievable sir. British Guiana 1856. It's the 4-cent black and blue. And it's initialled EDW, absolutely spot on, and got to be worth £30,000."

Klarkey sat there smugly. He was being told exactly what he already knew.

Twenty minutes had past and the five other gentlemen in the office had crowded around the table where Hadaway and Klarkey sat. Any stuffy inhibitions they may have had, left the building long ago, and a large pot of tea and bourbon biscuits was brought to sustain them.

Their excitement was two-fold. Firstly, there was a genuine rush of pleasure to observe and handle unique quality pieces. Secondly, there was a realistic understanding that the firm would receive 15% of what would clearly be a very significant sale.

Klarkey interrupted their gasps, "I would expect a sale exclusive to myself but I must emphasise that I don't want personal publicity. Call it…'Property of a Gentleman' in the catalogue forward."

"That would be no problem sir", Hadaway hurriedly agreed.

"I also rather believe I deserve an across the board 10% commission for the sale… don't you think?"

After much coughing and spluttering, Hadaway reluctantly agreed, knowing that a rival, most likely offering a better commission deal, would snap up a collection of this quality in seconds.

"Then if we could catalogue every item and agree estimates, I think we can do business together." Klarkey held out his hand and Hadaway quickly shook it.

The front door to the auction house had been locked some while before, and it remained closed for another four hours while nearly 350 lots were hastily catalogued, using Klarkey's own pre-typed schedule as a guide.

"I suppose we are looking at a lower estimate of £4 million up to a high estimate of about £4.75 million for the collection." Klarkey looked up from his calculator.

Everyone around quietly nodded and accepted him at his word.

Klarkey finally lifted himself out of the leather seat and stretched, dipping into his pocket to leave a calling card.

"Please call me on my mobile when you've fixed a date for the auction. Also make it no longer than about eight week's time. You can send the final list of the lots with estimates and the contract for me to sign to my hotel."

Klarkey closed his now empty briefcase, picked up his receipt direct from the computer's printer, and left the huddled group of men in a stunned silence.

Strutting out of the office and onto the pavement of the polluted Strand, Klarkey breathed in deeply. Shakespeare's Anthony and Cleopatra came to mind as he held his arm high hailing a cab, "His legs bestrid the ocean", Klarkey whispered. This was how Cleopatra described her Anthony, and at that moment Klarkey felt he knew exactly what she meant.

Passing Buckingham Palace and chasing past the traffic in the bus lanes, Klarkey's mind wandered aimlessly. For the first time in a long time he wasn't exactly sure what was to happen next in his life, but he knew that money equalled power, and whatever he wanted to do, he could use his cash to back any idea emanating from his sharp mind, to move into whatever direction life's tapestry should weave for him.

When Klarkey returned to the suite he knocked on Matisse's door and threw himself down on a Louis XV style chair, tossing his briefcase onto the floor. Matisse was lying on the bed, TV remote in hand, watching CNN and chewing on wine gums.

"You took SO long I didn't know what to do Klarkey," Matisse whined.

Klarkey looked at her, long dark hair tossed to one side and knew the reasons he saw her as just such a good friend. She was like a sister now.

"You know what I was doing and I can say with total pride that I achieved everything I needed to do, to secure our future."

"You mean they're going to sell the collection?"

"Of course they're going to sell the collection. I had them in the palm of my hands and they were like salivating bulldogs. They couldn't believe their luck. I could've just as easily gone to Sotheby's or Phillips or Bonham's but no, I chose Westminster, and they were eternally grateful for it."

"And when will the sale be?"

"In about two months. We can have some fun in the meantime. Then we can go to the sale, stand at the back, and watch our fortune rematerialise. I get such a buzz out of it all. I think I'm going to force myself to have a cold shower."

"OK cheri"

Klarkey closed the door between the two bedrooms, and stepped into his marble bathroom. Slipping off his clothes, he climbed into a cool shower. Soaping himself up and down, he looked at the fading white line below his belly button and made a mental note to lie in the sun at some stage soon. He knew sun worshipping wasn't too good for the skin, but a little every now and then helped to keep him looking fresh and young. Forty was barely more than a couple of years away and that scared him a little. Maybe he should visit his mother sometime in the South. Was it really nearly a year since he had been there last? What a different Klarkey he was then. He had always made an effort to speak to his mother every week or so, but recently he'd been lax. What news could he bring her? Stories of illegality, riches and who knows what? He knew that if he lied, he would have to remember his lies. Lies breed more lies and he squirmed at the thought of being dishonest to his mother, which he would have to do to stop her from worrying. He had settled on a white lie that meant he could share some of the truth with her. No mention of the Paris-London operation, just some gentle revelations about stamps and covers. He had told her that he found a rare cover in a flea market in northern Paris. This he had sold for a big profit and he had become a wheeler-dealer in postal history. She was impressed. It certainly had been worth buying him that stamp album when he was a child - he had at last used his knowledge to some benefit.

She therefore received some level of truth, and that satisfied them both. At least when they spoke their conversations had some basis of truth, rather than complete fantasy. How many sons grow bored with talking to their parents because they don't want to discuss the reality of their lives? At least this truthful part of Klarkey's life was exciting, and he enjoyed telling her about it. She would never know quite the value of Klarkey's collection, but that wasn't relevant. She only needed to know that his time was being occupied usefully and successfully. This knowledge would satisfy any mother.

Klarkey dressed quickly and slipped quietly back into Matisse's room. She hadn't moved.

"Matisse. Listen."

Klarkey then went on to explain what Matisse was going to see over the next couple of weeks. Klarkey would hire a car and drive to Salisbury and Stonehenge. They would stop in Bath and see the Roman remains and take the waters in the new spa. He would take her to Stratford-upon-Avon and walk through the garden of Anne Hathaway's Cottage and Shakespeare's birthplace, taking in a pub lunch or two. He would drive her to Blenheim, telling stories of code breaking during the Second World War. He would take her to Windsor Castle and to Runnymede where the Magna Carta was signed. He would drive down to Portsmouth and show her Nelson's *Victory*, and the remains of Henry VIII's *Mary Rose*. There was so much to do. He loved being back in England. He realised that you really only miss your own country and what it has to offer when you've been away. And he was going to enjoy the trips as much as he knew Matisse would gorge on thousands of years of history about to unfold.

"Klarkey, you are such a good friend to me. Thank you"

"Don't thank me. Let's just be happy that we found each other."

He kissed her on both cheeks and then threw himself down beside her on the bed, grabbing the TV handset and turning up the volume to listen to the latest news from another depressing place in the world where a reporter had set up a satellite dish to tell one more tragic story.

CHAPTER SIX   MEETING OF MINDS

Jamieson's transfer from Claybridge Police station to Enfield Prison was not untypical, as prisoner transfers go. He wasn't a paedophile or a child killer, so there wasn't a violent mob baying for his blood, banging on the side of the van, foaming at the mouth. The only commotion was coming from Jamieson himself, who was demanding that his human rights be respected.

"You bastards can't take me to bloody Enfield. OK, I don't expect to be near home in Southend, but why the hell can't you put me near to my Lorna or at least on the way to Essex. NOT IN BLOODY NORTH LONDON."

"Shut it Jamieson. You'll go where the system puts you", the custody sergeant barked to the prisoner, as he enthusiastically led him from the cells to the confines of the Police truck, which would take him on his journey from Surrey south of London, to north of the city in Enfield. The journey could be expected to take two hours at this time of day. For years, the sergeant had repeated former Home Secretary Michael Howard's words to hundreds of prisoners, and he delighted in doing so yet again to Jamieson.

"Jamieson son...*If you don't want the time; Don't do the crime.* Ha ha ha ha." It was sad to laugh at the same joke time and time again, but the sergeant took pleasure from these little moments of despair manifested on the faces of the criminals, and this was his way of rubbing their dirty noses their inevitable fate.

Following Jamieson's unoriginal expletive, "Piss off you pig", he was bundled into the Police vehicle to Enfield for what would certainly be a few months incarceration pending his court case.

*****

Enfield Prison was known as one of the old-school prisons. It was Victorian and terrifying. It was built for the purpose of keeping criminals away from anything that could be classed as "luxury", fulfilling its role in society, which views prison as an austere, unpleasant place. The public was generally against penal reform; not in favour of larger modern cells, with more space to walk around and prison gyms. Mr and Mrs Joe Public, for the most part, wished to see criminals suffer. They would prefer prisoners to be locked in single cells with more than two men confined in over-cramped conditions. They would happily see them only exercised for half an hour a day. They could accept them showering just once a week and remaining stinking. They wanted to see them deprived of television and newspapers. They certainly wanted them to suffer. Surveys suggested that most people considered such distress as just desserts for those who had found their way into prison. They did not understand why taxpayers' money should go towards making the lives of prisoners comfortable, when the hospitals needed attention, the streets were not cleaned enough, and schools continued to crumble. Most people have always accepted that prison acts as a college for crime, and few people believe prison is an effective solution to criminality. Nevertheless, those against prisons remain unable to offer alternative effective solutions that would overturn the public's desire to see criminals incarcerated and punished.

After processing, Jamieson lay in his cell pissed off. He was more annoyed with himself than with the System or even with the Police. Much as it grated him, he knew that everyone along the line was just doing his job. He almost broke the creases on his face with a smile when he supposed that by robbing the bank on the London Road he had just been doing his job too. He even started to believe that if people like him didn't go about their business, robbing banks and committing offences, there would be a whole lot of people in the Prison service made redundant. His smile widened. But the outside world didn't take the same view. Somehow he wasn't surprised.

He knew that it was highly likely that he would be left to rot in this dump for quite a few months before the trial. After that, if he was found guilty, he was sure to spend a five-year stretch resulting from the latest rematch of Regina Versus Jamieson. He was just SO pissed off. 'What a life' he thought, 'in and out of prison, trying to make a crust as and when I can. Then finally this place: somewhere nowhere near home, because as a policeman reminded him, "unfortunately Jamieson, Her Majesty can't find you a place anywhere else between London and Southend, so you'll be stuck up in Enfield."

Then the sergeant had the gall to say, "Think yourself lucky son, you could've ended up going to Wolverhampton, like some young lad did last week. Covered in tattoos, hard as nails he thought he was. Burst into tears he did."'

Jamieson rubbed his face then thought some more,
'Lucky! LUCKY? Why is it always when something bad happens, some clever-mouthed toe-rag suggests you're lucky? LUCKY? BOLLOCKS.'

He didn't have any mates in this place and that was going to make life hard. Usually there was someone you'd met over the years, but not in this place. Worse than that, he'd been told in no uncertain terms on arrival that there weren't any places for work. Work was the only thing that kept a prisoner from going insane in a place like Enfield. He loved the gardens or the kitchens, post room or warehouse…contrary to popular belief and gangster films, no one made mail sacks these days.

Enfield Prison certainly conformed to the public's image of a Victorian Prison. It did everything that the public expected and it looked the part. Nevertheless, the prison management did try to help the prisoners behind closed doors, by introducing some level of technology into an otherwise technophobic society. With a large percentage of inmates not even able to read and write properly, there was serious discussion among the authorities whether there was any point in introducing computer systems for the criminals to use. Information technology was the present and the future, and it made sense for prisoners to feel included rather than excluded from this phenomenon that had engulfed the world in recent years.

Prison reformers had argued that prisoners without access or knowledge of IT would be left behind on the scrap heap of life. They would be unable to communicate in a world that had moved so fast in the last decade; even those behind bars had a right to feel included.

Traditionalists wanted to see prisoners punished. Prisoners should be excluded from normal everyday things such as computers and the internet, therefore helping them recognise the error of their ways.

Such diversity of beliefs suggests a chasm that could never be gulfed. What came as a surprise to most people was an acceptable compromise that was agreed by all sides of the argument. A quiet, somewhat clever, junior civil servant happened upon a revolutionary idea that managed miraculously to marry the two schools of thought in a way previously considered impossible.

As a result, a top-secret memo was issued from the Home Office to all prison governors, and to Her Majesty's Inspectors of Prisons:

"It is the view of the Government that prisoners should have the right to feel included within society. Whilst the need for incarceration of prisoners is essential, it is also considered important and constructive, to encourage prisoners to become more inclusive as citizens within our society, rather than feeling socially excluded.

"Information technology has developed rapidly in recent years, to the extent that a high proportion of the population is able to access the internet and more e-mails pass through the system every day than items of ordinary mail are sent in one year. It is the Government's desire to include prisoners, to a limited extent, within this world of IT. It is the Government's wish to empower every prisoner with the ability to communicate through e-mail and to usefully engage in work through the use of computers.

"The Government recognises that some will consider the rights of prisoners secondary at all times to other members of society. Indeed, it is also the Government's opinion that schools, hospitals and other institutions not directly associated with criminals should always be prioritised.

"To this end, the Government has agreed at the highest level, to institute a new policy within prisons which will enable prisoners to benefit from the use of IT in new Internet Rooms, to be established in every prison. At the same time, the information gained from the use of the Internet Rooms will be made secretly available to Police, Security Services and HM Customs and other relevant agencies, which will have the full backing of the Government to act upon any information gained during the monitoring of the prisoners' activities.

"Since the disbanding of the IRA, the Government and the Security Services have actively sought to take all action necessary to combat the wider threat of terrorism and major crimes. Monitoring of internet activities by Police and Security Services will fulfil an important role in reducing crime and stopping the threat of terrorism in the United Kingdom. The Government has taken legal advice on the issues that could be raised by implementing this new policy and it is accepted that the powers already exist to proceed, under the Terrorism Act 2000 and the Anti-Terrorism, Crime & Security Act 2001.

"Finally, the Government believes the human rights of the prisoners will not be violated by intercepting messages and pages visited by prisoners, as the Government considers all prisoners' rights to privacy waived within prison, especially in rooms that are not cells."

This memo changed the way prison was perceived by both prisoners and authorities. Both sides were satisfied. Prisoners were able to learn about subjects they were studying or interested in by accessing relevant pages on the internet. They were able to send messages to friends and relatives across the globe without the need to buy phone cards, and they felt included in a world that was rapidly changing. A world just a few feet away, separated from them by a thick high grey wall.

Authorities were happy with the changes in mood that came about in prisons. But most of all, they were happy with their right to secretly read and study the activities of the criminals. Internet Monitoring Rooms (IMRs) were established in every prison, and secret statistics were starting to be assembled as to the number of crimes that were solved as a result of intercepting prisoners' e-mail. The prisoners of course were suspicious that their correspondence may be read, just as they had previously been concerned about telephone calls being intercepted, but none of them really understood the extent to which the authorities had elaborately and extensively created a network of IMRs to study the activities of the criminals. The authorities studied every second of every day when the internet connection was open in a prison.

Each prison was fitted with a state-of-the-art computer room. One computer in each room was connected to the internet. This computer was reserved in advance by any prisoner and was used for a maximum of 20 minutes per three days by each prisoner who chose to book it.

An IMR was fitted into the bowels of every prison. This was a room known only to prison governors and the authorities, and was usually accessed from outside the grounds of the prison, through a discrete doorway, seemingly not connected to the prison. The IMR became a nerve centre for the Police. Each IMR was fitted with a couple of desks, a toilet and a kitchenette. The computer screens were constantly switched on.

One of the computer screens, a 17-inch flat screen monitor was permanently networked to the internet-connected computer in the prison. Its display was recorded on tape and a rotation of IT-trained Police officers would study the screen for 10 hours every day.

*****

The first successful use of IMRs in prisons came just two weeks after the project had been fully installed. An exchange of e-mails between a convicted jewel thief in Barnsley Prison and his wife was being monitored, as it had been from the first day of installation. The cost of creating IMRs and the staffing involved to monitor them was enormous, but it was considered money well spent, compared to the level of surveillance that would be required to solve the same crimes using traditional methods of policing.

After two weeks of benign exchanges, they hit the jackpot. They needed to find out where a haul of stolen silver had been hidden, and there was no way any Police operation could warrant staking out the prisoner's family or their criminal contacts on an open-ended basis. The IMR provided them with the assistance they needed.

Anything cryptic would immediately ring alarm bells. A sufficiently cryptic message came from Barnsley to the wife, and that was enough to justify personal surveillance on her. This led them to the stash of silver and ultimately to a successful conviction.

The criminals and their accomplices had become used to using the internet, and in so doing had become sufficiently indiscreet. The Police for their part would simply confirm to the Press or any interested parties that

61

there had been "an ongoing extensive operation of surveillance on the suspects' contacts". No mention of the IMRs would ever be made in public.

Many crimes were either stopped before they could happen or solved more efficiently than they would have been under previous methods. Crime figures hadn't yet started to fall, but the rate of solving crimes had increased and those who knew why, hailed the covert project a success.

*****

Jamieson had nothing to reveal to the spying eyes in the IMR. Like so many of the inmates, he enjoyed an exchange every few days with people in various chat rooms. He enjoyed it. He could be anything and anyone in those rooms, and he loved not being a prisoner. Sometimes he was a painter and decorator living in Margate, or a builder from Dagenham. He never tried to over-fantasise about his occupation or lifestyle as he wanted to make sure he could carry off any conversation without stumbling. He was never tempted to say he was a lawyer or a doctor. He knew for sure that he would be caught out too quickly and that would spoil the fun.

*****

Klarkey also enjoyed playing the chat rooms. He'd sent Matisse off to a hair salon in Mayfair. He knew she'd delight in visiting one of those salons owned by one of the so-called celebrity hairdressers, where charges were extortionate. At such places customers were supposed to feel a million dollars because they'd paid nearly that price in charges for a cut and blow dry.

When Matisse had safely left the hotel in a cab, Klarkey pulled a new silver shiny thin laptop out of his bag. It had been preloaded with most programs that anyone could need and had also been made compatible for all internet browsers. He sat at the desk in the hotel with a glass of fresh orange juice and his laptop connected to the internal hotel network and he would play. In the last few days he had been dipping into London Wide chat rooms. Like Jamieson, he could also escape from his world. But he was now a man with a purpose. He had new vigour. This was something he'd not felt for months. He always had to have a project to plan, and he could feel the next one bubbling up inside him.

Entering AcrossTheDivide.org, Klarkey knew that it was time to make contact with some prisoners. He had a purpose and this new resolve had been in the planning for some time.

This website provided a link between prisoners and those on the outside. It created a lifeline to many prisoners, especially to the lifers, who would never escape incarceration, except through their fantasies created in internet chatrooms, fuelled by those on the outside. Some prisoners wanted news from the real world. Sometimes news specific to their town or family. Some wanted to get messages to loved ones, and some wanted old scores to be settled.

After several days of chat with various prisoners in Scotland, the Midlands and in the West Country, Klarkey happened across Jamieson.

Klarkey: *Where are you mate?*

Jamieson: *Inside north London. Hate it. Where's you?*

Klarkey: *London. Not inside. Done some dodgy deals in my time though. Spose I've been lucky not to have gone down.*

Klarkey knew that if he was going to befriend anyone, he had to appear to be one of them, without giving too much away about himself. He wasn't sure where this was going but he had his plan.

Klarkey: *So where inside are you mate?*

Jamieson: *Enfield worst luck. Can't stand it. Not made any friends.*

Bingo. Klarkey needed to make friends with someone in Enfield Prison and after several days of looking, he'd found one. Jamieson also needed a friend and he was happy to chat more than he normally would with a stranger.

Klarkey: *What you inside for then?*

Jamieson: *You ask a lot of questions. You're not old bill are you?*

Klarkey: *No way. Just interested. You don't have to say anything you don't want to. I just wanted to make sure you weren't a nonce.*

Jamieson: *Bloody hell m8, I'll sign off now if you're gonna accuse me of that shit.*

Klarkey: *Hold on hold on. I've just got a problem with nonces that's all.*

Jamieson: *Yeh, well…we've all got a problem with nonces mate. And I ain't a nonce. Armed robbery for me. Yet to be proven anyway. Besides, nonces aren't allowed on the internet. They've got no privileges.*

Klarkey: *Sorry my friend, I didn't know.*

Klarkey knew exactly the rules relating to the use of the internet. It just made good conversation to be contentious and it made him a friend more quickly.

Klarkey: *So what's your name? First name only I know. I'm Sam.* Klarkey lied.

Jamieson: *Yeh I'm John.*

Klarkey: *OK John. Cheers. Look, I don't want to sound like some do-gooder or whatever, but I'm only in this chat room because I've had mates that have been inside and I know sometimes it's good to have a chat.*

Jamieson: *What? Like to a social worker? Bugger that.*

Klarkey: *No I didn't mean like that. What I meant was to chat to someone who's not part of the system. I've got no side to me you see. No hidden agenda. Just a bloke on another computer miles away who you can have a laugh with.*

Jamieson: *There's no laughing in here I can tell you. Just a load of miserable bastards. And the arsehole I have to share a cell with stinks. Reckons he's allergic to water. I said he could borrow some aftershave my Lorna sent in for me. LOL.*

Klarkey: *At least you can have a laugh about that. So Lorna's your wife then?*

Jamieson: *Girlfriend. I really screwed that up. She could've been my wife... but before I could get the ring on her finger I got arrested. Seem to make a stupid habit of getting locked up when something good's gonna happen.*

Klarkey: *Maybe I could give her a message if you like?*

Jamieson: *Not sure mate. I speak to her once a week but she can't afford the internet.*

Klarkey: *I've given other blokes girlfriends' messages for them. If you want me to do that I'd be happy to.*

Jamieson: *I'm thinking about it....you won't piss me around will you?*

Klarkey: *I'll do what I promise. Really.*

Jamieson: *OK mate, cheers. Her number is 015394 9898984. Just tell her I'm sorry.*

Klarkey: *Is that all?*

Jamieson: *That's all for now. Really. Look, I gotta go now, my time's up. Wanna talk some more on Thursday? I can 't use the machine till then. Say about 5 ish.*

Klarkey: *No probs. I look forward to it mate. I'll pass on your message.*

And then Jamieson had to sign off. The next prisoner was already staring over his shoulder, ready to breath in his share of the outside world.

Klarkey had made the connection he needed to make. This was going to be the most difficult and treacherous journey he had ever made and the hairs on his arm stood up through goose bumps when he considered for a moment what could happen.

Just for now though, he had a call to make.

The phone rang in the mobile earpiece a few times.

"Yeh?" A tired female Essex voice answered.

"Hello, my name's Sam and…"

"Look mate I dunno who you are but we ain't buying any." She put the phone down.

Klarkey held the phone a foot away from his hand and stared at it with a perplexed sideways grin. He called again.

"Lorna…"

"Oh it's you again. Hold on! How did you know my name?"

"That's what I'm trying to say if you'll give me a chance! John asked me to call you?"

"You serious? What…you just got out or something?"

"No, we spoke on the internet. He made me promise to give you a message."

"So what is it then?"

"He says he's sorry. That's the only message."

Lorna started weeping.

"Just get lost will you? Wasting my time…" And then she hung up on Klarkey for a second time.

CHAPTER SEVEN   MATISSE'S STORY

Matisse Espère was the last child born to hard-working parents in a suburb of the Western French city of Tours. Monsieur Espère was a traditional baker who worked long hours and missed out on watching his family grow around him. Madame Espère worked part-time as a cleaner at the magnificent chateau, Chenonceux. Her area of expertise was fire-cleaning. She loved the historical full body height fires that dominated the rooms in the turreted historic chateau and never once considered giving up work to look after the children full-time. She knew she had her mother to help around the house, and with five children she certainly needed the money.

Matisse was the fifth child where the first four children had all been boys. Mr and Mme Espère were desperate for a girl when their fifth child was born, but they were to be sorely disappointed. Matisse was also a boy.

From birth, Matisse was dressed as a girl. A psychological analysis of the life of Matisse and his parents would probably have led to the prognosis that Mme Espère had suffered some kind of breakdown after the birth. It was a combination of post-natal depression and immense disappointment that Matisse was not female, that led the couple to bring Matisse up as a girl. It was not a question of sexuality, but one of gender.

Matisse enjoyed an idyllic childhood, albeit as a boy, dressed and treated as a girl. But as Matisse grew older, he realised the folly of his parents activities, whilst at the same time recognising that his life simply wasn't normal. Other boys and even girls picked on him at school, quickly recognising Matisse as an easy target, which led him to become an even more introvert child. He had been dressed in girls clothing up to the age of five, but when it was time to start school he was forced by the authorities to dress as a boy. This was where a deep confusion developed in

Matisse's mind. It is widely accepted that behaviour towards children from an early age impacts significantly on their future. This certainly was the case with Matisse, who became increasingly uncomfortable wearing boys clothes and behaving as a boy, and yet he became progressively eager to become a girl; to fully transform into a girl with all that entailed.

Then puberty came. This was like being hit over the head with a sledgehammer for Matisse Espère. He didn't want to grow hair on his face. He didn't want to grow a larger penis. He didn't want to find girls attractive – but at the same time he did not feel gay. The overwhelming feeling that swept over Matisse was not that he was attracted to boys, but that 'he' wanted to be a 'she'.

He struggled with these feelings for another two years, failing his exams at 16 years old and feeling desperately alone. He was certainly unable to talk to his parents. Usually he felt he hated them, despite the fact that it was his parents who were the most relaxed about Matisse being a girl. Matisse was fulfilling the dream of his parents. It was not that simple. Matisse knew his parents wanted a girl. That was clear. He could never forgive them for making his life so miserable and intolerable. He blamed them for his moods, for his depression and for his loneliness. He blamed them for his beatings at school and for his educational failure. They had sought to manipulate his life from the moment he was born and he felt suffocated by them. Yes, he wanted to be a girl, which was what they wanted. But he wanted to be a girl NOT because they wanted it, but because he believed he had truly been born into the body of the wrong gender. He believed that he was the epitome of a girl fighting in a boy's body, and he vowed to do something about it one day.

"Salut Mama" were his last words as he closed the door behind him one June afternoon, making his way into town towards Tours train station, to catch the TGV train to Paris,

never to see his parents again; to make a new life as a girl.
As a woman.

He became a she very quickly.

She bought new clothes inexpensively in the Boulevard
Montmartre, and headed straight towards Pigalle, where she
tried her luck as an exotic dancer in the Club Hirondelle.
Matisse pretended to be a girl as she had since she was a
baby, but the staff weren't convinced by this, despite her
slight figure and reasonably high voice. They'd seen more
transvestites and transsexuals in their life than they could
remember, but this one was different. Matisse really
believed she was a girl, and who were they to argue with
her passionate conviction. She quickly got the job and after
agreeing a nightly rate of pay. Matisse skipped down the
street celebrating, booking into a dive of a hotel between
Pigalle and Montmartre knowing and believing that she'd
stepped onto the first rung of a ladder in life as a woman.

Things worked out well at the Club Hirondelle and
Matisse was popular. At first she thought she should
change her name, she'd been used to being a boy at school
with this name and thought it sensible to make a complete
change. Claudine, the manager of the club thought
otherwise.

"Cherie darling your name is divine. Don't ever change
it! How wonderful to have been named after a painter.
Matisse it is and Matisse it must stay."

Matisse was now the name of a girl.

The club could be generously described as a drinking
club with exotic dancers as entertainment. Some would say
unkindly that it was a pick-up joint for punters and their
dancing whores. The truth was somewhere in the middle of
the two opinions.

Matisse was a good girl. She had found her gender – at
least she behaved within the gender she wanted to be. There
was one more serious piece of surgery that would have to
take place if she wanted to be a full woman. She had

started to see Dr Hervé, a leading sex change Doctor in Paris, and she was taking female hormones that made her breasts swell and the hair fall out from her chest and face. She was fortunate not to have been a hirsute boy and she was pleased there had never been any hair on her back.

Existing as a woman suited Matisse well. She didn't mind the leering and suggestions of sex from customers. She never fell into their laps or let them touch her…just in case they touched too much. Although she had been told that some men would pay a fortune if they knew she was a transvestite with a penis. These kinds of thoughts appalled her. Few people believed she was a virgin – but she was. In fact, if the truth about her virginity had been known, the price on her head, and every other part of her would certainly swell to more than double the going rate.

As she danced on her pole, up and down, round and round, she switched off from the smokey, stale scenario in which she existed. Her mind drifted back to the days of Chenonceux, sitting with her mother in the beautiful gardens, the orangery or staring at the waxwork images of Diane de Poitiers, mistress of Henry II, in her lavish 16th century costumes. Then she would dream of going to England, and seeing real English castles, like Windsor or the Tower of London. Becoming a real woman certainly was Matisse's most important dream, but her second was to visit England and appreciate the magnificence of its historic past.

To fulfil her English fantasy, Matisse took English lessons at the local lycée after regular school hours, where adults who had not learned a foreign language before could benefit from the teachers' expertise. She would smile to herself sitting at the desk at the school some early evenings, thinking how just a couple of years earlier she wouldn't be seen dead trying hard to study in a classroom environment.

Fulfilling her ultimate dream of becoming a woman was unquestionably going to happen. It was just a matter of timing and money. If she had the money she would go to Dr Van der Vogel in Amsterdam with no hesitation. It was just a matter of money. There was no question that she had made the wrong decision to have the full sex change operation. She had no desire to remain anatomically as a man and that dangling appendage between her legs simply had to go.

One particular Friday evening was the same as every other. Not too busy, but full of men who had clearly just left work, probably having made the excuse to their wives they were working late. It was a little too early for unpleasantness and drunkenness and Matisse was working the pole as usual, this time thinking about the Bloody Tower at the Tower of London, and the two young princes who were supposed to have died there.

She rarely looked into the faces of the wide-eyed men in the club. Their sad letching mouths often put her off her routine, but on this occasion, she noticed an attractive man sitting by himself, quietly, confidently drinking a bottle of beer, looking on with a face that seemed different to the others. Most men were alone and of a certain age, or in groups, or packs, younger and louder.

Matisse felt confident dancing towards this man, even looking into his eyes. He didn't seem threatening and she felt comfortable and confident near him. He smiled and held up his bottle of beer as if to greet her, and then gave a gentle applaud when she'd finished her routine. Since when did ANYONE ever give her a positive reception in this job? She had to go and talk to this man.

Usually Matisse would stay backstage in the cramped paint-peeling backroom that was an excuse for a dressing room. Teeming with girls in various stages of undress, swilling direct from bottles of spirits supplied by the management, or from bottles of champagne supplied by the customers who had overpaid heavily in the faint hope of some future liaison.

This time, after her routine, Matisse grabbed her towel from behind the tiny stage to wipe her forehead and hands, and for the first time, walked out through the tables at the front of the stage and stepped right up to the pleasant-faced man, a man in his thirties, who she had felt confident with earlier.

"Bonjour you," she started.

"Bonjour YOU," he responded confidently.

"Mind if I sit in this chair?" Matisse said in English, assuming an air of sophistication.

"I don't mind at all." The Englishman answered quickly.

"Matisse", she said extending her hand, delighted that he had answered in English.

"Klarkey," he said, noticing her well-manicured fingernails.

"You like my dance Klarkey?"

"Yes I do. Not that I expect anything more by the way. I just needed to get away from work for a little while."

"Don't worry, you and everyone else come here just to get away from work. What do you do?"

"I'm working on opening a language school."

"Are you serious? Is it English Language?"

"Of course...is there any other language worth learning apart from French?"

"I've been learning English at the lycée for some time now. My teacher says I have a gift."

"You're English is perfect. You're teacher's not wrong."

"Would you accept me for your school?"

Klarkey thought for a moment. This wasn't part of his plan. He needed to think of a way to put her off but at the same time not to hurt her feelings.

"I'm sorry Matisse, but you're far too advanced for my school, which is going to be strictly for beginners. Anyway, it hasn't even opened yet."

"OK Monsieur. Thank you for your compliment." And then Matisse took a swig of Klarkey's beer, threw a card down on the table, and swept through the now crowded tables back to the confines of the cramped dressing room.

Klarkey looked at the card: "Matisse Espère". Her number was local.

He intended to call.

*****

Several weeks later, and several meetings later, Klarkey and Matisse had become firm friends. There never was any sexual chemistry between them. Even if Klarkey had been tempted to think lustful thoughts, they disappeared after Matisse revealed that she had more to offer between her legs than most women. He didn't care though. He'd found a friend and she'd found a true companion who didn't judge her. Matisse felt somewhat exposed to Klarkey at times. Not in the physical sense, but in respect of what he knew about her; that he had discovered her working a pole in a dance club. She felt vulnerable. Klarkey knew that she felt exposed. He'd walked straight into her place of work – how could it be any other way? Matisse on the other hand knew very little about Klarkey's Grosvenor School of English. She wondered why he was so secretive about his work. She wanted to see what his school was like. She wanted to speak English with some of the pupils.

Klarkey had never told anyone about his school and it was due to open in a week's time. The teachers were employed; the building in Rue de la Chapelle had been transformed. The 'lines of enquiry' for students had been established and almost everything was in place. Everything except an appropriate front person.

"Matisse…" Klarkey said out of the blue after they had both been staring aimlessly at their double espressos for more than a minute.

"What cheri?"

"I've been thinking about talking to you more about my school"

Matisse pulled herself up into her seat and smoothed out her short skirt on the wicker chair,

"Tell me more Klarkey darling, you never talk about your school."

"The school opens its doors in about a week and I would like to offer you a job there."

"A job? But Klarkey I already have a job, and I'm not qualified as a teacher."

"No, not as a teacher. More as a..." he wanted to avoid the word 'receptionist', which may sound somewhat uninteresting,

"Student liaison and induction officer".

"A what? Even my English isn't quite good enough to understand the meaning of this."

Klarkey pushed on... "Let's say I need someone I can trust,"

"Yes",

"Someone who will be the front person at the School. Someone who the pupils will view as the face of the School when they arrive, when they are processed, and before they leave. Someone who will have responsibilities second only to me."

"My goodness Klarkey! You're offering me a management position? Are you sure?"

"Of course I'm sure. I think I'm a pretty good judge of character and I trust you. Though I suppose it's no good threatening you with cutting you're dick off if you misbehave because that might give you a licence to fool around!"

Matisse slapped Klarkey playfully across the face with a napkin. "Méchant méchant bad boy!!"

"I suppose we should talk about money." Klarkey said rather formally.

"Well you know exactly what I'm saving my money for, and I think somehow it would be hard to earn more money anywhere else than in the job I do now – however unpleasant it is becoming."

"How much are you earning now Matisse? If you don't mind me asking."

"I get about 2,500 Euros a week, and I work five nights a week. You won't be able to beat that."

"If I said to you that your operation just got closer because I'm prepared to pay you 3000 Euros per week would you take the job?"

"If you said you were going to pay me 3000 Euros per week I would wonder exactly what I was expected to do. Work 400 hours a week? Or do something illegal for my wages – what is it?"

"Hmm", Klarkey thought for a second. Then he proceeded to tell Matisse about his grand project. How he wanted to help people from across the world realise their dreams of living and working in the UK, and how in the process he was going to make his fortune. Matisse was mesmerised. She would flick her hair in disbelief as every new part of the story unfolded, and when he was finished, she remained silent for a few seconds. Then she started laughing.

"Klarkey! There was I, thinking you were a respectable language school owner, and all along you are a master criminal…I'm amazed!"

"Sshh…" Klarkey grabbed Matisse by the arm, threw down a 10 Euro note for the coffees, and dragged her outside of the café.

"Let's walk," he said firmly.

"You're hurting my arm…let go…you're scaring me"

"Look Matisse, I've told you very private, secret information. This could get all of us in a lot of trouble. You must keep this quiet and never talk out loud to arouse suspicion."

"OK OK. I'm quiet already."

And so they walked along the Quai by the River Seine, past the Animalerie stores with every dog and cat breed staring out at them, as if to say, "Buy me please": sad puppies and kittens, rats and rabbits, gerbils and lizards; countless types of tropical fish, parrots and other exotic birds; cockerels and hens, spiders and snakes.

Matisse loved the animals and they took her mind off the matter in hand just for a little while. Most Parisians believe that if you are from outside of the city you must have grown up on a farm with lots of animals. It is certainly true that much of France is very rural, but Matisse hardly ever saw any animals in the suburbs of Tours. Her family certainly never kept any pets.

"Look Klarkey, this grey cat is SO gorgeous."

'CHARTREUX - 1500 Euros' the sign read.

"Klarkey, can you believe how much those babies are? You know what? I'm going to take your job and buy myself a Chartreuse cat!"

"You're prepared to pay 1500 Euros for a kitten? You must be completely mad" Klarkey spat.

"I figure it this way. If the cat lives for 15 years, that's what? 100 Euros a year. So Klarkey that works out to only 2 Euros per week! Not so bad!"

And so their deal was sealed. In just a few minutes, Matisse had accepted a new job and had resolved to buy a cat. Klarkey hailed a taxi and they returned to Matisse's apartment to discuss the details of the job, which she was to start the following day. She could come back for the cat later.

From then on, Matisse would become an ex-dancer and had taken another step closer to her goal. That made her very happy.

CHAPTER EIGHT   KLARKEY AND CHARLOTTE

The structure of a person's life, his outlook, the way he treats people, his whole life's philosophy, will be moulded by the events of childhood. Infant memories and experiences become ingrained in the soul, leaving an indelible mark.

Klarkey's childhood memories of nearly thirty years earlier, continued to seriously trouble him. They would haunt him until death, and there was little he could do to change that.

Klarkey was seven years old. Seven is old enough to feel and understand the world around you and to be sensitive to it, yet too young to rationalise how to control those feelings. Klarkey's sister, Charlotte, was beautiful. She was two years older than him and he accepted her as his mentor and role model.

They lived an idyllic life in Kingston-upon-Thames, often walking along the river and spending time as a family, engaging in normal family activities: going to the zoo, eating in restaurants once a week and occasionally taking trips to the seaside, with buckets and spades, inflatable beds and blow-up arm bands.

On this particular day, Charlotte and Klarkey's parents had taken them on a trip to the seaside. He'd blocked it out of his mind exactly where, but the beach was sandy, not stony like other beaches they'd visited on the south coast. The sea went out a long, long way where you could wade out far, with hardly any wave, and the warmth of the day made it seem perfect, whether you were seven or seventy years old.

Charlotte wanted to go for a walk along the beach. Klarkey preferred to stay with his parents and play in the sand. His father was an English traditionalist, which meant he looked rather ridiculous to many people in his sandals and socks with trousers rolled up. His mother was à la carte

French, with a fine figure and happily topless. Other kids sniggered, but Klarkey didn't know why. They seemed like a normal family group to him. Certainly he didn't think it was strange for a woman to be topless. Even his sister was topless, but then she was only nine years old.

"Please Klarkey come for a walk with me," Charlotte whined.

"No. I want to play here. I'm going to make castles. Mummy and Daddy will live in a castle made by me one day. I'm going to be an architect." Klarkey was adamant.

"Darling...you want to be an architect? Last week you wanted to be an actor," Mother laughed.

"If you don't want to play with me I'll find someone else to play with."

And at that point, Charlotte turned on her flip-flopped heels and walked away towards the dunes higher up the beach.

"Don't go too far," mother called to her.

"La la la...la la la" Charlotte sang as she waved her arms in the air as if not to hear her mother's demand. Then she was gone, obscured by the long grass at the top of a dune.

The sun peeked out from behind a light cloud and mother lay down on her brushed mat, drawing one leg up to the other's knee, coating it with a fine layer of sun milk, whilst father, in a deck chair, closed his eyes, put his hands behind his head and let out a long exhaustive sigh, as if the cares of the world were exhaled in one breath.

Charlotte had been gone for a while, and the sun had passed in and out of several cloud formations. Klarkey had been for a gentle paddle in the sea and started to build his castle; mother had already coated her other leg with sun protection and father was now snoring loudly.

Klarkey patted his mother's stomach, "Mummy, I want to play with Charlotte, where is she?"

"Charlotte, Mon Dieu, where is she? DADDY!"
Mother called to father. He stirred and rubbed his eyes.

"I don't know," he said, "have I been asleep? What is it?

"Charlotte, she's been away for too long…"

"OK, I'll go and look for her."

"Yes please, I'll stay here with Klarkey."

"She went over that way daddy," Klarkey said, holding one hand to his mouth and pointing with the other towards the dunes at the rear of the beach.

Father took large strong strides towards the dunes and was gone in a few seconds. Klarkey started to cry.

"I should have stayed with Charlotte. Maybe she's lost." Klarkey whimpered, feeling responsible for the conduct of his sister.

Klarkey's memories of childhood died after this point. The most powerful of emotions would often overwhelm him. Usually under these circumstances he would play Górecki's Symphony of Sorrowful Songs on the CD player, and allow the waves of hatred, fear, anxiety and guilt to wash over him. He would often experience a recurring dream. As he closed his eyes he would start to fly. He would fly over land by the edge of the sea, occasionally swooping down to turn over giant boulders to peer below them. Underneath one was a nest of vipers; under another were a million maggots; under another a putrid-smelling swamp. Under the final rock he would find Charlotte, buried up to her neck in the sand, calling his name. He would scratch and scrape with his hands and nails at the sand to free her, exhausting himself until he was able to lift her out and cradle her in his arms. She would be wet and cold and sobbing, and Klarkey would take her hand and tell her that everything would be all right. The he would draw her upwards and upwards, higher into the air until they're flying together, and she would be scared, but Klarkey would tell her that everything will be all right. As they would go higher and higher, the cold wind would wash away the sand and dry out her hair and clothes, and Charlotte would look at him and say, "Thank you Klarkey for saving me. I love you." And then he would wake up.

This time, he woke from his daydream slumber; relieved to be in the Kensington hotel suite he now called home. He stepped into the bathroom and threw cold water over his face. Looking at his watch, he realised it was nearly one o'clock and he was hungry. It was time to kill two birds with one stone.

He knocked on Matisse's door.

"Come in, come in. I'm sorting out some clothes, that's all."

"I want to take you for lunch. I need to have a chat with you about something."

"That sounds serious"

"Well, kind of…it's just…let's just go and we can talk there."

Matisse dropped the clothes she was folding onto the bed and followed Klarkey down the stairs and along the cobbled mews into Kensington High Street.

"Let's go here," Klarkey pointed at a seafood restaurant with crisp white linen tablecloths.

"This looks nice. I like the name. 'L'huitre' sounds so much better in French than in English, The Oyster, don't you think?

"I suppose so." Klarkey wasn't really concentrating; his mind was on his distant painful yet ever-present past. This wasn't going to be easy. They sat at a window table.

"Hello Madame, sir, my name is Pierre" the cheerful Scottish waiter greeted them, presenting two menus. "Our starter special today is "Coquilles St Jacques", plump juicy salted scallops with button mushrooms, grilled, with white sauce and sprinkled with Parmesan cheese. Our main course special catch of the day is Padstow Lobster, served either grilled with fine herbs, or steamed with mayonnaise and served with various green leaf salad leaves. And here is your wine list…I'll give you a few minutes"

"If his real name is Pierre," Matisse laughed, "I was born with these size 36C tits!"

Klarkey wasn't in the mood to laugh. He stretched the left hand corner of his mouth, as if forcing a smile exhaling from his nose, then took a deep breath.

"I want to tell you about something. Something that's very important to me. Something that fundamentally makes me who I am."

"So profound Klarkey! Can we order first?"

"I guess so."

They sat in silence for a minute studying the menu. Klarkey looked up from the page, raised his eyebrows at the waiter, who scurried over to take the order.

Matisse chose first, "I would like a dozen Fines de Claires oysters to start, and then the Char-grilled sea bass please"

"And for me," Klarkey started, "seeing as you've gone for oysters from western France, I'll take the oysters from south-western England, and go for a dozen Fowey oysters, followed by a plain grilled skate wing with some mixed vegetables. Oh, and a bottle of the Chablis please."

"Very good", the waiter said as he took the menus and flew off to the kitchen.

Then they were alone.

"Matisse. This is really hard for me."

"You're not sending me back to France are you?"

"Of course not. Silly. No. This isn't about you. This is about me!"

"Oh…OK. I'm listening."

"I'm going back 28 years ago. Back to when I was seven years old. Something terrible happened that still haunts me to this day. I can't even say that time has mellowed the feelings because it hasn't.

"I was with my parents and my sister Charlotte."

"Oh, you never mentioned you had a sister…" Matisse interrupted but Klarkey continued, using his hands to gesture her not to stop his flow.

"…She was a couple of years older than me, and even though she was nine, she seemed very grown up. We went to the seaside for the day. It was lovely. Really warm and not busy with people. My father had discovered this beach that not so many people from outside of the area knew. I guess it was one of those locals' beaches, like you can occasionally find in Brittany, away from the crowds."

"Yes I know what you mean." Matisse rested her chin on her hands and stared into Klarkey's deep green eyes.

"I was playing with the sand. I loved to make sandcastles and dream of how one day I would design my own castle. I wanted to be an architect or a builder maybe. I don't remember exactly. Charlotte wanted to go for a walk along the beach but I didn't feel like it. I regret that forever now."

The waiter came across with the chilled bottle of Chablis, and Matisse broke her stare, and silence came over the table.

"Monsieur." The waiter said, pouring a sample of the crisp white wine in Klarkey's glass.

"Very good. Please…," he beckoned to his glass having taken a sip and wishing that the waiter would just leave them alone, which he finally did, having poured wine into both of their glasses.

"So Charlotte went for a walk. Nobody thought anything of it. Why should they? She wanted to go for a walk and she did." Klarkey's voice trembled as the memories flooded back.

"That was the last time I saw her."

"My God Klarkey…what happened to her?"

"We searched everywhere for her. Dad went looking all over the dunes. Mother grabbed me by the arm as tight as I'd ever been held before and she started sobbing. At first I didn't understand there was a problem. After all, Charlotte said she was going for a walk and as far as I was concerned that was where she was. The problem was that it was becoming dark, and we should have left for home by then, back to the quiet suburbia of Kingston, but we couldn't, because Charlotte was still missing.

Later on, I don't know what time it was, there were Police everywhere. I remember lots of flashing blue lights and bright yellow waistcoats. Dad had checked us into a small hotel near to the sea front and various men in uniforms came into the room to whisper quietly into my parent's ears. I don't know what they were saying but I remember being very frightened. I was confused and no one was telling me anything. I pushed my face into the pillow on the bed hoping everything would get back to normal. I kept saying, 'Charlotte's not here, where is she?' and then my mother would cry. I just didn't understand."

The waiter returned with their oysters, on beds of crushed ice on silver platters.

Klarkey grabbed a piece of lemon, and pressed his fork hard inside it, pouring juice all over the oysters and over his hands. Then he tipped Tabasco drops onto each oyster, before slurping the first juicy oyster into his mouth with a sharp gulp and wiping his hands on his napkin.

"A spat is what I had with Charlotte. A stupid spat is the last thing that we had together."

"What do you mean a spat?"

"I mean we had a stupid petty argument. Did you know the word 'spat' also means a baby oyster?" He gulped down his second oyster after adding more black pepper.

"You have so many English words that mean different things. It can be very confusing you know."

"I suppose you're right…I've never really thought about it."

"We have the Academie Française to decide what words we can use, but you're language grows from however people speak, it's very interesting." Matisse didn't want to draw the conversation back to the subject of Klarkey's sister, until he was ready to do so.

"It's typical of a bloody republic to demand that everyone speaks the same words."

"What do you mean a republic?," Matisse said defensively," The Academie was founded in 1635, well before France became a Republic!"

"OK, I stand corrected. You actually learned something in school then!"

Matisse flicked her napkin at Klarkey and they carried on eating their oysters in silence for a few more minutes.

Klarkey waited for the waiter to take away the discarded oyster shells before continuing.

"I loved my sister. And I never had the chance to tell her."

"You were just a child Klarkey. You shouldn't blame yourself. Was she ever found?"

"Oh yes. That's the worst part. She was found two days later, by a teenage boy walking his dog, about half a mile along the beach amongst the long grass. He must have had the shock of his life. She was part buried in the sand, naked and dead."

"My God Klarkey. I'm so sorry, I had no idea."

Klarkey held his face in his hands. The waiter then returned with their main courses, and noticing they were in deep conversation, at last, put the plates down with a hurried 'Bon Apetit' and left them alone to Klarkey's emotional outpouring.

Klarkey slid his knife between the skate and its bone, staring down at his plate.

"I didn't understand what had happened, but years later I read the press cuttings my mother had kept, and the whole truth was shockingly revealed.

Charlotte had been walking along the beach and had stumbled across a stranger. She was well trained, as we both were, in not talking to strangers, but obviously this bastard was clever, and knew exactly what he was doing. Either that, or he just forced her to go with him. I guess we'll never know. Anyway…" Klarkey took a mouthful of fish and then one of wine,

"She was just taken by this stranger. And then she was…abused. Then he… killed her."

"That's unbelievable". Matisse didn't know what else to say. She was disinclined to eat her sea bass, but felt compelled to eat it, as she didn't want to catch Klarkey's eyes at this sensitive moment.

"The newspaper said she was 'seriously sexually assaulted, then asphyxiated with some kind of leather strap, probably a belt'. In other words, she was raped and murdered by this animal.

"These were times before DNA tests and computer tracking of paedophiles. I don't even think most people knew the word paedophile in those days. We were devastated. I can't think of another word for it. I became a completely absorbed child, losing myself in books and my stamp collection; my parents became shadows of themselves and my father died within 9 months of Charlotte's death. He had a heart attack probably brought on by stress. I think he blamed himself for taking us out for the day to the seaside, but it wasn't his fault."

Silence once again came over the table and they took a moment to enjoy their food. Klarkey waved the empty wine bottle to the waiter, who quickly brought over another, draping the bottleneck in a napkin and plunging it into a bucket of iced water. Staring out at the traffic passing in the street, he continued.

"After my father died, my mother decided we would move out of England to the south of France, near to her family. We both needed a change as everything around us reminded us of Charlotte or of Dad. Not that we wanted to forget them of course, it was simply that life became very painful. It also co-incided with the end of the trial of the man that killed Charlotte."

"So they caught him?"

"Oh yes, I don't know how…perhaps he blabbed to someone when he'd had a few drinks. I don't know. Matthew Groucher was his name. He was a local man. A fisherman. Charlotte was in the wrong place at the wrong time.

"He was jailed for life. The press quoted the judge as saying 'this is one of the most serious crimes I have ever had to preside over in my 30 years on the bench' . Well of course it was! What I don't understand is why the system gives someone a life sentence if life doesn't mean life? I mean he took away my wonderful sister's precious life, before she'd had any chance of growing up. The judge recommended he serve 30 years in prison. I suppose to some people that would mean life. But if Charlotte had been alive at the end of such a prison sentence, she would still have only been 39 years old. Maybe she would have had kids of her own. I could've been an uncle! Who knows?

"Anyway. What I'm saying is that in a couple of year's time Groucher will probably be getting out of jail. And that makes me sick. Sick so deep in the stomach that I can't eat."

Klarkey pushed his plate out of the way and took a large mouthful of wine.

"Groucher was a petty criminal, in and out of prison, so the papers said. What they also said was he'd been accused by several local girls of attempted sexual assaults, before Charlotte's death, but nothing could be proven and no charges had previously been brought against him. The Police knew what this creature was like and he was left to roam in the district, finally preying on my darling sister, like a struggling trapped fish in one of his nets.

"Klarkey," Matisse wasn't really sure how to proceed, but she continued anyway, "why are you telling me this now…after all this time of knowing each other?"

"Matisse," Klarkey took her hand, "You are like my family now. There are some things that are so hard to share in our lives. We can either bottle them up and explode, or we can share them with those we care about and perhaps then think about how we're going to act."

"And how are you going to act? I know you can never forget these terrible things, but there's nothing more you can do? I know it's a cliché, but you can only let time be the healer, surely?"

"No Matisse. Time isn't going to heal THIS wound. When I was 13 years old, we had a school trip to London. It was great to come back to England and our English teachers took us to the Old Vic theatre to see a Shakespeare play, The Merchant of Venice. There was a wonderful husband and wife team playing the lead roles, I'm sure you've never heard of them, but they are very famous here: Prunella Scales and Timothy West. We sat in the second row and were covered in spit as the actors projected their voices towards the upper circle. It was an incredible experience. I will never forget one speech by the character Shylock. These few lines that Timothy West spoke have stuck in my mind forever:

'If you prick us, do we not bleed?
If you tickle us, do we not laugh?
If you poison us, do we not die?
And if you wrong us, SHALL WE NOT REVENGE?'

"Matisse, revenge is what I want against Groucher. I crave it. There's no way he's getting out of prison. He doesn't deserve freedom; he deserves pain. He deserves as much pain as my Charlotte must have felt all those years ago. Don't let the system try to convince you he's served his time. He deserves to die."

Matisse didn't know what to say. She wanted to tell Klarkey that he shouldn't stoop to Groucher's level. She wanted to warn Klarkey that he should not take the law into his own hands. She wanted to tell him not to let his heart rule his head.

In the end, "Shall we have coffee?" was all she could manage.

"Yes, let's have some coffee. And how about some chocolate cake while we're at it?"

Matisse managed a smile, unsure exactly how she planned to deal with Klarkey's story, and even less sure how Klarkey was intending to take revenge against the monster featured in it. Deciding that she, very unusually, felt uncomfortable in Klarkey's company, she excused herself to go to the toilet, leaving Klarkey to place the pudding order with the waiter who had raced back to the table to take advantage of a break in their intense conversation.

When Matisse returned to the table, two plates of chocolate cake and two double espressos were in place.

"So what can you possibly do?" Matisse ventured.

"I kind of have a plan"

"Kind of have? Even I know that's pretty bad English. What do you mean?"

"Look, do you think that it is right to take the moral high ground in certain situations? What I mean is, is it right to decide that you are right and someone else is wrong and as a result take action that could be construed as illegal or improper?"

"I don't know? Give me an example."

"OK. Let's go back to the Second World War. Say, for example, you were working in the French Resistance and there was a visit by Hitler to your city. And say for example, you had the opportunity, because you were a crack shot and also because you knew the layout of your own hometown, that you could get a direct shot at Hitler and kill him stone dead. Do you think that would be a proper thing to do? To change the course of history for the greater good." They both took their first spoonfuls of cake, speaking with their mouths full.

"I think you're talking about two very different things. Killing Hitler would have been to save the lives of millions that may die as a result of him staying alive. Somehow killing this guy Groucher, would be to avenge a death already taken place."

"But Matisse, that's where you're wrong, it's only with the benefit of hindsight that we know just how many people Hitler killed or whose deaths he was responsible for, right up to the end of the War. What we do NOT know, is how many deaths and destroyed lives could possibly be prevented, if the death of someone like Groucher was to happen sooner rather than later."

"I see what you mean. Because the future has not happened, we don't know whether he's changed his ways or will go back to the way he was."

"True. But I believe I can take the moral high ground and take a life… yes in revenge, if you like, but also as a prevention of this tragedy ever happening to someone else as a result of Groucher coming out of prison."

"So you think you can make a one man war?"

"War, crusade, mission. Call it what you like. Yes, I do think it's my personal war."

"You still haven't told me what you are thinking of doing."

"When are you going to Amsterdam for your final operation?"

"In two weeks time. But what's that got to do with any of this?"

"By the time you get back from Holland I think I will have put together my plan of action. Until then, I'll keep my thoughts to myself. Now let's finish our coffee and go for a walk in the park."

CHAPTER NINE   SHORE'S MOVE

DCI Shore was to become Detective Superintendent Shore - not before time as far as he was concerned. A man of 50 should probably already have made Commander or even Deputy Assistant Commissioner. Retirement age was supposed to be fifty-five so there weren't too many more years for him to progress through the ranks to increase his pension pot. Shore was a traditional Policeman and guessed that his passing over was more to do with positive discrimination towards minorities, including women, rather than his lack of ability to fill the role. Besides, part of him liked being more on the shop floor with his eager Inspector and the very capable sergeants and constables. He knew the more he climbed the promotional ladder, the more removed he would became from the reality of every day life and every day policing which he loved.

Shore wasn't particularly glad to leave Essex. He'd had some good times there, and he was also surprised to have made some real friends within the Force. He enjoyed summer days where scantily dressed young ladies would adorn the various sea fronts of the eastern coast. Yes, he loved the sea, 'and South Enfield Police Station certainly wasn't near to any water, unless you counted the covered reservoir next door to the station' he mused.

He was given the usual send-off at Southend, where the area Commander paid his respects in a speech about how the streets of coastline Essex were made safer as a result of his efforts. But as the lights dimmed and the hangover kicked in, he'd come to the realisation that the move to South Enfield not only meant a nice well-deserved pay rise, but also much more responsibility as the most senior head of CID. It would also give him the opportunity to address his past reticence in embracing new technology. Up until now he'd hidden behind the computer wizardry of the lower ranks, but now he had to face his technophobia head on.

The main reason for Shore's slower progress through the ranks was most certainly his rejection of new technology. He hadn't impressed one Commander after scoffing at the use of laser-beam recordings for taking fingerprints. He simply didn't feel comfortable unless the accused had his fingers and thumbs covered in black ink. Another senior officer turned against him when he'd said "DNA? Doesn't that stand for Dicks 'N' Arse sir?"

But now Shore had been given an irresistible opportunity. He had decided to embrace the idea of Internet Monitoring Rooms and would make it his priority to ensure that criminals were caught as a result. Of course, at first he had naturally rejected the idea of the internet having any use to Policing. It had taken a visit to his brother's house a few months earlier to change his mind. His niece Cheryl, a bubbly 15-year-old, had insisted on showing him how she could pretend to be a ballerina in a chat room and dragged her bored uncle up the stairs to her room towards the computer to demonstrate. Cheryl had broken her toe in a riding accident a couple of years earlier. Becoming a dancer had been her dream ever since she could remember, but the awkward fall from her horse had destroyed that ambition in a second. Shore sat next to her in her bedroom, fascinated by what unfolded on the flat screen in front of him. He couldn't believe that Cheryl not only had the gall and nerve to carry on a conversation with complete strangers across the world, but also that she could so blatantly lie about her circumstances, suggesting that she was in the Court de Ballet at the Royal Ballet, and that one day she would be a prima ballerina.

At first, Shore was concerned that his own niece might have been committing an offence, passing herself off as someone else, but then after further consideration, he realised the greater implications of her actions. Not that she was committing any offence, but that others could commit offences against her.

"Cheryl love, doesn't it bother you that you're lying to these people?"

"Don't worry Uncle Rob, it's just a laugh. Everyone's doing it and I don't think anyone tells the truth."

It was then in an instant, Shore realised the internet, whilst providing an infinite library of information for schools, was potentially a dangerous tool held in the wrong hands. It worried him that his 15-year-old niece could come into contact with who-knows-whom. From that point on, he decided to learn more about computers, the internet and their use. It was as a result of this study, that he obtained the promotion he'd been craving. The new job in South Enfield would have special duties over internet technologies and the Internet Monitoring Room of Enfield Prison.

Although it was effectively a management position, Shore insisted on visiting the IMR at Enfield Prison on a more regular basis than was expected - sometimes several times a week. He was amazed to watch the unfolding exploits of the prisoners, and he took the greatest pleasure in resolving a case, or preventing a crime from happening at all, by sanctioning operations directly resulting from the monitoring of prisoners. This was truly a wonderful advance in effective policing. Even he was ready to accept that fact.

During the first couple of months of his tenure, one particular case had given him the most pride, even fame. As far as the Public was concerned, it was good old-fashioned Policing that had won the day. The use of the IMR in crime solving was to remain strictly confidential and anyone involved now had to sign the Official Secrets Act.

Operation Tricorne was a sting totally under Shore's control. He had instigated it and co-ordinated it from its inception, to its ultimate conclusion. He had also been praised in the Press for its success, a rare feat for any Police officer to achieve.

Shore worked closely with SO6, and specifically the Arts and Antiques Unit within the Specialist Crime Operational Command Unit of the Metropolitan Police, based at Scotland Yard. Ordinarily, any case involving collectables or antiques would have been passed to this Unit, but the use of the IMR made things different. This was a new mode of Policing, and as the case was unfolding in South Enfield, it was Detective Superintendent Robert Shore who was going to take overall responsibility for its resolution.

Sergeant Morris had been 4 hours into his shift at the Enfield Prison IMR, when Johnny Graves, convicted fence or 'antique dealer to the stars' as he preferred to be known, took his 20 minute place on the computer connected to the internet in the Internet Room of the prison. The prisoners thought they were being clever by turning the monitor slightly so that it couldn't be viewed by passing officers. It was one of those slightly inferior flat screens that can only be properly viewed directly from the front. Only if someone was standing right besides or behind them could the contents on the screen be fully visible. Little did they know that every word, every image that was projected via 16 million colours of pixels onto the screen was in fact being closely watched by a Police officer in the basement of the jail. Behind a solid wall just a few yards from the kitchen where the prisoners' food was prepared, lay the IMR, the control room that represented the future of Policing.

Johnny Graves started his internet session harmlessly enough. At first he went to Sotheby's site and viewed the latest results from recent sales. His interests were wide and he was as happy to check on the status of Decorative Arts at Olympia, as he was viewing the Silver sales in Amsterdam or the Old Masters in Bond Street, London. Sometimes he would treat himself to an auction catalogue, and he'd often ingratiate himself with the other cons when he received catalogues with wide appeal, such as movie posters or football memorabilia, sharing them around and telling them about the value of all things rare. "Ten grand for an FA Cup winners medal, bloody hell!" and he knew they'd be a mate for life; at least for the life of his sentence anyway.

After viewing the Sotheby's site, he moved onto his e-mail account. There were twenty messages in his in-box. Four were from family members, his wife, two daughters and one from his son in Australia. He answered them all with the same style of message: loving yet matter of fact; looking forward to seeing them on the next visit; looking forward to getting out in fourteen months time, all being well. Fifteen messages contained the usual spam. Two from Nigeria looking to launder $38 million with his help, another five offering Viagra or penis enlargement, plus an assortment of prize draws, casino information, sex with dwarves and mortgage offers. He deleted them all.

The last message was from Archie McHarrigan, a virtual address not tied to anyone's home or workplace. The Police traced its origin to an internet café in central London.

"I've been offered something that may be interesting for you mate - do you want in? Reckon it's too specialist for me."

The sergeant saved this e-mail and sent it directly to the control room for internet operations at South Enfield.

"What do we know about Archie McHarrigan? Not exactly a common name." Shore was addressing his weekly IMR meeting.

DS Jones spoke first. "We've run a check on McHarrigan, and if it's the same bloke, he's got form sir. Petty stuff mostly. Theft of small artworks, antiques, the usual. Caught a couple of times on his way back from Bermondsey with some tasty silver bits and pieces in the back of his van."

"Good work. Keep a check on any further developments between McHarrigan and Graves. This could be interesting. Next on the agenda…"

Over the next few weeks the information gradually unfolded. Shore realised this was not only an opportunity to prove his abilities, but would also be a case that would cause a sensation throughout the media. It was a big one. He named it Operation Tricorne. The climactic day of the operation was one which started early with a full briefing to the team:

"Good morning everybody. After several weeks of monitoring the activities of Johnny Graves within Enfield Prison, and McHarrigan and other associates on the outside, Operation Tricorne today is coming to its conclusion. For those of you not up to speed with this operation, here are the details.

"Approximately 8 weeks ago, Graves was contacted by the known small-time criminal McHarrigan, who wanted to offer Graves a hat known as a tricorne. Unusual you may think, but this hat was rather special.

McHarrigan had made acquaintance with Italian criminals based in Rome who claimed to have discovered something significant. A three-cornered hat belonging to none other than the composer Mozart, with allegedly a manuscript of music rolled up into one of the three sides.

"At first, we naturally thought this was some kind of joke. That was until we contacted Commander Rodgers' brother, the Dean of Southwark Cathedral. He told me that in 1769, the composer Mozart, aged only 12, set out on the road on a 15-month tour of Italy with his father. By Easter 1770, they had arrived in Rome, and just like any other tourist, they visited St Peters, to celebrate the service and to listen to the famous Miserere, by the composer Allegri, sung in the Sistine Chapel. This piece of music was supposed to be so special, that the Pope had made it an offence for anyone to write the music down. That way, the only way the Miserere could be heard was at Easter in Rome. Anyway, to cut a longish story short, Mozart went back to their lodgings, wrote the music down that he had heard, then returned on Good Friday to make some corrections, storing the manuscript in his three-cornered tricorne hat. You can see where we're going now can't you?

"We know that he DID write the music down because a copy of a letter from Mozart's father Leopold to his wife, dated April 14th 1770 survives, and I have a translated copy of it here:

"You have often heard of the famous Miserere in Rome, which is so greatly prized that the performers are forbidden on pain of excommunication to take away a single part of it, or copy it or to give it to anyone. But we have it already. Wolfgang has written it down and we would have it sent to Salzburg in this letter if it were not necessary for us to be there to perform it. But it is in the manner of performance, which contributes more to its effect than the composition itself. Moreover, as it is one of the secrets of Rome, we do not wish to let it fall into other hands"

Shore placed the letter in the back of his cardboard file and continued.

"It has been suggested that a music historian, Sir Charles Burney took the manuscript from Mozart when they met, because following Burney's return to England the following year, the Miserere was printed several times. However, the truth is that the Mozart manuscript has never been found."

An inquisitive PC raised his hands nervously.

"Yes PC Roberts?"

"Sir, I just wondered, what would be the value of such a manuscript if it was found?"

"Good question. I can tell you that a few pages of the Marriage of Figaro sold in 2001 for over three-quarters of a million pounds, so it's not unreasonable to suggest that it could well approach a value of a million with this history attached. Not that most of the criminals we're dealing with know of the true value of what they're handling, of course. Graves certainly isn't letting on to his associates that he knows what the value could be. Perhaps he's keeping this close to his chest. I wouldn't be surprised.

"Or under his hat," DC Roberts piped in. Only he laughed.

"It appears that the tricorne hat, complete with the manuscript were found in a space behind a bedroom wall that was being pulled down, in a run-down hotel in central Rome. What seems to be the case is the manuscript was hidden by Mozart in his hat, because it was too hot to handle at the time. Excommunication from the church in those days was a serious matter. The Dean of Southwark supposes that Mozart was simply proving his abilities by writing down the piece that he heard in the Sistine Chapel, without thinking of the consequences at the time."

"So he was just a kid showing off?", another DC suggested.

Yeh, that's about right. He may have been a genius, but don't forget, he was only twelve years old. It's likely that his father made him hide the manuscript for collection at a later date, which of course he never did, for whatever reason.

"It's a fascinating story which has led the trail from a lodging house in Rome to our Johnny Graves in Enfield Prison. Operation Tricorne must result in the safe securing of the tricorne hat with manuscript and the custody of those persons responsible for the theft and smuggling of the manuscript. Needless to say we are working closely with the Arts and Antiques Unit at Scotland Yard, the Guardia Police in Rome and also the Vatican Police who have taken an interest in our operation.

"Who in the end has the right to ownership of the manuscript is not clear. I personally think the owner of the hotel has a pretty good claim. It seems the trail of discovery started with the builder in the hotel. But that's not for us to worry about."

In an operation that could never have been hatched had it not been for the Internet Monitoring Room, the Mozart Tricorne with manuscript was intercepted at Harwich harbour on a ferry from the Hook of Holland.

Archie McHarrigan was pretty smug. He boarded the ferry in Holland, knowing that in a few hours he would be meeting one of Graves' contacts who would exchange the little hat and manuscript stored in his sports bag, for a twenty grand bag of cash. 'Not bad for a single job' he thought.

Operation Tricorne had no jurisdiction to act in Holland or in the North Sea. Shore was determined to take McHarrigan and the manuscript successfully as soon as they landed in England. An advance team were sent ahead on the ferry: Detective Constable Jane Hobbs and Detective Sergeant Mark Ives. They knew that McHarrigan was taking the overnight ferry and it was likely that he would take a cabin. After all, he had a precious cargo to protect.

Jane Hobbs was absolutely beautiful. She knew it. Everyone knew it and Operation Tricorne was about to create a honey trap with a difference. They needed to separate McHarrigan from the manuscript in order to verify it was what they had hoped it would be.

The new ferries crossing the Channel and the North Sea were well equipped, even with swimming pool and steam room.

Jane Hobbs befriended McHarrigan as he was walking to the bar to collect a beer to take to his cabin. She bumped into him, as if by accident, and spilled her drink down her blouse. Immediately the pout, the red lips and the cleavage had him hooked. He was a fairly good-looking bloke, so why shouldn't this babe fancy him, he considered. He was on a roll.

"I'm so sorry dahlin'," he said. "Can I get you another drink, maybe help to clean up?"

"No it's OK," Jane pouted. "I don't really fancy another drink anyway. I split up with my boyfriend in Holland but I don't feel like getting drunk. Maybe something else…I haven't really looked around the boat yet."

"Oh yeh?" McHarrigan raised one eyebrow.

Suddenly composing herself, she worked her magic. "Look, I don't mean to be funny, but I don't know anyone on this bloody boat, do you fancy going for a swim downstairs?"

"What… in the pool?"

"Of course in the pool! I don't mean in the north sea."

As he stammered to find an answer, the adept female officer had already grabbed his arm and taken him towards the pool.

"I just fancy a swim with someone. And maybe a steam. That's all." She licked her lips.

They headed downstairs towards the pool and steam area, where they spent a happy 45 minutes swimming and steaming. 'Thank goodness there are kids in the steam room', DC Hobbs thought, 'at least McHarrigan won't be trying it on with me'.

During this time, Mark Ives of the specialist Art and Antiques Unit gained access to Grave's cabin.

"I'm in sir." He phoned back to South Enfield Police station on his satellite phone.

"I've found a sports bag and inside there are some clothes, toilet bag, a couple of dirty magazines, and…bingo. Here's the hat, in a carrier bag. It's really small, but then it's a kid's hat isn't it? Turning it over now. Hold on, I'm gonna put the phone down and see what's inside."

Ives turned the hat over and felt into the lining in each of the sides. The third time he got lucky, and pulled out a double width piece of handwritten music.

He picked the phone up.

"Bloody hell sir, this really looks like it. It's not signed. You wouldn't expect that like a painting, it doesn't even say Miserere at the top. That would be a bit of a giveaway. The words on the other hand...I had a close look at the Latin text of Psalm 51 yesterday, and it looks pretty much like it. It's also dated in the top corner. 1770."

"OK Ives, put it back, exactly as you found it and get out of there." Shore spluttered into the intercom that was echoing on loudspeaker in the office.

Jane Hobbs playfully flicked her white towel against McHarrigan and thanked him for showing her a good time, as she made her way towards the women's changing room.

"Don't you want a drink or something?" He called out to her.

Her work was done. She'd kept McHarrigan away from his cabin for long enough to know her colleague had checked out the goods. "No thanks. I'm feeling really tired now, I'll have a lie down in my cabin. Maybe see you later." She winked and walked away.

"You bet." McHarrigan was sure he was in there. He went to shower, tossed the towel into the basket, quickly dressed and returned to his cabin where he fell asleep in no time, dreaming of making his money and spending some of it on this woman who was clearly putty in his hands. Damn, he didn't even know her name.

From then on the operation was easy. McHarrigan became a sitting duck. The rest of the Tricorne team assembled at Harwich for the arrival of the ferry and promptly arrested McHarrigan with his historic bag of swag.

"How the fuck did you know?" McHarrigan spat at Shore.

Keen to protect the source of his success, Shore had no concerns about putting the cat amongst the pigeons.

"Let's just say one of your team's a grass. We've been following you for a while now McHarrigan. Get into the van. You're well and truly nicked."

The Press loved it. The story was sensational. *Police sting retrieves lost Mozart manuscript worth £1 million.* It ran and ran. In the meantime, Shore continued to use his internet monitoring team to greater and greater success - solving cases, preventing crimes and saving the nation a fortune in Police time. Everyone was happy except the criminals.

*****

Klarkey logged onto the AcrossTheDivide.org chatroom at the agreed time. Jamieson was waiting for him.

"Where you been?", Jamieson demanded.

"I'm not late am I?"

"No, you're alright, I'm just bored mate. And pissed off."

"What's up with you today?"

"Bloody Lorna's refusing to visit me. Can't even get any fags at the moment."

"That's a bummer. Look, how would you like me to visit you? I'm not doing any work at the moment and I could come up to Enfield easily enough. And I could bring you a carton of fags."

"What would you wanna do that for? Look mate, you've been good to me, chatting to me and all that. But I wouldn't have any way to pay you back. Not for a while yet anyway."

"Don't worry about that. To tell you the truth, I've been pretty bored myself lately. I wouldn't mind having something useful to do."

Klarkey persuaded Jamieson to think about sending him a Visiting Order. These weren't to be dished out to all and sundry. After all, he could only have one visitor per week, and he had to hold out hope that Lorna was going to come sometime soon. Even a visit from his mum would've been nice, but he hadn't seen her for a while. At least Klarkey could bring him in some prison currency - cigarettes.

Klarkey gave Jamieson the details he needed "*in case you want company*".

Jamieson signed off. Klarkey had found a way into Enfield Prison. His personal crusade was up and running.

CHAPTER TEN   VICTORY

It was a bright morning and the automatic telephone alarm woke Klarkey at 8.05 am. The radio kicked in and a rousing classical piece blared out. Klarkey had already given great consideration to the fact that 8.05 was better than 8 o'clock or 8.02, because at 8 he would wake up to the doom and gloom of the day from the morning news. 8.02 and the news would be finishing but the annoying adverts for selling endowment policies or for haemorrhoid treatments would ingratiate their jingles into his brain, refusing to leave his head for the rest of the day. So 8.05 was the perfect waking time; the news and adverts over, and only music to lead his mind from slumber to wake.

Klarkey slid out of bed, grabbed an orange juice from the mini bar and banged on Matisse's door hard, entering without waiting for an answer.

Matisse was spread out across the bed in an oversized Mickey Mouse T-shirt, hair spread in different directions as if her body had been connected to an electric current.

"Wake up Matisse, we're off to do YOUR day today."

"Huh?" She stirred.

"I said we're doing what YOU want to do today. We're going to see some history. Some old ships, the sea, whatever you want."

"Really?" Her eyebrows looked up but her eyes were still closed.

Klarkey turned around returning to his room as he spoke.

"We're going in 30 minutes. HURRY UP!"

Thirty-two minutes later, they were both dressed and ready to leave.

"What about breakfast? Klarkey, I'm hungry"

"We'll get something at the station."

"Station? You mean we're travelling by train? Will it ever arrive?"

"Don't be cheeky my love. British trains aren't that bad you know. And I'll tell you something for nothing: the stations are much better than in France. Give me Waterloo any day rather than crappy Paris Nord."

"Ppphhh" Matisse exhaled a typically French lip splutter, raising her arms at the same time. By now the pair were in the street and Klarkey whistled for a cab. Miraculously one arrived on cue.

Klarkey leaned through the front offside window, "Waterloo Station please."

"Jump in", the driver said.

Fortunately the driver left them to their own conversation as they weaved in and out of the bus lanes during the twenty-minute journey to the station. If Klarkey heard another cab driver's conversation about politics, the problems of being overrun by asylum seekers or which celebrity he'd had in the back of his cab...

Fortunately the next words the driver said were "That'll be ten pounds eighty please my friend."

Klarkey was pleased to give the driver a generous fifteen pounds just for the pleasure of a peaceful journey.

Waterloo was a station Klarkey knew well. After all, it had been the receiving point for his people smuggling operation. That seemed an age away, even though he'd closed it down just a few months ago. The station was huge, not only accommodating the European trains, but also a vast array of south of England trains fanning out from the Victorian part of this south London hub. St Pancras in north London was still a long way from becoming the new terminus for the European trains. Klarkey led Matisse along the concourse to check on the times of the trains. They had about 25 minutes to wait before the next fast train to Portsmouth Harbour.

"Let's get our tickets and have some breakfast."

"I thought you'd never let me eat. Do I look like I need to fast?" She put her hands round her waist as if to express pride in her slightness.

Coffee and various almond and chocolate croissants later, Klarkey and Matisse headed towards the train, boarding the first class carriage.

"You know…train travel in this country is SO expensive Klarkey. Here we are in first class and for three times the price of the second class ticket you get a few less seats and a white tea towel over the head rest."

"Have you finished?"

Matisse tutted as they sat down opposite a petite elegant-looking woman in her 30s.

"I suppose at least there are no kids here in first class."

The woman opposite smiled and half looked up.

"Sorry did my tactless friend offend you?" Klarkey said apologetically to the woman.

"No not at all. I'm a teacher. That's why I'm travelling first class today. It's a treat. To avoid sitting amongst lots of children. Your friend caught my mood exactly."

"That's OK then. I'm Klarkey and this is Matisse Espère." They both extended their hands and laughed at the same time.

"Pleased to meet you. I'm Roberta Green."

Roberta looked smart in a twin-set lavender suit. A high street tailored suit which she was perhaps a little young to wear. Klarkey's eyes lingered on her face. Matisse noticed her shoes. They were expensive. Slim, small feet in zebra print sling-backs. Maybe Manolo but could be Prada. One thing Matisse couldn't change about herself was her feet. She was always a little jealous of women with small feet. She had read in one of her magazines about a new Los Angeles trend for foot surgery. She made a mental note to investigate at a later time.

Matisse was quite happy to get into conversation with a new person. It made a change to speak to someone other than Klarkey. But she was keen to steer the conversation away from work issues. Whilst the woman had already revealed she was a teacher, Matisse hadn't considered exactly what she should tell people she did for a living. She was certainly not an exotic dancer any more, nor a receptionist. Companion perhaps, or maybe just personal assistant. Her exact position was something she had avoided discussing even with Klarkey. She loved the English expression "going with the flow", as that was exactly what she had been doing for the past few months.

"How long is the journey to Portsmouth Harbour?" Matisse finally settled on the subject of travel.

"Oh, it's about one hour and forty minutes. Not too long. My stop is just before, at Portsmouth and Southsea. I'm on my way home from having done some research at the National Gallery. I teach art at the sixth form college."

"We're going to see the ships in the harbour. Have you been?"

"Oh yes!" Roberta enthused. "The exhibition is excellent. You'll really enjoy it."

The next hour and a half was spent enthusing about the history locked inside the cities outside of London. Meanwhile, Woking, Guildford and Petersfield stations flew past them. Matisse went to the lavatory a couple of times, and each time Klarkey found himself lustfully staring and chatting with Roberta. He didn't feel shy with her, but at the same time he didn't have the confidence to ask her out. Before long they had arrived at Portsmouth and Southsea Station.

"Well this is me. It was so nice to meet you. Goodbye."

Roberta shook both of their hands and climbed out of the train, waving goodbye as she walked along the platform.

"Nice lady" Matisse said.

"Yes, very nice." Klarkey nodded, stretching his lower lip up into his upper lip, keeping his stare fixed on Roberta walking along the platform.

"I think you liked her, no?"

"Matisse! She was just nice to talk to." Klarkey released a rare half-blush.

"OK. Whatever!"

The train moved off and a few minutes later they arrived at Portsmouth Harbour.

"Oh look," Matisse cooed, bouncing up and down on her knees on her seat like an excited schoolgirl, "I can see the masts of a ship!"

"You'll see more of that a bit later. Let's grab a cab to the hotel and we'll come back here when we've off-loaded our bags."

Another few minutes later, the cab arrived at the Queens Hotel on the sea front.

"This is nice, look at the ceiling Klarkey."

They sat down in the reception area next to a large pane of etched glass.

"You see this image on the glass Matisse, it's The Victory. That's the ship that Admiral Nelson fought and died on, against the French I'm afraid, and that's the ship you saw in the harbour."

"It's so exciting."

"Over two hundred years of history. You'll see."

After freshening up in their rooms, they walked towards the seafront.

"Matisse," Klarkey said unusually tentatively,

"Yes darling?"

"Have you ever felt so mad you could kill someone?"

"What?! Where on earth did that come from?"

"No I'm serious. Has anyone ever bothered you so much that you feel you have the right or at least the passionate desire to kill someone?"

"I'm not sure. I don't think so. Haven't we been here before?"

They continued walking, past young children eating candyfloss and their parents tucking into paper bags of seaside fudge.

"What I'm really saying, is: Do you think that killing someone could ever be justified? Let's look back to the Second World War again. If you knew that killing Hitler and his cabinet in 1939 could have stopped the invasion of France do you think it would be justified?"

"Well if you put it like that. I suppose so. But don't you think we make these opinions only with the benefit of hindsight. Perhaps my grandparents in France during 1939 did not have had such a bad opinion of Hitler. It was really only after the invasion, and then especially after the war that we realised how bad the Germans truly were."

They passed a group of lads playing football on the Common, and walked towards the screams emanating from the rides within the funfair.

"So what do you think of revenge? Didn't the mobs go after the collaborators in France after the war? Didn't they shave the heads of the women that slept with the German officers and string them up? Isn't it right to take revenge on those that do ill to us."

Matisse laughed. "If I was a good Catholic I would say that we should forgive those that do ill towards us. But it's not so easy is it? Sometimes we have to take actions because of how we feel."

"That's true. I've come to believe that I have the right to take revenge upon those that do us harm. But also I believe that sometimes we must take control of a situation and act to prevent some people from doing things that will harm us or our communities."

"Klarkey, that's pretty deep. But I think I see where you're coming from. Is this anything to do with your sister?"

"I'm sorry to bring it up again. Does this kind of talk bother you?"

"It's not such a problem. If it wasn't anything to do with your sister I'd be worried you were some kind of psychopath."

They turned into the harbour where the historical dockyard and its maritime museum presented in from of them.

Klarkey paid the entrance fee and they passed through the turnstile, taking a left turn towards HMS Warrior.

"It's like a prison down here," Klarkey ventured as clunkety-clunk they walked below the deck.

Along with a few other visitors who had gathered, a member of the crew met them,

"Good morning ladies and gentlemen and welcome to HMS Warrior, Britain's first iron-hulled, armoured battleship. Launched in December 1860, during one of the Kingdom's coldest Winters, the ship refused to budge through the frozen waters of the dockyard, which had to be pulled by extra tugs and hydraulics to free her by rocking the ship from side to side."

Klarkey and Matisse listened and moved on. The internal areas of the ship didn't particularly impress them.

"I suppose this must have been amazing in its time, but it just looks like a load of metal with rivets to me. I can't say I'm excited by it."

"OK, let's go somewhere else"

They left the Warrior and made their way towards HMS Victory.

"This is more like it," Matisse gasped. "A wooden ship… so magnificent."

"Even if it did beat off the French?" Klarkey laughed.

"Let's get on board."

The first thing they both sensed when they boarded was the smell.

"Mmm". Klarkey twitched his nose.

"Oh, can you smell old age?"

"I can smell wood and old rope I think, plus maybe an old sooty kind of smell."

"Do you think that could be the guns? After all these years?"

"Look how low the ceilings are. They must have been very short people in those days."

"Well your Napoleon was short. I'm sure our people were just as tiny."

Matisse nodded.

They took their time to look around the ship, marvelling at the capstan, the huge anchors and the miles of rope and sails. They observed the spot deep below deck where Lord Nelson died, and took a moment to observe the plaque on the open deck indicating where he first fell.

"This is so amazing, I'm fascinated by the history of this ship and Nelson. The whole romantic story of Lady Hamilton and Nelson's bravery." Matisse was genuinely enthralled.

"I'm sure Lady Nelson didn't think it was so romantic."

Klarkey had to wrench Matisse away from the ship. With a large sigh, they sat down together on a bench tucking into a 99 ice cream with a double flake.

"Were you serious about revenge and taking action against those that harm you?"

"Of course." Klarkey picked one of the flakes out of the cream and sucked the end to create a spear shape.

"So what do you intend to do?"

"I have every intention of killing the bastard that killed my sister. And if anyone else gets killed in the process, that's too bad."

"You're not serious! It doesn't seem in your nature to behave in that way."

Klarkey licked the escaping ice cream from the edge of his cone and tried to speak at the same time.

"How do you know what's in my nature?"

"Calm down darling. Why are you so argumentative today?"

"I don't know, I have lots on my mind."

"Well you can stop talking about killing people to start with. I was with you 100 per cent when you chose to help people through the Grosvenor School. Yes it was illegal, but we helped people who really wanted to make something of their lives. But if you start talking about killing people, I don't know how I'll react." She shook her head.

"Let's leave it for now. Come on, you HAVE to see the Mary Rose."

He stood up from the bench he was straddling and tossed the base of the ice cream cone into the bin. "It was King Henry's warship and was raised from the bottom of the harbour. They're still spraying it with a fine mist of water to preserve it.

"So much history, my God."

Matisse wiped her hands on a handkerchief and headed towards the Mary Rose exhibition.

Inside, they peered through the steamed up plastic sheeting and marvelled at the 400 year old warship that sunk in the harbour close by.

"It was overloaded you know, and couldn't cope."

"That sounds like your mind at the moment. I'm really worried about you."

A chattering family with a teenage son in a wheelchair squeezed past them, staring at the mist pouring around the ancient timbers.

"Let's not talk here any more. We'll discuss this later."

They took the exit and squinted as they came back into sunlight. Two hours had passed and their legs were tiring.

"Why don't we go to the loo and then have a look at the museum before we go back to the hotel," suggested Klarkey.

Matisse sat down in the cubicle and looked forward to the day when she would pee like a real woman. This was something almost everyone in the world took for granted but it was different for her. She looked down at her genitals and dreamed of the day when they would be transformed. She hated looking down there, but she was distracted by Klarkey's line of conversation earlier. She knew that when Klarkey became fixated about doing something there was no stopping him. Mon Dieu, what was he going to do? She shuddered with the thought, blew her nose with some toilet paper, and washed her hands before meeting Klarkey outside.

"I've just been looking at the map of the museums here and I think the Nelson exhibition is definitely for you."

Passing into the Royal Naval Museum, Matisse was inspired by the Nelson collection.

"Klarkey! I have decided I am going to become a collector of Nelsoniana."

"A what?"

"A Nelsoniana collector. That's someone who collects memorabilia related to Nelson. Look at these wonderful pieces. There are mugs and plates, paintings and fantastic miniatures. Klarkey, look at the miniatures." She gushed.

Klarkey appreciated the pieces were very nice. This was without question. But he found it difficult to get too excited over them. It just wasn't his thing.

"Honey," Matisse continued, " I've never really owned anything of real beauty in my life, apart from my cat which you made me leave in France, DON'T FORGET. I've never really collected anything or been interested in collecting anything. At least you can appreciate I now have an interest?"

"OK, ok, I do," Klarkey smiled and acknowledged her insistence. After all, he could hardly reject her passion for the museum pieces when he had been such a dedicated postal history collector: a subject he knew most people would find completely dull. Furthermore, he considered Nelsoniana was likely to increase in value over time, so he came to accept his best friend's new passion. Matisse pulled a face.

"I really DO," Klarkey emphasised. "Let's see if we can find you something in London. Now can we go?"

With a spring in her step, Matisse grabbed Klarkey's arm and they made their way out of the dockyard to find a cab to take them back to the hotel.

*****

The sun started to fade over the harbour and Matisse and Klarkey decided upon a walk-and-talk, fish-and-chip dinner along the sea front. They smiled at each other as they ate. The waves crashed onto the old castle ramparts and the Isle of Wight hovercraft mounted and departed the stony beach close by.

As the evening became a little chillier, they headed back towards the hotel and into their suite where Matisse slid onto the sofa and switched on the television to catch the late evening news. Klarkey went straight into the bathroom to remove the lingering smell of tomato sauce from his fingers.

"KLARKEY KLARKEY." Matisse shrieked.

Klarkey bounded into the room with his hands dripping, nearly tripping over the white towel that he was holding in his right hand.

"Look!"

They both stared at the screen listening intently, looking at a photograph of Roberta Green, pasted to the corner of the screen behind the newsreader.

"...and the victim has been confirmed as local teacher, Roberta Green, the subject of the latest vicious attack in the precinct this morning, following her arrival on a train from London. Despite being in broad daylight, a gang of bag-snatchers attacked Ms Green from behind and it appears a struggle ensued. Whilst Ms Green is in a critical condition at Queen Mary Hospital, she is now stable. Police inform

113

us that these incidents are becoming all too regular, and whilst they hope to apprehend those responsible, they say resources are stretched to the limit and it remains difficult to Police all areas of the City effectively. Portsmouth City Council has now approved CCTV installation and it is hoped these attacks will come to an end when the cameras becomes operational. Now we go over to Jeremy at the sports desk for the latest football update, and then we will return to the national news."

Klarkey grabbed the handset, switched off the TV with the standby button and banged his hand down on the top of the writing desk behind the sofa.

"SSHHIITTT!"

"I just don't believe it. She was so nice. Is so nice." Matisse put her palms to her forehead.

Klarkey was shaking. He ripped his mobile phone from his belt and screamed to Matisse to pass him the telephone book by the side of one of the beds. He vigorously turned the pages, ripping some of them as he forced his way to the letter Q. On finding the number for the hospital, he dialled the number and waited.

"Come on...come on....why do they take so long to answer these...Oh hello, I need to find out how Ms Roberta Green is please...no I'm not a relative...I'm a friend. What does stable mean? OK OK. Can I visit her? Is that possible? Oh I see. I see. Thank you very much." He clicked off.

"Well?"

"Only her closest family are allowed there. She's stable. They won't say what that means... just that she's not getting worse. They won't let us see her."

"We should call again tomorrow, maybe there will be more news then."

"Maybe. There's no way I'm going to be able to sleep now. I'm going to the gym."

Klarkey threw open his case and dug out a pair of shorts and a pair of red football socks, not just in homage to Paris St Germain, but also a colour that reflected the rage he felt at that moment. He dressed, pulling on a loose T-shirt and took strides down the corridor towards the in-house gym.

He started with the multi-gym weights; shoulder presses pushing and pushing upwards, jerking the bar in anger; veins in the side of his head, popping out; sweat pouring into his T-shirt and down his legs. Staring ahead, he tried not to think of anything, nor how angry he was feeling.

After making his way around the machines and feeling slightly light-headed as he got up, he asked the receptionist if he could take a sun bed. Fortunately it was available. Most people were retired to their rooms by now and the gym was ready to close.

Klarkey threw his towel onto the wicker chair in the corner, grabbed a handful of paper towels from the dispenser and sprayed with disinfectant, the Perspex bed on which he was about to lie. After wiping the flatbed clean, he slipped off his T-shirt, trainers and socks and lay motionless on the cold slab. Pressing the start button and closing his eyes, the machine powered up and the individual long UV lights ping-pinged into action above and below him. He took a deep breath and let himself drift into thought for the first time since he'd seen the local news on the television thirty-five minutes earlier.

At first he couldn't think of what happened to Roberta. His mind drifted back many years to his childhood. To the pain he felt when he lost his sister, and to the anger he felt at not being able to do anything practical. His chest felt tight and uncomfortable, but this was eased slightly as the light tubes heated his bed, giving his skin a warm glow.

He had already decided what to do about his sister's killer, but he now considered taking action elsewhere.

Revenge, justice, punishment. It was time to make those criminals, who inflict pain and suffering on others, become victims themselves. Make them feel real pain. Stop them laughing.

He had already considered how he would test run his attack on his sister's killer. He had also already worked out how he would revenge a terrifying ordeal that two of his old university friends had experienced some months earlier outside a nightclub in south London.

He now had a third mission to make. He would revenge the attack on Roberta. Perhaps then she may even come to love him? He could take care of her.

Klarkey sighed, and then clenched his fists in anticipation of planning his next series of exploits. The sun bed clicked off and the lights faded down. Klarkey lay there for a few seconds without moving, but as the pools of sweat behind his back and calves started to cool, he swung himself round and wiped himself, then the bed with his towel. Gathering his things, he nodded to the receptionist, who was pursing her lips and jangling her keys clearly desperate to close up, and then he returned to the room, ready to sleep, comfortable in the knowledge that the basis of a plan of action had been made. Tomorrow he would start to work out how he could achieve his goals and get away with it. He knew with the right planning, he could do anything. And he believed he held the moral high ground, so felt no qualms in hurting others. As he bounded up the stairs towards his room his resolve was strengthened as he thought of his teenage bible studies, *"...thou shalt give life for life, eye for eye, tooth for tooth, hand for hand, foot for foot, burning for burning, wound for wound, stripe for stripe."*

CHAPTER ELEVEN   THE VISIT

Klarkey had set up an anonymous post office box when he came to London. He wasn't sure where he was going to live in the long term; also it removed any identification of his true whereabouts. That was important to him.

Earlier that week he had travelled as usual to the non-descript Holborn address where he would pick up his mail from time-to-time, and there it was: A single item of mail in a cheap manila envelope with an EN postcode. Enfield. He didn't know anyone in Enfield and knew instantly it was from Jamieson in the prison.

Klarkey had been corresponding by e-mail messenger for a few weeks now, and had become quite close to his new friend, so Jamieson believed. Klarkey despised him. But he knew that his friendship with Jamieson had a purpose. Jamieson was going to help him and he wasn't even aware of it. Jamieson was going to provide him with information and a route to achieve his goal.

"Thanks Mr Stevens." The receptionist waved at Klarkey as he bounded out of the door with his letter.

Klarkey had called himself Sam Stevens for the purposes of mail collection and in his discussions with prisoners on the internet. There was no sense in leading a trail to his real name. 'Leave no stone unturned' was one of his many mottos. Sam Stevens was in homage to his favourite TV programme that he watched as a child, *Bewitched*. This was the series where an earthly witch, Samantha Stevens, would twitch her nose and perform spells at a seconds notice. She had the power to transform herself through time, become animals or objects, move into any location on the planet, and even become invisible. 'A little bit of power like that could come in very handy' he often thought. This was one of the many television series whose memories stayed with a person forever, forming part of someone's cultural background. It was one of those elements that united people of a similar age when discussing childhood. For Klarkey, it was also one of the few American TV series that he saw in Kingston as a child, then again in France, dubbed into French. It really did leave a lasting impression. So for mail purposes he would become Sam Stevens - he could hardly call himself Samantha Stevens, so he settled on Sam.

As he left the building and passed down the steps back into High Holborn, he thought about this area of central London, where he'd spent of a lot of time in one of his summer holidays as a teenager. He looked down towards Aldwych along Kingsway, and smiled, thinking how hard he worked studying the births, marriages and death records when he had exorcised a fixation about researching his family tree. Day after day in St Catherine's House checking through the huge volumes of births and marriages, in the hand-scribed vellum pages from 1837 onwards, then popping across the road into Kingsway to Alexandra House to view the black volumes of deaths. All that had changed now. The records were all combined in the swanky Family Records Office in Islington. They could even be accessed on the internet. He shook his head and smiled. Part of him was simply amazed how studious he was in those days - even in the summer holidays. Another part of him wished he'd been a little wayward like his contemporaries and not such a geek.

By now he was on a bus heading west and he'd opened the envelope. Sure enough it was the expected Visiting Order from Jamieson.

Klarkey's mobile buzzed and tweeted with the sound of an incoming text. *Still Shopping.* He didn't need to check whether Matisse sent the message. That was plainly obvious.

He stared out of the window of the bus. Trafalgar Square, the Houses of Parliament and back into Kensington.

His eyelids were heavy and he was flying again. Charlotte was holding his hand and she was free.

He opened his eyes and refocused.

What was he going to say to Jamieson? Had he really become such a cold and calculating person as this? He would have to stay focused. Fixed on his ultimate mission of revenge. Damn whoever got hurt on the way.

*****

Matisse wasn't really out shopping today. It was certainly true that most days were filled with shopping, but today was her regular visit to a specialist beauty centre. It was electrolysis day.

Marj was a well-built woman, in her twenties wearing fashionable spectacles. She had a warm smile.

"Nice to see you Matisse. Please have a seat."

"Thank you." Matisse lay on the couch.

Marj studied her paperwork. "So today we're going to give you a facial and genital electrolysis session. Is that right?"

"Yes. Can you do my face first?"

"Naturally. Have you been having the procedure for very long?"

"Oh for about 8 months or so in France. You can see my hairs now are very fine. There are hardly any course ones left."

Marj stared closely at her face with an additional eyeglass over one of her lenses.

"Yes I can see that quite clearly. Not too much work to do. I presume you've had some anaesthetic cream on for a while?"

"I live just around the corner and I've had the cream on for about an hour."

"Good." Marj nodded with a clipped voice. She then set about her business. Each hair in Matisse's face was individually plucked and burned with the specialist instrument down to the root of the follicle.

After about an hour, red-faced, Matisse took a deep breath and prepared for the remainder of her treatment.

Two chains hung from the ceiling towards the end of the couch. At the end of each chain were cuffs for the ankles. Matisse could only think of some of the museums of torture fashionable in many of the capitals of Europe. Having removed her lower clothing, Matisse raised her legs and Marj gently placed the ankles into the cuffs and closed the buckle. Then she went back to work, removing the hairs from the small testicles and penis that Matisse looked forward to having removed.

Marj gave Matisse a hand-towel and she patted her perspiring face. Despite the anaesthetic cream, she still felt much pain.

*****

The day for the prison visit arrived, and Klarkey treated himself to a hire car for the day. BMW delivered a smart new 5 series to the door: Black sapphire metallic paintwork, black Dakota leather seats, xenon headlights and a smart navigation system that would take him to wherever he wanted at his command. Klarkey loved the luxuries in life - occasionally. He would never describe himself as an extravagant person, however much money he had, although he did enjoy the finer things in life from time to time. It was his choice to appreciate certain luxuries on rare occasions, so he could really appreciate them. This day was one of those times. He slid into the vehicle, set the seat adjustment to fit his body, placed Beethoven's Emperor piano concerto into the CD player, and glided out of the parking space into the chaotic London traffic.

The I-drive navigator had told him the journey would be 14.3 miles. At his current speed the vehicle estimated the journey would take about an hour and a half.

An hour and twenty minutes later, Klarkey pulled up outside the austere outer walls of the Victorian Enfield Prison, feeling relaxed and able to face what lay ahead. He needed to tune his mind to remembering every aspect of this visit.

A private prison road ran alongside the tall prison walls, at the end of which was the public entrance. Before passing down this road he went into a newsagents opposite the prison and purchased a carton of Benson and Hedges cigarettes to satisfy Jamieson. Prison currency. He picked up some dark chocolate while he was there for the visit. 'Everyone likes chocolate don't they?' he thought.

Then Klarkey walked down the road towards the entrance. The sound of the road echoed against the tall grey bulbous-topped wall running along the side of the prison, and he passed some depressing looking flats on the other side that he assumed were for the prison officers who lived on site. 'Poor bastards', he thought.

Approaching the public entrance he passed through a double door, then an airport type X-ray machine. An officer instructed him to place his jacket and the parcel he'd brought in for Jamieson onto the rubber conveyor belt.

"This is for my friend," Klarkey said pointing at the carton of cigarettes.

"Don't worry mate, we'll see he gets it." The booming Glaswegian officer yelled at him, speaking from the corner of his mouth. "Can I see your visiting order please sir?"

Klarkey showed the officer the green piece of paper.

"OK my friend. We'll pass these onto Jamieson. Let's hope he stops moping around after he gets them."

"I've brought some chocolate to have during the visit if that's ok?"

"Nae bother, just put it on the belt and walk forward through the door frame."

Klarkey looked a little quizzical. What? Did they think he'd secreted a nail file into a small bar of Bourneville? He did as he was told nevertheless.

He was then led into a large well-lit room, and instructed to sit at a booth set in a long curved line of booths, where about 15 were occupied, mostly by women, some with young children, and a couple with crying babies.

Just as he sat down on the hard grey plastic seat, a group of men, dressed in jeans and striped blue shirts, passed through black iron gates from behind the line of booths, led by two officers. Everyone knew where to go and whom they were meeting. Jamieson was led towards Klarkey and they shook hands. He didn't want to give the impression to the officers that he didn't know Jamieson. They had spoken many times across a typed screen, but no photographs were exchanged so they had no idea what each other looked like.

Klarkey eyed him up very quickly. He noticed Jamieson was slightly taller than he was, and thicker set. His hair was long, pulled back into a ponytail and he had one of those goatee beards that used to be popular, but probably still were in the fashion-free world of prison.

"Sit down mate. Cheers for coming." Jamieson beckoned towards Klarkey's chair.

"No problem." Klarkey smiled, trying to be friendly, but not really caring about Jamieson at all.

"Did you bring me fags?"

"Yeh I did." Klarkey pointed to the entrance of the room. "They took them off me when I came in but said you'd get them."

"Cheers for that. Was it a carton?"

"Of course."

"Nice one. B & H?"

"Yep." Klarkey nodded.

"Thanks mate. It's really good of you." Jamieson extended his hand and Klarkey shook it. There was silence for a couple of seconds.

"Do you want some chocolate? I thought we could have some during the visit."

"Wicked. You're a real mate you know Sam."

"Don't mention it."

They tucked into the chocolate. Jamieson carefully bit round each square, like he was biting a fingernail, savouring every miniscule bite of the nectar that it was.

"Did you call Lorna for me?"

"I did yes. It took a couple of goes before she'd listen to me. But I passed on your message. She didn't say much except...well, she started crying. She's not been to see you I suppose?"

"No. I hoped she'd come today. No offence mind. I just thought she might have come by now."

"Don't worry mate. She will."

Despite their many conversations over the internet, this first meeting was as if they'd never spoken before. Speaking through typing was clearly no substitute for a meeting face to face. After about fifteen minutes of small talk about prison food, Lorna, using the internet in prison and more Lorna, Klarkey felt able to aim the conversation towards his goal.

"So what are the other blokes like in here then? They treat you alright?"

"Yeh, not too bad at all." Jamieson nodded and raised his eyebrows at the same time, which made his ponytail bob up and down as if he was a horse preparing to make a jump. "Coz I robbed a bank they give me respect." He lowered his voice "Pathetic ain't it? But I'm not complaining. Better that than being shat on coz you've done a kid or beaten up an old dear."

"Are there many people here that have done kids? Nonces I mean."

"Not too many. They keep them away from all of us lot anyway."

"I s'pose most of them are lifers aren't they?"

"I s'pose so. The ones that killed anyway."

Klarkey decided to seize his chance.

"You get much trouble with the nonces then?"

"Why you so bloody interested in the nonces?"

"Just interested that's all"

"Well you know some of them are famous. Some get fucking fan mail. Can you believe that?"

"You're joking."

"No really. There's that Singh geezer who killed the white lad that stabbed his son. He's always getting mail. Then there's Groucher, he's always getting visitors. I told my cellmate that I reckon he's going for parole but he's got no chance. Bloody child killer."

Klarkey felt sick. He almost had to stop himself from running outside for air, but he held himself together. It was very strange to hear someone, anyone else talking about Groucher as a real person. Up until now he had been quite remote; a mythical character that had torn apart his family; someone who was written about and locked away. He certainly didn't consider Groucher having feelings or behaving like any normal human being.

"This Groucher," Klarkey started tentatively, "does anyone think he'll get out?"

"He's supposed to be out in a couple of years so I don't reckon he'll be out early, but they have to do what they call 'rehabilitation'. That's just bollocks for making sure he don't kill again and learns how to buy a pint of milk in the local shop without upsetting anyone."

"How can anyone be sure he won't kill again? Is that possible?"

"I don't bloody know. That's like saying how does anyone know I won't rob a bank again. Even I can't be sure of that."

"You mean anyone might re-offend if they become desperate enough?"

"I suppose. I'd rob if I was desperate for money, same as Groucher might do a kid if he was needing to perv."

Klarkey really was going to be sick now.

"Look mate, I've got to go. I reckon I had a dodgy prawn sandwich and it's gone to my guts," Klarkey started out of his chair and Jamieson stood up.

"OK Sam, cheers for coming and thanks for the fags, come again yeh?"

"Oh yeh, you can be sure of that."

Klarkey rushed to the doors, pushed his way through the security doors and into the fresh air. He vomited against the sidewall into a drain. He couldn't help himself. A tall young woman with a baby strapped to her in a papoose was about to enter the prison for a visit. She came over to Klarkey and handed him a tissue pulled from the sleeve of her cardigan.

"Here you are love, it gets to you sometimes don't it?"

"Yeh thanks." Klarkey looked up through bloodshot eyes and blew his nose. The woman went inside and Klarkey made his way back to the car.

This had been a cathartic experience, but rather than bringing closure to his inner pain, it gave him more of a resolve than ever to continue with his plan.

CHAPTER TWELVE   TIME FOR CHANGE

Matisse kissed Klarkey on three cheeks: Dutch style. Then they hugged. It was a chilly but sunny autumnal day, and the night's rain was now reflecting off the cobbled stones in the small mews street they called home.

"I'll call you every day Matisse. I'm sure everything will go smoothly."

"Let's hope the surgeon gives me a beautiful crotch huh?"

"Matisse! I'm glad you can see the funny side of this. It's such a big step."

"Ah...but that's where you're wrong. You may screw your face up in horror at the thought of what I'm doing, but for me it's the most natural thing in the world."

The black cab pulled up in front of the hotel, announcing itself with screeching brakes, despite driving slowly.

"I wish YOU luck too Klarkey. Let's hope your auction makes you lots of lovely money."

Klarkey opened the rear door of the cab whilst the driver lifted Matisse's red Samsonite into the front luggage space.

"If I'm honest, I would say I'm pretty nervous about the sale."

Matisse playfully rubbed Klarkey's head through the window with her left hand, while her right buckled the seatbelt into place.

"I'd have to admit to being anxious too, " she whispered. Then turning to the driver, "Heathrow Terminal 4 please."

The cab drove off and Klarkey waved to Matisse like a child would see off a loving relative. He shivered realising he was only dressed in a short-sleeved shirt, and then rushed inside the hotel, up to their suite, tossing his shoes and trousers onto the floor going straight to bed whilst wrapping the duvet tight around himself to regain body heat. He contemplated briefly how important the next day was for both of them, and decided not to worry any more, drifting slowly back to sleep, letting images of the warm sea by his mother's cottage fill his dreaming mind.

The journey to Heathrow was uneventful and quick.

It never ceased to amaze Matisse that so many different cultures were so close together in Europe, separated by aeroplane journeys of less than an hour. It seemed like the KLM flight had only just reached its cruising altitude, only to start its descent towards Schiphol Airport near Amsterdam.

Despite being a small country, The Netherlands was blessed with a huge hub in Schiphol. It competed well in the international battle for airport supremacy, in size, passenger numbers and shopping opportunities.

Matisse made a mental note to buy or certainly to have a look at the diamonds at the Diamant counter on her way back to London. 'If I'm going to kill time at an airport I might as well spend it shopping for diamonds', she thought to herself as the black Mercedes cab pulled away from the airport heading towards the spidery network of canals that was central Amsterdam.

Matisse was looking forward to meeting Dr Van der Vogel again. Although she'd only met him once in Dr Hervé's practice in Paris, she felt confident in him because he had a warm smile and soft hands. These qualities satisfied Matisse and the fact that no one had ever died on his operating table was also a comfort. Dr Van der Vogel worked out of a small private hospital on the Prinsengracht, not far from Anne Frank's house, and Matisse looked forward to settling into her room and completing her transformation.

On arrival at the Queen Wilhelmina Hospital, Matisse felt a sense of dread. She knew what was to come and the thought had started to give her butterflies deep in her stomach. She wasn't having second thoughts, just apprehensions about the operation and how her life might be following it. There was no going back - this wasn't a vasectomy that could be reversed. This was the fundamental removal of the penis, castration and restructuring of the scrotum to form a vagina. There was no euphemistic way to express what was about to happen and the seriousness of this situation finally hit Matisse as she took the six steps up to the entrance of the red-brick hospital.

A beaming blonde nurse wearing a crisp white uniform took Matisse to her room.

" It's beautiful, like a hotel. And the view!" Matisse was genuinely delighted.

"Oh yes. It is more like a hotel in this hospital. It is our policy to make you as comfortable as possible. The Doctor will see you shortly. Then you can take a walk if you like outside. After all you will be here in this room for about 7 days."

Matisse gazed out of the window at the canal, fixing her eyes on a young couple riding pedaloes on the water.

"If you need anything, dial 100 on your phone."

The nurse left the room and Matisse sat down on the bed and spoke out loud to herself.

"It's really happening. At last!"

Matisse opened her leather handbag and pulled from it a small box that used to carry expensive dark chocolates. Carefully opening the lid she looked inside and smiled. She hadn't many possessions left from her youth, and she ran her hands over the beautiful amber necklace with its matching earrings that used to belong to her grandmother. She had vowed to wear them when she became a complete woman. Until then she refused even to try them on. She closed the box and her stomach felt a little settled.

Knock knock.

"Come in. Oh, Doctor Van der Vogel, so good to see you." Matisse extended both hands into his. She recalled that he was a tall man, with a full head of grey hair and good looks, probably in his early 40s. She thought he had the look of President Clinton about him.

" I have some questions to ask you before we proceed, Matisse. Is that OK?"

"Oh yes Doctor, please ask whatever you like."

"OK. Last time I saw you at Dr Hervé's clinic we established that you had been taking the hormone treatment oestrogen for over 6 months. Did you stop two weeks ago like I told you?"

"Yes Doctor, and I haven't smoked for 2 years and I haven't had any aspirin for a long time."

"OK that's good. What about your diet for the last two days."

"Just soup Doctor. We don't want me shitting the bed do we?"

"No indeed Matisse. Your operation will be at midday tomorrow and it is very important you don't have anything to eat or drink in the morning. Is that clear?"

"Yes".

"And are you perfectly clear what is involved with this Gender Reassignment Surgery?"

"I think it's pretty obvious."

"OK. As I said to you in Paris, we should produce a perfectly normal looking vagina and clitoris after a couple of months, but in the meantime it's very important you follow the instructions in order to make everything work as it should. In fact the stimulation you will be able to obtain through the new clitoris will be very real as I will create it from part of the glans of the penis."

"After the Penile Inversion Vaginoplasty you will have a pack of surgical gauze placed into the new vagina, this will help retain the tissues in their proper locations for about five days while healing proceeds. During this time you'll be on bed rest and a clear fluid-only diet to avoid the possibility of bowel movement, which could damage the vagina or disturb the pack. You'll be catheterised for 7 days to allow the urethra to heal. You must dilate the new vagina at least 3 times per day otherwise you'll have real problems. We'll take the stitches out after about 12 days."

"That's clear Doctor. Can I stay here for the 12 days?"

"Of course, but you may prefer to stay in a hotel after a week. The hospital costs are somewhat more expensive."

"If it's OK with you I'd prefer to stay here."

"No problem, I'll have reception book the room out to you. So have a little walk along the canals, come back for some soup and rest up ready for your big day tomorrow. Yes?"

"Yes Doctor," Matisse felt relaxed for the first time since arriving at the hospital. Excitement had overtaken her nervousness and she decided to take a walk along the elegant Prinsengracht.

Taking a brush from her bag, she tugged at her long curly hair. She knew she was lucky to have such good hair, and all her own with no extensions. She applied some lipstick, smoothed out the creases in her jeans, changed her trainers to a pair of flat-heeled black shoes, threw a small handbag over her shoulder and made her way down to the canal.

The water was still and the road running along the edge of the canal was quiet, despite being crammed with parked cars. A heavy man cycled passed her, ringing his bell, cigarette hanging from his mouth. He blew her a kiss. She liked that. She couldn't understand why so many women were offended by the attentions of men. As far as Matisse was concerned it was confirmation that she was a woman. By the end of tomorrow she would be more of a woman than she was today.

Matisse turned right into a side street and stumbled across a clutch of art and antique shops, typical of those found all over the centre of Amsterdam. She marvelled at every window, looking at old clocks and sculptures, crazy modern art and old masters side by side, 18th Century tiles and delft pottery. Then she stopped in front of a beautiful portrait of a woman. It reminded her of a portrait of Lady Hamilton she had seen in a television programme about the Frick Collection of art in New York. The woman looked so graceful with a dog in her arms and an innocent ruddy expression that concealed her true nature. Then Matisse started to cry. She cried thinking of the beautiful day she had spent with Klarkey in the Nelson museum in Portsmouth. She cried with the thought that she too was to become a true woman. She cried when she considered how long it was since she had spoken with her parents. She hadn't cried for a long time; nor had she reflected so much on her past. The final teardrops only ceased when she reached the steps of the hospital and she climbed the stairs to her room for her last evening in the male gender.

*****

Klarkey jumped out of the cab about 100 metres from the entrance to Westminster Auctions. Diagonally from the other side of the street he could secretly observe the arrivals at his postal history sale. He was well aware that auction prices realised were only as good as the people in the room. When he saw some of the most important figures in the industry arrive, he allowed himself a smile. There was Larry Solenski from New York, Corbin F Fitzgerald from Chicago and Saul Erlich from San Francisco. The Americans were by far the biggest players with the most money, but European buyers and others were not to be ignored. He bought himself a coffee to keep warm on the street and then noticed Herman Keiditch from Frankfurt, Greta Zeitz from Geneva who was one of the few women and a couple of Columbians whose names he had forgotten. He wondered if they had come to launder drugs money.

Matisse rose early and felt hungry and thirsty. She rolled some water around her mouth but made sure not to swallow. The television was to be her only companion for the next couple of hours. Then the nurse arrived: a stout black woman who wouldn't stop talking.

"Take your clothes off my dear and change into this theatre gown please. Are you from Paris?"

"I live in London at the moment."

"Oh, I love London, but I learned English in New York. I'm from Surinam. My name's Grace."

Matisse slipped on the gown. "Where's Surinam?"

"It's on the coast of South America my dear. Did you know it was owned by the British and they exchanged it with the Dutch for New York?"

"Really?"

"Well that's what they say. Matisse, I'm going to give you your pre-med injection now to prepare you for your general anaesthetic and operation. You'll feel a little drowsy and dreamy, but don't worry, that's normal. I'll collect you in about an hour and you'll be taken to theatre."

"Thank you nurse."

*****

Klarkey slipped through the door marked "Private", located on the floor directly below the main auction room. He was familiar with this room as this was where he had first come to offer his postal history collection for sale.

"Ah, Mr. Klarke, I wasn't sure if you would come."

"I couldn't really resist. Don't forget what I requested Mr Hadaway."

"I understand. Mum's the word eh?"

"I just thought I would come round to wish you well for the sale."

"Don't worry Mr Klarke, there are some expert buyers in today, as I'm sure you are well aware. I'm certain you'll do very well."

Klarkey shook Hadaway's hand.

"Thank you and I'll see you later."

Klarkey made his way out of the office and up the front stairs into the main room.

Finally the sale was about to start and Hadaway, who had entered the auctioneers' platform from a rear staircase, was now testing the microphone with the air of a judge arriving in his courtroom. The saleroom was full and a baritone hum permeated the air. Hadaway had strict instructions from Klarkey to ignore him if he entered the auction room. As far as everyone was concerned, Klarkey was just another buyer and was not identified as the vendor.

*****

Matisse was alone again. She looked down for the last time at her genitals, and said goodbye. She felt rather disoriented, as the nurse suggested she might, and it felt strange to be addressing parts of her body. She enjoyed looking at her growing curves and now fully developed breasts. She took a vanity mirror in her hands and shakily held it against her shrivelled testicles and penis. In her opinion there was nothing attractive about what she had between her legs. The parts didn't have any sentimental value. She closed her eyes and hoped it would all be over soon.

Matisse heard a bang at the door and nurse Grace entered.

"It's time honey." Grace supported Matisse to the door so that she didn't fall and helped her onto a hospital trolley.

*****

The hundred or so people in the London auction room had travelled from all parts of the world. There was a bank

133

of four telephonists on the sidewall, discreetly dialling their clients, and Hadaway stood high on the dais, ready to commence proceedings.

"Good afternoon ladies and gentlemen. Welcome to this October sale of fine postal history at Westminster Auctions,"

Klarkey opened the catalogue to the title page. "Property of a European Gentleman" the central text indicated. A hundred people turned to the next page.

"We'll commence most appropriately with Lot One," and silence hit the room.

"Shown here," the brown-overall wearing porter exclaimed,

"A fine cover from Antigua dated 1872 to London, six penny blue green. Will someone start me at £1000?"

Klarkey bit his nails. He hadn't partaken in that bad habit for years, but the tension was suddenly getting to him. The estimate for Lot 1 was £4000-£6000.

Finally someone raised his bidding paddle.

"Thank you sir. Any advance on £1000?"

Finally hands started to rise.

"£1200, £1400. Thank you sir. £1600, £1800." Hadaway was gently pointing to bidders and the price rose to £3200. Klarkey knew the reserve for this lot was £3000 but had hoped he would make £5000.

"At £4000 for the last time, anyone else." BANG. The gavel came down hard on the rostrum and the first item was sold. Klarkey winced. He hoped this wouldn't be the shape of things to come.

Hadaway was getting into his stride now.

"Lot 2 is a startling £2 black and rose Australian cover postmarked 1913. Can we start at £5000?" Klarkey noticed the estimate was £7000-£10000. He held his breath.

A paddle in the second row was raised confidently. Klarkey strained his eyes. It was the man from the Australia Mint in Sydney. Perfect.

More paddles hit the air.

"6000 and 7, 8 thousand and 9. 9 thousand and 10. At ten thousand pounds, do I hear any advance on ten thousand? And 11…and 12…and 13 thousand. Any more bids?" Klarkey felt as if his bladder was about to explode with the tension.

"At thirteen thousand pounds, sold to bidder number 715. Thank you."

Klarkey turned around, striding out of the front door, flying down the steps and into the Pig and Whistle pub next door. He ordered a large Whiskey and hoped that Lot 2 might be the start of a very successful afternoon's sale. He took the glass in hand, swirling the amber liquid, and looking at his thumbnail that was now almost bleeding around the cuticle.

*****

Matisse was drowsy but lay still, attempting to focus her eyes on the cornicing around the edge of the ceiling of the hospital corridor. She could tell that two porters were leading the trolley, and she felt almost naked in the loose fitting theatre gown she was made to wear.

She arrived shortly in the operating theatre, which seemed to her to look like a cluttered room. It was nothing like what she expected. Equipment surrounded her and several heads with face masks stared down at her. She recognised a friendly voice. It was Dr Van der Vogel.

"Hello Matisse. Well this is it. Miss Claes here is our anaesthetist and she will guide you through the next process, where you will be put to sleep for a while. OK?"

Matisse nodded. She had waited for this moment all her life and knew that by the end of the day she would be a new person.

"Matisse…hello. I'm Helena. I'm going to put a butterfly clamp on your hand that will be used to pass the anaesthetic into your body. I want you to count from 10 to 1."

The clamp was fitted and Miss Claes tapped Matisse's hand.

"Dix…neuf…huit…sept…six…cinq…"

Matisse was asleep. Miss Claes nodded at Dr Van der Vogel. The scalpel in his hand glinted as it reflected the powerful operating theatre lights. Then he made his first incision.

CHAPTER THIRTEEN   TRIDENT PLANS

Matisse was still away in Amsterdam. She'd been gone for a week and Klarkey had only spoken to her on the phone for the first time last night. She was sore but was going to be fine. It was now time for Klarkey to get to work.

Dragan Kradij was from Bosnia. A tall, slightly effeminate boy of 22, he'd been one of Klarkey's first successes in the people smuggling operation. And he was immensely thankful. He stayed in touch with Klarkey and was more than happy to help him with his project when he received the call at his studio flat in Leicester. And the £2000 Klarkey promised to pay him in cash would also be very helpful.

Kradij was ex-army, albeit a chef. He was also a sharp shooter. He was desperate for a new life in England and jumped at the opportunity. His family offered their life savings to bring him through Paris and into the UK with Klarkey's help. He would be eternally grateful to him and to them.

Klarkey had seen Kradij just once in recent weeks. He had briefed him with the plan and he had prepared him for his role in what he called Operation Rat Control.

He was now driving Kradij to Guildford, through the south London traffic and onto the A3, all the time confirming the details of the operation, leaving no stone unturned.

Kradij was dressed in women's clothing, carrying a bag with his own clothing inside. Klarkey had to admit that the boy was quite convincing as a woman. Kradij had no intention to become a woman, like Matisse. He certainly wasn't a transvestite and definitely wasn't gay. To him, this was just a job. And this job demanded Kradij to be dressed as a woman to fulfil the role. As Klarkey had said, there were rats to control.

"Let's be absolutely clear what you have to do Dragan."

"OK Klarkey, but we have been through this more than four times now." Dragan was tired yet running high on adrenalin.

"Dragan, it must be done right. You tell me the plan so that I can know for sure you have it firmly in your mind."

"OK. We're driving to Guildford Station, which is on the line to Portsmouth. I take the first train to Portsmouth, which arrives at Portsmouth and Southsea station at 5 o'clock. I make sure I get off at that stop otherwise I end up at the Harbour. From Portsmouth and Southsea station I walk up through Commercial Road, very slowly. I wait to see what happens."

"So far so good Dragan. If nothing happens, you walk back down Commercial Road and then back up, UNTIL something happens. Carry on."

"It is likely that I may be mugged by a gang operating in the area targeting women. That is why I'm dressed as a woman. If a Policeman walks past me I shouldn't catch his eye…"

Klarkey laughed. "You don't want him to think you're a prostitute on the hunt for a sailor!"

"I keep my gun available in the slip pocket at the back of my skirt and shoot if I am attacked. No questions asked. If I do shoot I should walk to the top of Commercial Road, take off my wig and heels in the derelict doorway of the old cinema, slip my own shoes and raincoat on, wipe my face of make-up and make my way to your car which will be parked in front of the church. Then we leave."

"Bloody hell it sounds so simple. Let's just hope nothing goes wrong."

"Don't worry Klarkey. I was in Special Forces for the Bosnian army, I can deal with any situation that might arise."

"Dragan! You were a bloody cook."

"Ah yes, but we had to cook in unbelievable circumstances. Always on our toes; constantly aware the enemy was around us. You know, I always say it was more difficult for me in the army feeding the men, carrying odd shaped pots and food on our backs than it was for the fighting men simply carrying regular supplies and guns."

"OK OK. Whatever you say. You know what you have to do and you know you have to do it quickly and efficiently. We have to flush out the rats and you're going to shake them out of their sewer."

"You make this sound like some kind of war."

"In a way it is. It really is."

*****

The next day was Friday. Louis and Amelie Jabood were a handsome couple from Algeria. Educated, elegant and desperate for a new life in England, they had jumped at the opportunity to come to the UK with Klarkey's help. Louis and Amelie were struggling. Things hadn't quite worked out in Birmingham, and the last few months had been an uphill battle. If it wasn't for the help of the local Algerian community they would probably have been starving. When Klarkey called them to "do a little job", they jumped at the idea of earning £4000 for a night's work. Especially when they were both offered new outfits to wear on top of the cash.

Klarkey had taken the Jaboods to Kensington High Street and bought them new clothes and furs. They had such a good time shopping, yet at the same time they couldn't fully relax, knowing their day would ultimately end in horror. They had already been briefed with the work they were supposed to do and it wasn't something they would be proud of. Nevertheless, they trusted Klarkey's judgement and had even more faith in the money he would give them after the job was done.

They entered The Scorpion Club in south London at about 11pm. They waited patiently in the queue and having paid to go inside they made their way upstairs to the coat check, where they checked in their fox coats and a sports bag.

It was difficult to relax, and they felt somewhat out of place. Everyone seemed very young, very sweaty and very...deranged.

"Why is it that everyone seems so crazy?"

"This is what they call club culture Amelie."

One hour passed and their heads were aching. If only they could have arrived much later, but this went against the strict instructions they'd been given.

"Louis, I'm not happy about what we are doing. It's not right."

"Amelie," Louis hissed, with half an eye on a near naked girl brushing past him, "we don't have much choice. We have to trust Klarkey. The man we seek is bad, evil. Klarkey knows the truth and whatever the reason, we're taking the law into our own hands because we trust him. Like we did back home for ourselves. Remember?"

"You were a Policemen back home Louis. That was different. Here you are just an Arab asylum seeker. You are nothing."

"Enough Amelie." Louis raised his hand as if to strike her, but he held back.

Amelie knew she was beaten, if not by her husband's hands, then by his words. She could provide no realistic alternative to secure their financial future, and felt compelled to comply with what she thought was a despicable act. They sat in silence in the coffee shop, drinking vile weak coffee, waiting for the appointed time to leave.

Hours passed and the club was due to close at 6am Saturday morning. At 5.45am Louis and Amelie made their way to the coat check, collected their coats and sports bag and as soberly as they had entered the building, made their way downstairs towards the front entrance where the cars were double-parked across the road, waiting to take the

clubbers home, or in some cases, onto the next den of
iniquity.

A huge black man with a clipboard asked them if they
wanted a cab.

"No thank you. We're waiting for our friend to pick us
up."

They stood slightly to one side so as not to get in the
way of the customers who wanted to pick up a legitimate
cab.

Right on cue their target arrived. Screeching to a halt in
an old Ford Sierra, an illegal touting mini-cab pulled up in
front of Louis and Amelie.

"Yes sir yes madam, would you like a cab? I can give
you best price. Cab boss? Jump in."

Louis and Amelie were happy to oblige. They had a job
to do.

Amelie frowned as she made herself comfortable on the
back seat. Just for a second she was disgusted at something
else besides the horror of what was about to happen. Ugly
white and grey dog hairs clinging to the back seat of the car
were now attaching themselves to her new coat.
'Revolting', she thought.

Louis had asked to go to Camden, but he knew the
driver would never take them there. He felt into the sports
bag and opened up the fluffy white towel inside in which
the gun was hidden. He looked up and the early morning
sun was bouncing off Millbank Tower and his mind focused
on the job in hand. His palms were lightly sweating and his
heart was beating faster and faster. Amelie started to feel
sick. The driver was oblivious to their feelings.

They leaned into the tight turn around the roundabout at
the bottom of Westminster Bridge and then stared up at the
London Eye to their left. They knew they were close.

Shooting past the Imax cinema, south of Waterloo
Bridge and across towards Blackfriars, Louis noticed the
driver glancing into his rear view mirror at them. The

driver was waiting to be asked why he'd not gone over the bridge, but Louis stayed silent. He wiped his sweating hand on the towel in the bag and breathed long careful breaths.

Now at the bottom of Blackfriars Bridge the driver made a series of twists and turns and in seconds was parked in a faceless estate.

The driver had assumed wrongly that his two passengers were so out of their minds on drugs they'd no idea he'd taken a wrong turn. His over confidence led him to misread the moment.

Five seconds after pulling a knife on them he was dead.

Louis put the gun back into the sports bag and silently pointed to Amelie to get out of the car. He then carefully wiped the door handles with the towel. They walked towards Southwark tube that had opened about half an hour before.

"I feel sick", she said approaching the station.

"Don't you dare be sick. You can't leave evidence of who we are at the scene? Let's go. Quick."

Klarkey had already paid them their money. They had been instructed never to contact him again. They had been given exact details of the wheelie bin that the sports bag was to be thrown into. They were happy to shut the front door of their home in Birmingham behind them and to condemn the events of that night to a forgotten past.

*****

Three days later, Yousef Al-Rashid met Klarkey in the restaurant at the top of John Lewis's Oxford Street Store. Despite protestations from the store management of how the central London congestion charge had severely dented business, Klarkey and Yousef struggled to find a table to chat discreetly about the plan ahead of them.

Yousef was a well-built twenty-something man from Iraq. Before the war, he'd been in Baghdad studying history of art and drama. His family were Marsh Arabs.

He'd been the lucky one. Escaping Saddam's draining of the marshes meant a future for him in the city. His family wasn't so lucky. Following their deaths, principally through hunger, he made his way to England, with Klarkey's help, and then onto Glasgow. He'd settled into his new surroundings with few difficulties, even adopting a Scottish accent quite quickly. He utilised his acting skills to smooth the process of fitting in, although professionally he was could only find work in a coffee shop. When he received the call from Klarkey, he knew that he no choice but to respond positively. The seductive draw of £4000 for an evening's work was also irresistible.

Klarkey had brought with him 3 cans of lager. These were not ordinary cans. Matisse had brought them to London from Amsterdam during her pre-op trip to Dr Van der Vogel. The cans were bought in the red light district of Amsterdam, and did not contain lager at all. Among the hemp, pipe and sex toy-filled stores of Amsterdam, were a selection of containers that had been remodelled, ostensibly for storing drugs. These 'stash cans' were cleverly altered. The ring pull on the top was intact, but a cut had been made just below the rim of each can. The liquid removed, these cans were then fitted with an invisible screw top and internal container, weighted down to give the impression of a full can, but in fact containing nothing but drugs or anything else the owner would secrete into it. They were often marketed as containers for storing valuables including jewellery.

Klarkey had removed the internal containers from each can, leaving the screw top in place and the ring pull intact. He then filled each can with highly concentrated sulphuric acid: drain cleaner easily obtained over the counter from any plumber's merchant. He screwed the tops back into place, leaving no prints as he'd used rubber gloves and put them into his sports bag ready to give to Yousef.

Yousef had been given his instructions. They took the first bite out of their chocolate crêpes and Klarkey handed Yousef the cans, which he put into his own bag. An old lady looked up and tutted. She hoped they wouldn't be drinking beer here in John Lewis.

"Here are your instructions Yousef. You need to ensure you find homeless vagrants in one of the doorways and offer them these drinks. Don't take no for an answer, just look like you're doing them a favour."

"OK Klarkey. I understand."

"In this envelope is your money, plus details of where you are to stay. Use your UK passport for ID."

Yousef, looked into the envelope and saw the bundle of fifty-pound notes. He took out an A4 piece of paper, and read the typed instructions.

Go to Luton airport by train from Kings Cross, leaving London at 3pm taking the 3 cans of lager with you. Keep them upright at all times. Wear gloves whenever touching them.

Arrive at Luton airport and check in at the Easyjet desk for the Aberdeen flight.

Use UK passport for ID.

Arrive Aberdeen at 7pm and take a taxi to central Aberdeen on Union Street.

Locate homeless drunks living in a doorway but do not approach.

Break for dinner at any fast food restaurant.

Approach the vagrants in a friendly manner and give them a can of lager each.

Walk away from them quickly and do not look back. Take a taxi from the cab rank to central Dundee.

From Dundee, take another taxi to Glasgow. Pay cash for each taxi and arrange the price in advance. Do not argue over the price. Ensure the final taxi takes you to no closer than one mile from where you live in Glasgow. Walk the rest of the way home.

When you are safely back home, destroy this piece of paper by burning. Do not contact me ever again.

Yousef's command of English was excellent, but nevertheless, he took his time to read the instructions. Then he read them a second time.

"I don't understand…" he started.

"Yousef. You don't have to understand anything. You simply have to do a job for me. If you perform it, you have earned your money. If you fail, I will find you and take the money back. It's your choice. Will you do it?"

"Yes of course. How can I refuse? It would take me five months to earn this kind of money in the job that I do."

Yousef stood up, pushing his plate away from him. Klarkey grabbed him tightly around the wrist and stared into his eyes.

"Don't let me down."

"I d'Nae have a choice do I?", Yousef said, emphasising his Scottish accent.

Yousef pulled his arm free and walked off towards the exit. Klarkey finished his coffee and made his own way out of the store five minutes later. He smiled. His three small operations had been put into place. He could relax until it was time to read about them in the newspapers. He looked forward to how the incidents would be reported. They would make no sense to anyone but himself.

It was 1.30pm on Tuesday afternoon and he had a visit to make. He took the hire car keys from his pocket, and sped down the stairs into the underground car park. A slow crawl through central, then through south London, led him past Wimbledon and onto the A3. He hated most of this dull road and decided to take the turn onto the A325 for part of the journey, a slower route to Portsmouth but much prettier and greener. The beauty of the route even made up for occasionally being stuck behind a tractor or an army truck, on its way to Borden or Aldershot barracks.

Two hours later, Klarkey had reached the outskirts of Portsmouth. He switched on the I-Drive, which gave him clear instructions, how to reach Roberta's front door.

She lived in a flat-fronted two-bedroom terrace house. And she lived alone.

Klarkey rang the bell. His chest felt tight. He was picking at his fingers and he could sense his face breaking out into heat lumps, despite the fact that it was a chilly autumn afternoon.

"You're lucky to catch me, I've just got in from school," she beamed as he stood over the threshold.

"Can I come in?"

Roberta waved her arm forward and Klarkey followed her into the sitting room.

"Coffee?"

"Thanks."

He sat in silence as he looked around the living room noticing plain walls painted yellow with a modest fireplace and laminated wooden floors and various pictures: all prints. He forgot how little teachers earned. The kettle whistled and clicked off. Seconds later, Roberta brought in a tray with coffee mugs, sugar, milk and butter biscuits. Klarkey thought she looked great, even if she was still a little bruised from her ordeal.

"I don't know why you're back at school already. Don't you think you should've taken a proper break after the attack?"

"Now you're sounding like my mother! I'm quite ready to go to work and try to get back to normal."

Klarkey put a sugary embossed piece of biscuit onto a plate and took Roberta's hand in his. To his relief, she didn't withdraw.

"Roberta...."

"Yes?"

"I've been thinking about you a lot...since I saw you on the train...and then since the attack."

"I've been thinking about you too. It's been good of you to call me so often."

She took his hand, and Klarkey lent over to kiss her cheek. The plate fell to the floor.

"Sorry..."

"Don't worry, I'll deal with it."

She picked up the plate and broken biscuit crumbs from the floor, kneeling by the side of the coffee table. He noticed she had a fine figure, a long slender neck and very attractive legs. As she finished fussing, Klarkey stretched out his hands to both of her arms and pulled her towards him. She let out a sigh, as if to yield to him. He pulled her closer to him and she was then on his lap. He pushed her hair to one side and kissed her neck.

"Klarkey?"

"Yes," he said, surfacing for air.

"Do you believe in fate?"

"I suppose I do. Except sometimes you make your own fate. Your own destiny. But if you're talking about us, then why not? Let's face it, if I didn't get into the train carriage that you were in, I wouldn't be here now."

"Maybe you'd be with someone else if you had!"

"Maybe...but I'm not. I'm here with you. And that makes me VERY happy."

And what about Matisse?"

"Matisse is my friend. She's like my sister and best friend rolled into one. We're not close like this..."

Roberta undid the top buttons of Klarkey's shirt and slid her hand against his slightly hairy chest. She gently squeezed his nipple.

"If we're going to get to know each other I should tell you that they don't work!"

"Maybe you should try mine. Because I can tell you...they most certainly DO work."

147

Klarkey smiled, lifted Roberta up off the sofa, and took her mock kicking-and-screaming up the stairs to the bedroom. He stayed the night.

*****

Klarkey woke with a smile like a Muppet toy with an endlessly wide mouth. There was no stopping him. They had made love the previous night, just one, slow, wonderful time, but that was enough for both of them.

"Are you awake?"

"No" Roberta said.

"Can I make you a drink?"

"If you like."

Klarkey bounded out of bed, kissing her on the way, threw on his shorts and made his way down to the kitchen. Finding his way around the cupboards and drawers, he brought upstairs two glasses of orange juice and two coffees.

"I could get used to this," Roberta spoke with a smile and stretched her body, fingernails digging into the headboard.

"And so you should."

Klarkey handed Roberta her juice and coffee, then put the tray by the side of the bed on the floor. He noticed the local newspaper from a couple of days earlier, unable to avoid the screaming headline on the front page: GANG-SHOOTING IN TOWN CENTRE. Roberta took her first sip of coffee and noticed Klarkey reading avidly.

"You see," she said pointing at the paper, "There is some justice in the world. It looks like the thugs who attacked me got their just desserts."

Klarkey looked up, and fell back down onto the bed, whispering with an adrenalin driven smile into his lover's ear…"Maybe it was fated."

CHAPTER FOURTEEN   GUINNESS

The operational test run in Aberdeen had passed off smoothly. The vagrants had drunk their alcohol replacement and Klarkey had proved to himself that he could do whatever, wherever.

Except events in Aberdeen were not as straightforward as Klarkey had hoped or imagined.

Harriet McWerter was a TV producer from the smart West End side of town. At just twenty-four years old, and 5 feet 2 inches tall, she felt she had a lot to prove, not least because it was the hardest thing in the world to command respect when young and petite, but also because most people in the profession believed she'd reached this point in her career thanks to her parents money. She was certainly young and short, but her parents hadn't helped her financially during her adult life. They believed it was important for their daughter to make her own way in the world: to prove herself. Although she didn't really agree with this policy when she was young, as she became more established in her chosen field of work, she came to accept and understand their opinion. She knew that all of her achievements were thanks to her own hard work, despite some people supposing otherwise. Since university, Harriet McWerter had adopted the nickname Guinness, not because of any propensity towards drink or student drinking games, but simply because she shared the surname of the great Scottish founders of the Guinness Book of Records, Norris and Ross McWerter. Guinness had stuck for no other reason.

Guinness was making a hard-hitting documentary. For two weeks, she had been camping out in a hotel room in central Aberdeen, with a rotating crew of cameramen. Her reporter, Richie Brakes, had been living the life of a homeless person. Brakes had spent several days unwashed and poorly dressed, visiting soup kitchens in Aberdeen and meeting with other vagrants. He had tried to sell the Big Issue but had been beaten up by other homeless persons who felt he was encroaching on their territory. After that, two middle-aged drunken tramps had taken pity on him, and allowed Brakes to spend time with them. He was inwardly horrified how miserable a person's life could become on the streets. Some passers by would spit on him, others would give him a little small change. Children abused him, yet grandmothers took pity on him. He was the star of Guinness's documentary on the life and times of a down-and-out in Aberdeen.

Every move he made was recorded on camera.

This October evening was like most others in recent days. Guinness was starting to worry about how she would justify to the television production company the amount of tape being used to record events and the amount of time in hotels and the cost of crew. The cameraman had discreetly followed the three tramps, including Richie Brakes, drinking from early in the morning; wandering from square to square and falling into the harbour area where they would sleep for another few hours; here one of them would score some crack cocaine and lie deranged next to the others.

Later still they returned to their night time accommodation in front of SofaSoGood. It was hardly as comfortable as a hostel bed, but they considered it safer: not surrounded by twenty crazies on heroin or schizophrenics who they considered should be securely locked away. They may have been out of their minds on drink and drugs, but at least they knew they could trust each other's company. They felt as safe as they could living on the streets.

Guinness had set up the static tripod camera from the hotel room and switched it to infrared. It was set to record Brakes and his new friends through the night, and would provide a backdrop for their daytime activities: a recurring piece to round off each segment of the report.

Guinness woke up with a start in the minutes before daybreak. "Those bloody seagulls" were her first words to herself. She knew that if she tried to get back to sleep, she'd be woken by a cameraman starting his shift at 7am, so it wasn't really worth even trying to sleep some more. It was better to get up, to gulp down a strong coffee, shower and to throw some clothes on. She couldn't cope with a beefy cameraman staring at her in her nightdress. She needed to try to look her best for work, even if the workplace was her hotel bedroom.

Guinness glanced through the camera lens and saw the three tramps asleep. 'Nicely framed', she thought. The next twenty-five minutes were spent drinking sachet coffee and getting ready for another day following the life of her undercover roving reporter.

Thump Thump Thump. The door of her room was being banged far too hard for this time of the morning.

"All right Des, hold your horses, I'm coming."

Des was her favourite - a stocky cameraman, who fell, somewhat breathless into the doorway as soon as Guinness has opened it.

"You have to take a look downstairs," he spluttered, "There's something going on. The Police are everywhere. Something's not right."

"OK Des, just calm down. Sit on the bed and I'll take a look."

Guinness suddenly felt awake and very alert. She didn't know what to expect, but the adrenalin was flowing through her faster than ever. She knew this was an indication that the direction of her film was to take an altogether different turn. Her thoughts were justified. Guinness opened the curtains and looked through the lens of the camera.

"Oh...my...God." She scraped both her hands through her hair towards the back of her head. "Oh...my...God."

"I told you something was going down." Des piped in, moving his head from side to side, hoping to look through the lens.

Guinness had momentarily forgotten that Des was sitting on her bed behind her, and his voice gave her a start. She looked up.

"The Police are putting a cordon round them. I couldn't see Richie, or the other two properly. Maybe they're being arrested. Or…I don't know." She rubbed her palm hard over her eyebrow and across her forehead.

"At least the camera's been running all night."

"Yes," Guinness started with a new forthright, Director-takes-control type of behaviour. "Set up the daytime camera. Stick with it and follow every movement you can. We may not be digital, but thank Christ we've got video and not film. Let's look at the night tape in a wee bit and see what happened before the Police turned up."

"OK boss." Des recognised her authority and was happy to obey.

"I'm going downstairs to find out what's going on and to see if I can help Richie without blowing his cover."

"No problem Guinness. Hey, be careful."

She was already out of the door. Ignoring the lift and racing down three flights of stairs, she opened the hotel front door and took a deep breath. It was cold and she'd forgotten to bring a coat. She crossed the road, dodging the handful of cars now passing along Union Street, and rushed towards the scene. She needed to find out what was going on, but at the same time knew it was crucial to protect Richie Brake's cover, as well as staying out of the camera shot. It was a lot to think about, but a decision was already made for her. She couldn't get as close as she wanted, and as she approached the shop doorways, two ambulances screamed around the corner and blocked the street. Police tape was blocking any way to get closer. Suddenly she thought it might be a good idea to buy a couple of bacon rolls from the bakers next door to SofaSoGood. She knew Des would appreciate that. He seemed to be constantly eating and his expanding waist demonstrated this. 'Why was it always acceptable for men to eat as much as they liked AND to get fat, yet for women, putting on weight is seen as a kind of crime against nature?' She's had to leave that thought for a while 'maybe it could become the basis for a new TV documentary. Make a mental note'. Now she was across the road.

The bakers had been open. The lights were on but nobody was inside. She put her hands on her hips and drew a blank. Other people had started to gather around. These were early morning workers and locals who'd popped out for a newspaper, only to discover intense Police activity. The public loved to stare, even when nothing was going on. She smiled as she thought of the American illusionist who spent 44 days suspended in a glass box by Tower Bridge in London doing ABSOLUTELY NOTHING. And still the people came to watch. Her mind went off on another tangent, 'The TV companies certainly made a fortune from it. Perhaps there was something in that. Something else to store away for the future.'

This, however, was a scene she was already filming. It was by now turning into something. 'Oh...my...God', she thought. 'The ambulances are really needed and the three guys are being put into them'. Now her heart was pounding. She felt helpless, ignorant, but also had a sense of being totally involved. After all, whatever happened must have been recorded on her camera. She had to get back upstairs and review last night's recording. Before she did, she grabbed the arm of the first Policeman she could find.

"Please...officer...can you tell me what's happened here?" She was desperate for information about her friend, but knew she couldn't reveal this to the officer.

"Sorry miss there's nothing to tell. Just three dead drunks found in a doorway. Nothing to see. Please move along now."

Guinness was silent. She broke off her grip of the officer and backed herself into the first shop doorway that was not covered by Police tape, shivering intensely as she slid her back down the plate glass where her backside rested on the cold pavement. She held her hands to her face and tried to cry. She couldn't. She didn't know what to think. Suddenly with a sharp intake of breath, she ran as fast as she could across the road and into the hotel and up to her room.

"I'm getting it all Guinness. Whatever, IT is."

Guinness took a few breaths so that she could speak without panting.

"They're dead. The Policeman said they're all fucking dead Des!"

Des let go of the camera, tightening the tripod on which it was sitting and rushed over to Guinness. She burst into tears into his chest.

He tried his best to comfort her. "Look, we're in this together. Why don't we see if we can find out exactly what's going on?"

"Oh…my…God," she looked up, "Richie's got a young family. His wife. Kids. Shit Des, what am I going to do? How am I going to tell them?"

"I don't mean to state the obvious, but I don't think you've got any choice but to tell them the truth."

"They didn't even know what he was working on. It was all completely hush-hush. You know I've been working on this for months. Richie's been away from his family for weeks. I think he told them he was going abroad to work undercover."

"I'm not sure I even know Richie's wife's name. We've got to find out exactly what happened. Let's check back over the tape."

The next hour was spent reviewing the previous night's recording, as documented by the infrared camera. Des's finger hovered over the rewind button, going backwards into the night, searching for any action that might be of interest. Half an hour into this process, Guinness glanced through the window and noticed the pavement was clear except for the Police tape still cordoning off the scene of whatever crime had been committed.

"I reckon we're going to have to go all the way to the beginning of the tape at this rate." Des was getting impatient to see something on the screen; all he had seen for the last hour were three shapeless, lifeless bodies in their sleeping bags in the doorway of SofaSoGood. "I suppose their either dead already or asleep. I don't know what to think."

Guinness sighed, "You know it was Richie's only worry that some bastard was gonna set light to them in the night or something. Otherwise he was as confident as you could be with the project. Oh Des...I feel terrible. I feel so responsible"

"Well I'm pretty sure that no-one set light to them. But something sure as hell happened here last night."

"STOP" Guinness shouted. "I just saw something. Go back five minutes and press play."

Des did as he was instructed. Guinness started to give a running commentary of what she was seeing:

"So there are the three of them. Kind of moving about. Well one of them is. They're definitely not in the position we saw them in this morning. Now. Here we go...There's someone approaching them. It's a man, but I can't see any more clearly than that. Bloody infrared. He's having a word with one of them. He's reaching into what looks like a carrier bag. He's taking something out, maybe a chocolate bar...the other two are waking up now. No it's too big for a bar of chocolate. Not a sandwich. Could be a drink of something, maybe a bottle, or a can. He's giving each of

them the same thing. Now he's off. Richie's in the middle.
He's holding whatever the man gave him in the air before
taking a swig. He must be thanking him. Oh…my…God.
Look Des, it's horrible…even without sound. You can tell
that whatever was in that drink was some kind of poison.
Shit man. Richie's been murdered."

"Oh my God," said Des.

*****

Guinness sprang into action. She sent Des to make a
copy of the night-time tape and turned the camera on
herself, sitting in a chair in the corner of her room, speaking
to camera for the first time, in what she felt was one of the
most important moments of her televisual life so far.

*Last night, sometime in the late evening, but before the
dead of night, our courageous reporter Richie Brakes, and
two of his newly befriended homeless pals were brutally
murdered. A stranger offered them some kind of drink that
resulted in their appalling deaths. This film has sought to
highlight the plight of the homeless. No one, especially me,
could have predicted how tragically this documentary
would end. No one could have imagined the brutality of
snuffing out the lives of three innocent men. They may have
been homeless, but they were men, with families and stories
to tell. With all my heart I intend that these men's poor
lives were not given in vain. My report will continue and I
will not rest until I find answers to what happened here on
this cold Aberdeen Autumn evening.*

Guinness bowed her head, took a breath and then got up
to switch the camera off.

She had a lot to think about. She needed to contact
Richie's family, but she didn't want to compromise her
investigation. She knew she had to speak to the Police - she
must not be exposed to being accused of withholding
evidence, especially when it related to such a serious crime.
After a few minutes thought, she decided to speak to the
Police first, then she would call the Press anonymously, but

she would not call Richie Brake's family. That job should be for the Police, who after all would be trained in breaking such news to families.

*****

Guinness lay down on her bed and started to hyperventilate. She pulled herself up quickly, making herself dizzy, and threw open the door of the mini-bar. She'd vowed never to drink from the hotel mini-bar, but she felt it was time to break one of her own rules. Another rule was never to drink before midday. It was 8am and she was drinking brandy, neat from a miniature bottle. She certainly felt she needed it.

Carefully lying back down on the bed, Guinness sobbed into her hands, and lay still, unable to think. She fell asleep, only to be woken again by Des banging on the door.

Guinness stumbled across the floor, tripping over the empty brandy miniature and opened the door to Des,

"Hi Guinness, you still feeling like shit? You certainly look it."

"Thanks Des."

"I got two copies of the tape," he passed them to her, "Have you decided what you're going to do yet?"

"I reckon I have. I'm going to have to go to the Police. But I'm damn well going to carry on my own investigation alongside. This is too important for me to let go."

"Fair enough. Oh, by the way, I just picked up the Evening Express on the way up. Look's like the shit's hit the fan."

Guinness grabbed the newspaper and wiped her eyes.

"ROUGH SLEEPERS MURDERED WITH KILLER BEER"

She blew out a large puff of air and stared up into Des's eyes.

"I want you to go home for now. I'm going to the Police."

"Don't expect me to leave you alone now."

157

"Thanks all the same Des, but there's stuff I need to do myself."

Des squeezed her shoulder and made his way out of the hotel room, and Guinness hurried to put on her shoes. She threw cold water on her face and took one of the tapes under her arm. The walk along Union Street towards Grampian Police headquarters was only a five-minute one, but it seemed like forever as she kept going over and over the moment when the three men took the drink and then collapsed. As she passed the doorway where the previous night's action had taken place, all that remained was a flailing piece of Police tape, and nothing more. It was as if this most significant event had never happened.

Guinness wasn't used to being in Police stations and Queen Street provided its usual mix of drunks, shoplifters and solicitors waiting to see their clients. As Guinness sat in the semi-circular reception area, she waited for her name to be called.

A tall handsome uniformed officer opened a side door.

"Miss McWerter?"

"Yes?" She looked up.

"This way please."

Guinness followed the officer into a side interview room.

"Miss McWerter, I'm Sergeant Robinson and I'm one of the investigating officers dealing with the attacks in Union Street. I believe you have some information that may be of assistance to us."

Guinness proceeded to tell the full circumstances that brought her to be filming the incident. She then handed over the tape.

She thought that she would feel better by telling the Police everything. She certainly did not. If anything, she felt worse. It made her feel more responsible for the incident. She felt responsible for Richie's death and there was nothing that make that feeling go away.

"Miss McWerter, we will be needing Mr. Brake's family's details."

"I know. I really don't feel up to speaking with his wife just now."

"Don't worry; we'll give her the news. A specially trained bereavement councillor will be on hand to assist the family. It would also be better if you didn't tell anyone about the tape for the time being. I presume your report will be put on hold?"

"Oh…yes, yes of course," she half-lied. Guinness certainly wasn't going to inform the world she had made a tape of the incident, but she was more resolved than ever that her investigations still had a long way to go.

"May I leave now please?"

"Yes, that'll be all for now, but please stay in Aberdeen so that we can find you again if we need to ask you some more questions."

Guinness rose from her chair and was shown out into the daylight. The streets were now busy, full with women and children, overburdened with shopping bags. Guinness wanted to scream. She mumbled to herself,

"Why is it that everything seems so bloody normal?"

Sergeant Robinson made his way into the CID office. The phone rang, but it was lunchtime, and few staff were in attendance.

"Get that will you," an officer shouted across the room.

"Sergeant Robinson," he answered.

"Mervyn MacFarlane here. The post-mortems have been completed on the three white males brought to us this morning. I'll have my full report to you by the morning, but I can tell you for sure they died sometime between 8pm and midnight. All three of them certainly died of wounds resulting from the consumption of undiluted sulphuric acid. Very nasty. Very nasty indeed."

"Thank you Doctor. I'll pass the information on to the investigating team."

CHAPTER FIFTEEN

It was time for Matisse to return to London. She arrived at Heathrow, glowing, but sore from the operation two weeks earlier. As she stroked the amber necklace hanging down between her breasts she felt revitalised.

She was determined to mix with other people. Matisse needed to see if people looked at her in a different way; whether they treated her more like a lady. She was inclined to take the underground back to the hotel, but common sense prevailed and she took a taxi.

She didn't perceive anyone looking at her in a strange way. Nor did she detect anyone projecting negative thoughts towards her. Then reality dawned on her: she was simply another woman on a plane; or walking along a travelator; or taking a cab. No one considered her in any particular way. It was Matisse who acknowledged a change in herself. It was Matisse recognising she was a fully-fledged woman, and not a man dressed as a woman. She had fulfilled her dream and she was happy - happier than she had ever been in her life.

She arrived back at the hotel through the usual heavy traffic of West London. During the journey from the airport it had become dark.

Matisse arrived at the front door of their suite, took a deep breath and opened the door. Klarkey was standing facing outwards against the Georgian window, hands spread-eagled across the windowsill. He was clearly lost in thought as he hadn't even noticed Matisse enter the room.

"Bonjour You..." she ventured quietly.

Klarkey took a sharp intake of air. "Bonjour You too! You're back! Matisse I missed you so much."

Klarkey ran over to her and hugged her hard.

"You are ok aren't you?"

"Of course I am. Everything was fine."

Matisse slipped her coat onto the sofa and wheeled her case into her room, still talking with Klarkey behind her.

"The doctors and nurses were so kind and helpful. Amsterdam was so peaceful. I told you I had a room overlooking the Prinsengracht. It was so pretty. Watching the pedaloes and the comings and goings from the houseboats. I couldn't have been in better hands. Anyway, enough about me. Did you get the results of the sale?"

Klarkey sat down on the end of Matisse's bed, whilst she went into her en-suite to freshen up.

"Hadaway e-mailed me from the auction house yesterday. They took a little time to get the final figures for me because they allow an extra week for dealers to make offers on the unsold lots. In the end there were only about six unsold lots and you'll never guess how much we've raised.

"How much?" Matisse gurgled through a froth of toothpaste.

"Six and a half million."

Matisse dropped her hand towel to the floor.

"Pounds?"

"Of course Pounds."

"Before or after commission?"

"After commission Matisse. I have got six and a half million pounds winging its way into an offshore account some time in the next hour or so and I don't know whether to laugh or cry."

Matisse started to laugh, then to cry. "I'm so happy for you. It's what you deserve and have worked so hard for." She hugged him, dribbling toothpaste onto his shoulder.

"Hey, it's not just for me. It's for both of us to enjoy. You're an important special part of my life and I'll always be there for you."

Matisse rinsed her mouth out with cold water. "Klarkey you're so kind. You know, when I was walking onto the plane, then through the airport, I was looking around, wondering if people would stare at me, thinking that people would assume I was some kind of freak. Of course, no one bothered me. You're the only person I know for sure has never judged me. I love you for that."

"OK. I'll accept that." Klarkey smiled out of the side of his mouth and wiggled his shoulders proudly.

They laughed and fell into each other's arms.

Matisse stood up.

"Would you like to see...you know?"

"Come again?"

"You know what I'm saying. And I mean this in a friendly way, not in some kind of 'you show me yours' kids sort of game."

"Well Matisse...err...OK."

Matisse undid the buttons on her hipster pants, slipped her knickers over the top of the trousers and put her hands on her hips.

"Well? What do you think?"

Klarkey laughed through nervousness. No one had ever asked him an opinion about the look of his or her private parts before. He certainly didn't know the appropriate response.

"It's very...nice." He shook his head recognising his response was as limp as it could have been.

"Nice? I suppose it's not yet looking at its best, but give it a few more weeks and it will be wonderful."

"Matisse, don't forget I never saw what you looked like before. It's a bit embarrassing...showing your new vagina to your best mate."

"Ppphhh," Matisse exhaled in her typical French style. She did up her trousers and went back into the bathroom.

Klarkey shouted after her. "I'm sorry Matisse, but I just didn't know what to say."

Matisse put her head around the bathroom door. She wasn't angry. "That's OK darling, I'm sure given time I will find many people to appreciate it."

With Matisse's head still peeping from behind the bathroom door, the main door to the bedroom opened. Roberta walked in.

"Oh I'm sorry honey. I heard voices and I wondered where you were. Excuse me." Roberta hurriedly made her way back into Klarkey's room and sat in a corner chair powdering her nose from a small compact.

Matisse screamed. She thought Roberta had seen her naked but was mistaken.

"Why didn't you tell me that woman was here? She has invaded my private space. Klarkey...KLARKEY."

Klarkey rose from the bed and went to the door.

"I suggest you calm down Matisse. Roberta is my guest here and we have become... pretty close."

"So close you couldn't tell me you were seeing her?"

"I didn't want to say anything until I was sure that we would be seeing more of each other."

"So you ARE seeing her?"

"Matisse, are you jealous?"

"Of course not. I think I will take a bath and do some of my exercises now."

"Exercises?"

"Yes exercises...you know...down there." She pointed to her groin.

"Oh...OH" Klarkey suddenly realised what Matisse was talking about and made a hasty exit from the room.

Matisse closed the door behind Klarkey. This wasn't the kind of welcome home she had been expecting. She knew that Klarkey and her would be nothing more than friends, but she believed they had a special bond between them. This was something that made them soul mates. She was desperately worried that this relationship could now be under threat.

*****

Sgt. Robinson had replayed the tape several times over the last few days. He had made a copy and sent the original off to forensics for analysis. It had been given top priority. He had to discover the identity of the man who had given the lethal drinks to the three men in the Union Street doorway. Perhaps equally importantly, he had to know why.

The sergeant sat in the dark, with the images from the tape lighting his face with a flickering reflection. He was miles away, but sharpened himself up when the door knocked three times.

"Sarge?"

"What is it Bennet?"

The blonde Police constable had some good news.

"Sarge, forensics have just called. They've made a clean image of the man on the tape."

"That's excellent Bennet. Call them straight away and ask them to e-mail me the best image of the man they can get."

"Already requested Sarge. Should be on its way now." Bennet closed the door behind her and left Sgt. Robinson in the dark.

He pressed the standby button on the video remote control and stood up. Twisting the bar on the Venetian blinds to let the light in, he realised that despite being only 3.30pm, it was already dark. He re-closed the blinds and flicked the main light switch on the wall. The strip-light buzz-buzzed into life and Robinson squinted to get used to the harsh light.

He sat down at his desk, stretched his elbows backwards, shook his fingers, and then clicked the 'send & receive' button to check his e-mails. He had eight messages: one from his sister in South Africa that he would read later, another two offering miracle penis enlargement remedies, another four offering various pills to cure penile dysfunction, and then finally the message he'd been waiting for.

Sgt,

I am delighted to attach an image of a man on your tape who allegedly supplied the drinks that led to the deaths of three white males last week. Our team has spent a lot of time enhancing the image and I hope it is of sufficient quality for you to take your enquiries further.

Our image analysts have assembled additional information that may be of assistance to you. Whilst their information is not guaranteed, it should be used as a guide to discovering the identity of the man.

Key points gleaned from the study of the tape are as follows:

1. We suggest the man is of Mediterranean or Middle Eastern extraction. His facial features and skin texture combine to give us this hypothesis.

2. The man is of medium build, neither overweight nor slim.

3. The man is approximately aged between 22 and 30.

4. Using various points of reference on Union Street, we estimate the man's height to be between 5'8" and 5'10".

If you require any further assistance, please do not hesitate to contact me.

Sincerely,

Dr Hamish Parsons, Senior Forensic Scientist, Grampian Police.

Robinson was impressed with the work of the forensics department. He had already received the results from the lab, which proved conclusively the victims had been drinking acid. Staring hard at the computer screen, he realised he was looking at the face of a murderer. This man had to be found. He decided against making the image available to the press and television after a discussion with the Superintendent. This was a hard but complicated decision to take, but one Robinson thought was right in the circumstances. This man looked middle-Eastern and the last thing the Police wanted was every racist in Scotland phoning their local station with the names and addresses of any asylum seeker who they had taken exception to. Other measures would have to be taken to trace the suspect.

*****

Guinness had abandoned the hotel room that she had come to call home and returned to the McWerter house a mile to the west. Although she had her own one-bedroom flat just a few streets away, she felt the need for family home comforts. Her father was a cold distant man: a well-respected surgeon at a private hospital, who rarely spent time with his family. Her mother was a large, soft character, who provided the hugs that Guinness needed following the shock of the death of her friend.

Guinness had hidden herself away in her former bedroom for three days without emerging. She had hardly eaten anything and her mother had become seriously worried about her.

On the fourth day, she woke having cried herself to sleep again. She stared into her dressing-table mirror and wiped the black craters under her eyes. She sighed deeply and slouched into the bathroom, dragging her dressing-gown belt along the floor.

"Would you like some breakfast today dear?" He mother called out to her.

"Yes please mum."

Mrs McWerter smiled, hoping this was the beginning of the end of her daughter's grief.

After a breakfast of porridge and toast with jam, Guinness, dressed herself and left the house with the tape that held the key to the deaths of Richie and the two others.

She took her mobile phone from her pocket and walked towards the town centre.

"Des? It's me. Guinness. I'm fine. Really. Listen, we need to meet. We've got to do something about Richie and I'm not prepared to leave it to the Police."

Des, her cameraman listened hard. He had wanted to do something about the deaths and had been waiting for Guinness to take the lead. He knew she was a strong woman and was happy to assist. They agreed to meet in a coffee shop in twenty minutes.

As Guinness walked purposefully along the street, she gripped the tape hard in her hand, and rubbed her teeth over her lips nervously. She was thinking carefully how to approach the next stage.

Reaching the coffee shop in 15 minutes, Guinness ordered two large cappuccinos and waited for Des. She found a table in the front of the shop, facing out onto the street and away from prying ears. It was still early and well before the lunchtime rush.

Des walked in and waved a big hand at her.

"Hiya darlin' how you doing?"

"I've been better."

"Aye. I know what you mean. What's the plan of action?"

Guinness pushed a steaming cup of coffee towards him with one hand and waved the tape above the table in the other.

"This tape has got to provide the answers Des. I have to finish the story, for the sake of Richie and his family. I have to get to the bottom of this and you're as much a part of this as I am."

"And what do the Police say?"

"Obviously they want to solve this case too. But they're not emotionally involved like we are. The way I figure it is this: if we can find out some information leading to the killer, we follow it up. Of course we won't withhold evidence from the Police…it's just a matter of timing. We will decide when we to give any information to the Police."

"You sure that's legal?"

"What? You think the Police will do us for withholding evidence if we supply them with information they were too useless to find themselves? I don't think so."

"OK. Guinness, I've been thinking, and tell me if you think this is a waste of time."

"Go on…"

"I've got a mate who works at Aberdeen Airport in security. It's all a bit hush-hush at the moment, but they're doing iris scanning at the airport. It's going on at a couple of English airports as well, but I know it's happening at Aberdeen."

"So?"

"Well don't you see, if our man came through the airport, his iris will have been scanned."

"…and his passport and ID recorded somewhere?"

"Well I reckon so. I could find out. My man owes me a favour. I lied for him when he was cheating on his wife not so long ago."

"Oh I see…honour among scumbags eh?"

"I suppose you could put it like that. You saying I'm no angel?"

"I know you're no angel Des, I've seen you in action." Guinness passed Des the tape.

"Take the tape Des and get that image checked out. It's our only hope to find the man who did this."

Des took the tape and finished licking the froth at the bottom of his cup. "OK Guinness, I'll give you a call if I find something out. It might take a couple of days."

"No problem. It's not like I'm going anywhere."

Des left the coffee shop and headed straight to the airport. He knew that time was of the essence and for a refreshing change, he was happy to be using his own initiative to help with the investigation.

*****

Klarkey had taken his cordless laptop down to the small back garden of the hotel. He hadn't really spent any time in this outside space before, but hoped that being away from the suite for a few minutes would calm things down between Matisse and Roberta. This was a man's simple perception of complicated situations between women. Klarkey had other things on his mind.

He quickly connected to the internet through the wireless connection and opened a browser. Clicking straight to his Bahamian bank account, he entered his username and password. For the next 15 minutes he repeatedly pressed the 'refresh' button and stared blankly at the screen.

After some time, on his twentieth refresh, a cold sweat criss-crossed his body. The Collective Bank of Bahamas account balance increased by £6,500,000 in front of his eyes. The money from the auction had been received safely.

He then proceeded to make six transfers of £1 million each into accounts in six countries across the world: to France, USA, Australia, Switzerland, Israel and Canada. These dormant accounts at six different banks were now activated, rapidly accepting the new funds and converting them into Euros, US Dollars, Australian Dollars, Swiss Francs, Shekels and Canadian Dollars. Klarkey smiled and rubbed his hands that had become cold. He now had access to funds internationally.

Meanwhile, in the suite, smiles were the last things on the minds of Matisse and Roberta. They had come out of their respective bedrooms and faced each other in the sitting room. Matisse spoke first.

"Have you come to take my best friend away from me? Is that your little plan?"

"Matisse I don't have a plan. I don't even know you. Why would I want to do anything to upset you? Perhaps you're in love with him?"

"Don't be ridiculous" Matisse turned away and slammed the door of her bedroom.

Klarkey returned to the suite to find Roberta standing alone in the sitting room.

"Is everything alright?"

"Oh yes, everything's just fine."

*****

Des was running from the high security area at Aberdeen Airport, past the haggis and gift shop and out towards the revolving exit door.

He had to push past several waiting taxi drivers, credit card salesmen and shoe-shine touts, but once he was outside, he rushed towards the taxi queue and jumped in the first Mercedes to take him back into the centre of town.

Out of breath he called Guinness. She answered quickly, seeing Des's name flash up on the display screen of her phone.

"Des? How are you getting on?"

"I'm leaving the airport just now. I've got some news. Meet me in the middle of Golden Square in 15 minutes. I don't want anyone to hear this." The taxi driver cocked his ears, but there was nothing more Des was going to say until he met with Guinness.

"Just take me to Golden Square will you," he barked to the cab driver.

Seventeen minutes later, Des arrived at the circular road within the square to find Guinness pacing up and down, hot breath coming out of her nostrils, rubbing her gloved hands together.

Des slammed the car door behind him. "You're not going to believe this, but my mate has really come up trumps."

"Well?"

"They've been testing this iris-scanning equipment for about 2 months now. Only the most senior Police know about it locally. It's described as the latest tool in the war against terrorism. They're using it up here because they think the oil rigs might be at risk."

"And?" Guinness was getting impatient.

"It turns out our man on the tape matches a chap who came in through the airport on the day of the murder."

"What?" Guinness held her hands to her face.

"No listen, it gets better. We've got a name. The iris scan is linked to the passport the man was travelling on. His name is Hussein Nizar Al-Jamil."

"Hussein Nizar Al-Jamil? That's a bit of a mouthful. Are you sure that's his name?"

Des shrugged. "That's the name on your man's passport."

Guinness squeezed Des's arm. "You've done a bloody good job. I'm impressed."

"So what next?"

"We'd better see if WE can find this Al-Jamil."

"Don't you reckon we should go to the Police with this information?"

"Are you kidding? I promise I will go to the Police. I'm not going to be accused of withholding evidence. I feel that I owe it to Richie to do some digging first."

Guinness grabbed Des's arm and they started walking.

Guinness stared up at Des's face. "I'm going to start by checking things out with my contact in Social Security. You can call your mate in immigration."

Des was a cameraman, but he had been making investigative documentaries for more than 20 years, and had collected a healthy contact book along the way. He knew it was time to call in some favours.

CHAPTER SIXTEEN   YOUSEF'S HEIST

Yousef was happy to accept a £4000 pay packet from Klarkey; earnings for a visit to Aberdeen and one evening's work. He wasn't going to ask any questions and he certainly wasn't prepared to consider the consequences of any actions he had taken. He had become hardened over the years, perhaps even psychologically disturbed. To Yousef, £4000 meant more than anything at that time. He was barely surviving in a boring job, in a country that didn't particularly welcome him. He had been a model citizen among his people back in Iraq: the only member of his family to make it to Baghdad to study. He adored art history and he had dreamed of working in the Iraqi National Museum, protecting the priceless antiquities of his culture. When Saddam drained the marshes, his people were decimated.

The marshes region, some 20,000 square kilometres located at the confluence of the Tigris and Euphrates rivers in south-eastern Iraq, is the site of some of the country's richest oil deposits. . The area once constituted the largest wetlands ecosystem in the Middle East, and the United Nations called its destruction one of the world's greatest environmental disasters. For Yousef, the calamity that fell upon the marshes was a personal tragedy. Like so many, he had lost all of his family. The systematic bombardment of villages, widespread arbitrary arrests, torture, 'disappearances', summary executions, and forced displacement reduced the Marsh Arabs from a population of more than 250,000 to fewer than 40,000. Yousef was safe in Baghdad, but his family had perished.

This annihilation led a gentle, loving and patriotic Yousef, to turn into a cold, bitter and isolated man, desperate to leave Iraq to start a new life elsewhere. He felt unable to remain in a country where his roots had been destroyed, his family murdered and where his future was destined to be hopeless.

Yousef's journey began on an oil transporter from the outskirts of Baghdad on the road to Jordan. As a student, he had successfully been able to obtain a passport from the Government. This would serve him well through Arab nations, but he had no idea whether he would be able to pass through non-Arab countries with as much ease. In fact, he hadn't even thought how far his travels would take him. Many people at his University had dreamed of travelling to the USA, but this had not been his goal. His art history led him to crave for a destination rich in the history or Art. He yearned to see the Louvre in Paris or the British Museum in London. Western Europe was his goal, but he had no idea how to achieve this, while he passed along the dusty road through the Syrian Desert in western Iraq towards the border with Jordan.

Crossing the border with Jordan was simpler than he had expected. Yousef had befriended the tanker driver and told stories of the history of ancient Mesopotamia. When they arrived at the border, the tanker was waved through. This was before the Iraqi War and border controls were light.

As the long road curved in a north westerly direction through the central zone of Jordan, Yousef had resolved to leave the tanker on the other side of the Syrian border and make his own way towards Turkey. He knew that a significant advantage of remaining in middle-eastern countries was that he could blend into the background, especially because everyone spoke Arabic. He shuddered to think how he would approach European countries, where people spoke a myriad of strange foreign languages.

Passing through the town of Al Mafraq in northern Jordan, the tanker crossed the Syrian border, again with no difficulty, and headed north towards its destination city, Damascus. Yousef said goodbye to the driver in the centre of Damascus. He was used to the heat and pollution of a busy city, but knew that after a meal and water he would need to move on, towards Turkey and then onto Europe. He had limited funds, but enough US currency to get him as far as southern Europe. Teaching art history to the young sons of wealthy Baghdadi families had provided him with some essential hard currency. Beyond the edges of Europe, his future was unclear.

He took his first train journey from Damascus, travelling north through Aleppo and into Turkey. He was lucky again. The border guards at Turkey were Muslim and they also spoke Arabic. They accepted his story that he was an art student seeking to visit the mosques of Istanbul. The guards were far more interested in searching visitors for weapons and Yousef had a backpack full of books and clothes. The train snaked north then west, and Yousef slept comfortably for the first time in the train's smelly and cramped carriage. In his dreams he cried for his family and for the plight of the marshes. He woke with a start and vowed never to cry again. It wasn't helpful to show weakness. From now on he resolved to remain tough. He would depend upon no one but himself, always putting himself first, whatever the consequences of his actions on others.

Arriving in Istanbul was inspirational. Yousef was torn between wanting to enjoy the sights as a tourist, and conserving his dwindling funds in order to reach Western Europe. He decided to visit the 17th Century blue mosque with its six minarets and then to find a way to reach Greece.

The journey was arduous and not without risk, but a series of boats took Yousef from Istanbul to Greece, from Greece to Italy and from Italy to Barcelona. Here in the Catalonian capital he had almost run out of money. He was exhausted and needed to take a proper rest. Barcelona was fascinating. He marvelled that this was a Catholic country teeming with Moorish Arab influences. He recognised many elements in the architecture that reminded him of home. He quickly learned to eat from the stalls of the street-traders, where he would usually find an Arab speaker ready to help him on his onward journey. On an April day in Barcelona, he found a Lebanese falafel seller who was to provide him with a stable home and job. The trader had a brother in nearby Sitges who owned a Lebanese restaurant and was looking for staff. Yousef took the thirty minutes train ride to coastal Sitges and walked another 20 minutes to the seafront restaurant that was to become his workplace and home for the next 6 months. He worked 18-hour days and saved almost every penny of his wages. In his short breaks during the day, he would stumble sweating into the impressive museums on the city walls, staring at the art, dreaming of moving onto Paris. He would look in a bewildered way at the topless women on the beach or the men holding hands along the promenade, often feeling isolated and removed from the strange activities of this Western world.

When the season was at an end, his services were dispensed with and he stowed away on a truck bound for France, knowing that his Arab papers were no longer of any use to him. Before setting out on this new journey, he sat on the beach, watching the sun go down and created a fire for his passport and other papers. He fought back the tears, remembering his promise to himself that he would never cry again, always to look forward. Yousef had become accustomed to working hard and living in one place for several months, but he knew his time had come to move on once again.

The long journey by road, surrounded by large containers of bottled water bound for Paris was uncomfortable, but also a relief. He had made few friends in the restaurant, although he was treated fairly well. The decision to move on was right and timely.

Yousef awoke from his sleep to the sound of car horns coming from all directions. He peered from under the tarpaulin and realised he was travelling around a grand arch. He had arrived at the Arch de Triomphe in central Paris. This was a spectacular first view of the city of his dreams. He wiped the sleep from his eyes, cut one of the bottles of water from the tightly packed container and poured the contents into his mouth and over his body. He was ready to face his next challenge, in another city with another alien language.

By the time he had composed himself and co-ordinated a safe dismount from the truck, he was at the Paris Nord station. He had no idea where the vehicle was heading, but he couldn't risk being discovered. As he walked out from under the raised metro railway line, he approached a run-down parade of shops, many of which had Arabic and French signs. One of them caught his eye. In Arabic the sign said: "Arab Care – We are here to help you."

Three men were sitting inside the store, drinking tea and smoking, talking Arabic with a French lilt in the accent. He guessed they were from north Africa.

Yousef excitedly told them of his travels, and his plans to see the sights of Paris. The men were unimpressed. They had heard his story many times from stowaways, migrants and refugees. To them, Yousef was another brother far from home, with the same dreams of bettering himself in a land that was unfamiliar and in their opinion, unwelcoming. Nevertheless, Arab Care helped Yousef to find a somewhere to stay and a place to work.

Yousef worked hard in the hospital. He was a porter alongside many other Arab and African men. On his days off he visited the Louvre and Montmartre. He marvelled at the Eiffel Tower and spent hours studying the frescos around the doorways of Notre Dame Cathedral. For the first time in a long time he was happy, although he did not feel completely welcome in this new land. Far right politics dominated the agenda in France and he was always aware that his Arab features, unshaven beard and lack of papers, could get him into serious trouble.

It was springtime before Yousef was able to take a decision about making the journey to the UK. It also took many months before he could save the money required to pay the smugglers. Klarkey's Grosvenor School of English was legendary among the hospital workers. At first, Yousef had no interest in travelling to England. He had travelled enough and was enjoying Paris. Time passed and he became disillusioned with Parisians. The problem was not related to any specific incident, or anything that had been said to him. He simply felt that he was looked down upon, like a second-class citizen. He knew in his heart there was no guarantee that life in England would be any better, but after several months he determined to make travelling there his next goal. He enrolled at the Grosvenor School and threw himself into his studies. He met like-minded people and became more confident that his decision to leave Paris was the right one. He continued working at the hospital on the night shift, going to the college by day, and sleeping in the late afternoon and early evening.

When he finally arrived in the UK, with a new passport and a new name, he was shocked to find that his journey was to end in Glasgow. He was resigned to his destiny and from then on he decided to style himself as an Arabic Scotsman. He developed new loyalties and rivalries, favouring Scotland over England, and supporting Glasgow Rangers football team. His English was improving rapidly and he was cultivating a Scottish accent. He even considered having a special kilt made for himself one day. It wasn't a wonderful life, but it was a safe life.

Yousef was now a different person to the carefree, excitable student in Baghdad. He had felt pain and grew hard from his experiences. He certainly did not want to end his days washing dishes in a back street restaurant in

Glasgow. Since living in Sitges he had been planning a strategy that could bring him wealth and freedom. When he returned to Glasgow from Aberdeen with £4000 in cash, his thoughts were not about what he had done for the money, but what he could do for himself with the money.

This would be the seed money for a crime in a place that he had come to know well. He was going to return to Sitges. He had a job to do and he hoped it would lead him to a new life wherever he chose to finally settle. His new persona of Hussein Nizar Al-Jamil would allow him to pass across borders with a British passport. After several weeks of preparation, he set his plan into motion.

It started with an argument at work. This was planned. The chef was French and was easily led into a rage. Yousef spent the evening knocking food from the work surfaces and knives onto the floor. As the demands from the front of house became greater, the temperature in the kitchen rose to boiling point.

"Get out of my kitchen you Arab bastard. You are useless and I never want to see you again. Pick up your P45 and your money on the way out. OUT. Get OUT."

Yousef wanted to be sacked. He did not want to voluntarily walk out, with questions unanswered as to why he chose to go. This way, there were no loose ends. He went home and slept soundly, dreaming of himself dressed as an Arab prince, with a beautiful girl on his arm. He hoped one day to find a wife. Perhaps his money making plan would help to make him more attractive to the opposite sex. It was different back in the country of his birth. In Iraq, a man married who he was told to marry, or who was good for the family. In this strange land, money and handsome looks were the key for getting the right wife. He was poor and considered himself not very good-looking. He hoped his new found wealth would create the attraction to women he craved.

The following morning he took £3000 from the under-floor hiding place in his small flat and took a taxi to Glasgow Airport. The flight to Barcelona, via Birmingham was not very busy and he was easily able to buy a ticket. He laughed to himself as he travelled through passport control in Barcelona. Then he shook his head. Memories flooded back of how immensely difficult his previous journey had been to reach this Catalan city. It had taken him months to make it this far. Today it had taken him half a day, thanks to his new name and passport in the name Hussein Nizar Al-Jamil. Armed with information from when he previously lived in Catalonia, he knew exactly where he was going and he had a new found confidence to complete his task with precision and complete success. He had made only one real friend while he worked in Sitges two years earlier. Khamal was still working in the restaurant whose kitchen sink they had shared for many months. He was surprised to receive the call from Yousef, but at the same time was intrigued by his mysterious request. Khamal was to meet Yousef before work at about 5pm on the Passeig de la Ribera, in front of the beaches. They met with a firm hug as if they were long lost brothers. Khamal squeezed his friend so tightly that the carrier bag Yousef was holding, fell to the ground. Yousef broke the embrace and stuffed the protruding rope back into the bag.

"Khamal my dear friend. I have a job for you to do."

"A job? But I already have a job."

"This job will take just a couple of hours. Trust me. You will be back into work by 7 o'clock and I will give you 1000 Euros for your help."

"Yousef. I don't like the sound of this. I can't do anything that might risk me getting deported. That won't happen will it?"

"Not if you do exactly as I say. Trust me. You want to earn some real money don't you?"

"Of course I do."

Yousef led Khamal along the sea front to where small boats were rented out to tourists. Yousef negotiated a price for two small boats and instructed Khamal to follow him.

Despite being an autumnal day, the sea was surprisingly still. The small motors on the boats hummed as they bounced on the waves, and Yousef led Khamal to the side of the great walls below the old church.

"Wait here for me. Put down your anchor and do not go anywhere."

Khamal was confused, but ready to take instructions nevertheless. "OK."

It was 5.45pm. Yousef sped off towards the St Sebastian beach two hundred metres to the east, stepped out of the boat, and climbed the steps by the old walls in the direction of the centre of the town. He passed alongside the pretty houses through the cobbled streets that were now deserted. This was siesta time and the busy summer season was over. If he had been in the same spot three months earlier the streets would have been overflowing with tourists. His destination was in sight. It was 5.55pm.

Yousef entered the Museu Cau Ferrat. The museum was the late 19th century home and studio of artist Santiago Rusiñol. He noticed, as he had done on several occasions before, an old man and woman were the only staff working at this time, and the last visiting member of the public was just leaving. He picked up a brochure by the solid wood front door and started reading:

Artists have always been attracted to and fascinated by Sitges. Late 19th century painters, painting in the open air were drawn to Sitges because of its sea and its light.

The last tourist left the building and the old man looked at his watch. Yousef's heart was pounding and he could feel the veins on his forehead standing to attention with every beat. He pushed shut the front door with his shoulder and put his hand into the bottom of the carrier bag, pulling out a gun. It was a replica, but the old man and woman were not to know this. They were scared and this slightly unnerved Yousef. For a second he considered the layers of lines on their faces, stretching with fear. Then he dismissed their distress and continued. They placed their hands in the air and Yousef drew out two pairs of handcuffs from the bag. The museum was famous for Rusiñol's collection of wrought iron objects and he used the largest closest heavy cabinet to join the old couple with the cuffs. He placed his finger to his lips and made his only noise.

"Sshhh"

The couple looked at each other in horror. They didn't know what would happen next. Yousef bolted the front door, knowing that any passers-by would expect the museum to be closed at this time. It would not reopen until the following morning. He then cut the telephone cables and proceeded to make progress on the plan that he had conceived over many nights when he previously lived in this sleepy town.

His love of art had first drawn him to this museum. It was a beautiful place, topped by a vaulted wooden roof and its walls over two floors were covered with paintings collected by Rusiñol. Yousef made his way to the ground floor room where four small Picassos hung with little dignity. He knew they were worth much money in England and he selected his favourite two. Then he made his way up the stairs and into the cathedral-like chamber filled with ironwork, glass, statues and pictures.

This room never ceased to fill Yousef with joy, and although he had seen it many times before, and despite being in the middle of a serious criminal act, he took a few moments to appreciate the space and to stare.

"Domenicos Theotocopoulos" he said quietly, squinting as he stared at the two El Greco paintings ahead of him. He lifted the Mary Magdalene Repentant from the wall and struggled with this and the Picassos to the window at the rear of the room. He opened the window and stared down at the boat bobbing up and down on the sea below.

"Khamal. I'm here."

Khamal looked up, startled. He had been looking in the direction of Yousef's departing boat and had not expected to rediscover him from above.

Yousef took a rope ladder from his bag and attached it to the window. He then proceeded to take four mailbags from his now empty bag. The Picassos fitted into one bag; the others were cut open and wrapped around the El Greco. He then tied them up and lowered the pictures down to Khamal, who took possession of the artworks without comprehending the severity of what was happening. Once the pictures were safely in the boat, Yousef lowered himself down using the rope ladder and fell from the last step into the boat. He grazed his leathery left hand along the ancient wall. He was bleeding.

"Drive!" Yousef commanded and Khamal did as he was told. Khamal had so many questions but he felt it was easier to say nothing except "Is your hand OK?" Yousef nodded, then leaned over the side of the boat as it bobbed up and down on the waves, letting his bleeding hand drag in the refreshing, yet cold seawater.

After about 20 minutes, Yousef ordered Khamal to stop. Yousef's hand was almost blue, but the bleeding had stopped.

"Yousef, what kind of person have you become?"

"The same person that I ever was: someone who wants to better himself without anyone getting in the way. Now do you want your money or not?"

"Of course."

"So stop asking questions and help me out of the boat with these pictures."

Khamal helped Yousef with his bag and the pictures. The coastline was craggy and quiet at this point and there was a small coastal road with a Mitsubishi Space wagon parked on the grass verge.

"Here's my car, I left it here earlier. You can leave me here. I want you to take the boat back to the harbour. Then return to the beach and take the other boat back."

Yousef put his hand into the inside zipped pocket of his leather jacket and withdrew a wad of notes.

"Here's your 1000 Euros. Now go! And don't ever speak of this again."

Khamal took the money and returned to the boat.

"Good luck my friend" Khamal shouted to Yousef as he was climbing into the driver's seat, having loaded the pictures into the rear of the vehicle out of sight. Yousef waved but did not look at his friend. He knew he would never see him again.

Meticulous planning had been Yousef's strong point so far. He had to occupy his mind with something during the long evenings of washing up in the restaurant, or when he was sitting at home watching television.

The next stage of his plan had to be put into action.

He drove straight to Barcelona, where he purchased several planks of wood, nails, bubble wrap and heavy-duty string. Leaning against the opened back hatch door of his hire car, he nailed together a box to house the pictures. He was completely ignored by the handful of people on the streets. It was only 9pm and the locals wouldn't be stepping out of their homes to eat for at least another hour.

The pictures were wrapped in bubble-wrap, then sealed inside the wooden box. He had practised making such a box on several occasions back in Glasgow. He had perfected the technique that produced a sturdy secure housing for the treasure he intended to take back to Scotland.

He drove to the airport and checked in the car at the hire company's office. He had hired the car in Sitges but returned it to the airport. He didn't want anyone to have seen the car in Sitges while he was working in the Museu. He tried to take actions that would leave few trails.

Yousef briefly considered the welfare of the old couple in the Museu. 'They would be fine until morning' he dismissed. He needed this time to return safely to the UK without any unnecessary examination of passengers on flights leaving Barcelona.

He handed over the wooden box at the 'fragile' loading bay, then checked himself in at the desk. His heart was thumping. He had always felt in control but now he considered that his fate was in the hands of others: the airlines and the airport security. He had to stay calm. He wiped his brow with a tissue and coughed as if he was suffering from a cold.

He returned to Glasgow without any difficulty. Despite stopping at Birmingham en route, the change in time zone meant that he walked through Glasgow customs not long after midnight. He picked up the large wooden box from the carousel and tucked the string over his shoulder. He walked straight through the blue channel; there was no one to greet him and no one in uniform to stop him.

*****

Guinness had been sitting in the reception of the Police station in Queen Street for over twenty minutes. She was biting the ends of her hair and felt a little unsure exactly how she might create an appropriate working relationship with the Police. As a journalist she was experiencing the age-old dilemma: whether to be the first to reveal a story to the public, or to perform her civic duty to report to the authorities any information pertinent to a case. She knew she had to strike a compromise, but she had to carefully consider what information she would give the Police and whether she could glean any useful leads from them in return.

A man in a pin-striped suit opened one of the doors into the waiting area.

"Miss McWerter? I'm Detective Inspector Rey-Smith, will you come with me please?"

Guinness followed the officer.

"I was speaking to Sergeant Robinson last time. Is he not here today?"

"Aye he's here, but the case is with MIT now. I'm one of the officers on the Murder Investigation Team and you'll be liaising with me if you have any further matters to discuss relating to the case."

"Oh I see. Do you know if the Sergeant spoke with Richie's family?"

"I believe he did. We're still trying to trace the families of the other men, but their identities are proving difficult to ascertain at the moment."

Rey-Smith held the door open to a room off a long corridor. Someone was banging and moaning against a wall on the opposite side.

"Not enough cells and too many bodies." Rey-Smith spoke in explanation of the noise.

"I'll come straight to the point," Guinness started, "and this is off the record, so no statements today please."

"No bother, carry on." The DI had taken his jacket off and cupped his hands with his chin resting on his knuckles.

Guinness moved awkwardly in her chair, unsure exactly how to approach this delicate situation.

"I may have a lead to help with the case."

"Go on."

"Naturally I can't reveal my sources."

"Naturally."

"But it might be possible that after a little more investigation, I may have a name of the person who might be responsible for the murders."

"Oh really?" Rey-Smith raised an eyebrow in a somewhat disbelieving way. He stood up. His six foot three frame dwarfed Guinness, and she was supposed to feel belittled. In fact, she started to become more confident.

"DI Rey-Smith. I said that I MIGHT be in a position to offer you the name of the person involved in the murders of the three men. Is this something we can talk about or not?"

Rey-Smith sat down.

"What do you mean talk about?"

"Detective Inspector, I am a reporter. I want to get the story. I also want to find the killer of my friend – the two parts go hand in hand for me. What I'm asking is a favour in exchange for a favour. If I find the killer and give you the information, will you allow me to interview him before you make the arrest? I'm willing to co-operate fully and not put myself or the investigation at risk. All I'm asking is your help for mine. What do you say?"

"Miss McWerter, I don't know what kind of investigation you think I'm running here, but if you have any information that could lead to the arrest of this man or person's involved then I expect you to give it to me, or I'll come down on you so damn hard that you'll never be making a bloody documentary or whatever it is you do, again. Do I make myself clear?"

"Perfectly. Can I go now please?" Guinness was crushed and angry.

"Aye you can. Here's my card. Call me if you have anything concrete to tell me."

They both stood up and silently made their way to the Police reception.

Guinness was furious with Rey-Smith's refusal to consider any kind of deal.

CHAPTER SEVENTEEN

Klarkey walked through St. James's, along the London streets just behind Piccadilly and stared into the windows of the elegant art and antique shops. He was desperate for Roberta and Matisse to get along, but it was clear that Matisse had more of a problem with Roberta than the other way around. Matisse, he felt, was acting like a spoilt child who had to concede to the arrival of a new baby. He considered the best way to deal with her jealousy was to buy her a present.

A teapot and stand caught his eye in the window of one of the Georgian shops that he was browsing.

An Important Chamberlain's Worcester 'Nelson Service' teapot, cover and stand, circa 1802-05.

'Perfect', Klarkey thought. 'Something terribly English and a piece of Nelsoniana for Matisse's collection'. He hoped her frosty mood would thaw when she saw it.

Klarkey pushed open the door and a bell rang with an old fashioned 'ting' when he entered. Klarkey expected to see a bespectacled man behind the old counter, but instead, a pretty forty-something blonde woman, with a silk scarf around her neck, greeted him as he entered.

"May I help you sir?

"Yes, the teapot with stand in the window. How much is it please?"

"Oh a marvellous choice sir. Painted and gilt in the Imari style and elaborately embellished on both sides with the Admiral's coat of arms, flanked by supporters below two coronets." She picked the teapot up to show Klarkey.

"Yes, I see…but how much is the piece please?"

"You see sir, the oval stand is painted with a jardinière of flowers, the border with panels of flowers, a crest and two coronets."

"Yes…but…"

"This was from a service, sir, named Horatia, and is mentioned in Lady Hamilton's diary after she placed the order with the factory in August 1802."

Klarkey waited until she had stopped talking. "And this would be…how much?"

"Thirty-five thousand pounds sir."

Klarkey coughed and his mouth remained open. "For one teapot and stand?"

"Indeed sir. It is most rare."

Klarkey felt a rush of blood to his head. "I'll take it. And I hope she appreciates it."

"I'm sure Madame will be most satisfied sir."

Klarkey pulled from his wallet a black charge card and considered briefly by how much his American bank account would be depleted by the purchase.

*****

Yousef had been sitting quietly at home in Glasgow for 3 days. He sat in a battered armchair in the semi-dark, drinking his eighth strong coffee of the day. Opposite him, lying on top of the cushions of a brown 1970s ripped sofa, was an El Greco painting, worth about £4 million and two small Picassos, worth around £250,000 each. He was waiting for the phone to ring.

*****

DS Robert Shore was making a regular visit to the Internet Monitoring Room at Enfield Prison. He had enjoyed spectacular successes from the surveillance work of the IMR and he was keen to keep the pressure on the inmates. The prisoners' conduct had improved extraordinarily because they were led to believe the use of the internet was a perk for good behaviour. This was privilege they did not want to have withdrawn.

"What have you got for me today Constable that's so urgent to pull me away from my morning briefing?"

"Sorry sir," the PC started, "I knew you would want to come over as soon as I picked up this conversation."

"Go on,"

"Graves the fence seems to be up to his old tricks again. He's been talking with someone called 'Prakash' for the last twenty minutes."

"And what does this Prakash want with our old friend Johnny Graves?"

"Well sir, it seems that Prakash is offering Graves a couple of valuable paintings he says a friend has got hold of from Spain."

"From Spain eh? Do we know what the paintings are?"

"Not yet sir, just that he says they're worth four and half million, and Graves says that if it's true, he'll give this Prakash four hundred and fifty grand for them."

"How generous. 10% of the true value and I suppose our Johnny plans to make another 10% on top. No doubt someone will buy the goods knowing they've got a bargain and won't be bothered about asking about the provenance."

"The what sir?"

"The HISTORY of the pictures you Philistine."

"Sorry Sir."

"Don't worry, let's set up an obbo and see where this leads to."

"OK Sir, what will the name of the operation be?"

"Operation…Philistine, don't you think?"

"Thank you sir."

*****

Yousef's phone rang. It was his friend Prakash calling from Kings Cross in central London, four hundred miles away. Prakash was a Pakistani who had come to the UK in the same group as Yousef. They had got to know each other well in the weeks leading up to their arrival in London, at the Grosvenor School in Paris. Prakash had connections with the criminal underworld in London, and it was to him that Yousef turned in his effort to turn the stolen paintings into hard cash.

"Prakash, I've been waiting for ages for you to call me, what's happening?"

"Yousef my man, relax. Chill. Everything's just fine. I've made the connection and it looks like you're gonna get some hard cash man. That is if the pictures are genuine."

"I tell you they're genuine. I lifted them from the walls myself."

"OK man. Too much information."

"How much am I going to get for them? I need to know."

"You know it's only a handful of people that will take them off you don't you? Not everyone wants to buy stolen paintings."

"Yes but those that do, don't mind paying a fraction of the true value. I know how these things work. How much am I going to get Prakash?"

"It's difficult to say to be honest man, but if they're really worth four and a half, then you should get about two hundred and fifty thousand."

"Two hundred and fifty thousand! One of the smaller pictures is worth that on its own."

"Yousef, Yousef my man, cool it will you. In your position you don't have many options. I'm the one with the connections and these blokes have a lot of expenses to take care of. If I were you I'd take what I can get, man. You could always find yourself another buyer."

"OK, ok. What do I have to do."

"I think you'd better bring the merchandise to London and stay at mine. Don't write my address down. I'll give it to you now and you can come in a couple of days.

*****

Roberta had returned to Portsmouth after an exhausting weekend. She loved her teaching job and no persuading by

Klarkey would convince her into giving it up. She didn't feel totally comfortable leaving Matisse and Klarkey alone, but they were friends and she had to trust them. Roberta planned to stay in touch with Klarkey every day by telephone and would look forward to the Christmas holiday, when they could spend more precious time together. She knew she was falling in love.

Matisse sat quietly in the sitting room of their suite, playing with her hair. She had seen Klarkey passing through the front door of the building after taking Roberta to Waterloo.

"Good riddance" she said into the air.

Klarkey opened the door of the suite and closed it with his hands behind his back.

"I'm sorry to see her go, but at least we can spend some quality time together." Klarkey was in the mood for reconciliation and could not bear a fight. He had bigger, more serious matters on his mind.

"Klarkey I am so sorry for being such a cow."

"No I'm sorry Matisse for being insensitive. I should have warned you that Roberta would be here when you got back from Amsterdam. It wasn't fair and I really am sorry."

Matisse held out her arms and they embraced. "Apology happily accepted"

Klarkey pulled away slowly. "Matisse...I've bought you a present. You know how I love to buy you things."

"Oh Klarkey, I'm excited now. What is it? What is it?"

Klarkey pulled down the flap of a wooden bureau and gave Matisse an expensively wrapped package.

Matisse opened the wrapping and stared. Then her eyes welled with water and she grabbed a tissue from the coffee table, wiping her eyes with one hand and holding onto the teapot with the other.

"Klarkey, I don't know what to say. Thank you so much. This is the first main piece of my collection of

Nelsoniana.   It's beautiful.   Tell me about it."   They sat down.

"Well it cost a fortune,"

"Yes…"

"and it was made for Lord Nelson…"

"Of course.."

"and it was part of a breakfast service made in 1802. I can't remember the rest. If you look in the bag you'll see a card with the information on it."

"Klarkey, this is the most wonderful present you could ever buy me. Thank you so much."

"Let this be the start of a valuable exciting collection for you Matisse."

Klarkey stood up and kissed her on the head.

"You know, it is possible for a man to have a relationship with two women."

Matisse looked straight into his eyes. "I know you will always be a best friend to me. Thank you."

*****

"Ladies and gents, let's have a bit of hush for Detective Superintendent Shore.. Thank you. Sir."

"Thank you Sergeant, " Shore began.

"As you know, we have enjoyed several high profile successes following the use of information obtained through use of the Internet Monitoring Room connected to Enfield nick. This week, we have been following leads out of the IMR, which have caused a new operation to be instigated: Operation Philistine."

A hum went around the room of Police officers.

"Quiet down please. So far, information is thin on the ground. We are sharing what we have with Strathclyde Police because we think the stolen goods are located somewhere in the Glasgow area. However our best course of action is to sit tight and wait until the goods come south, as we believe they will, and make our interception when our inside man reveals where his contact is going to meet the goods.

"The reason for briefing you this early in the operation is so that you keep your eyes and ears open for anyone making any connection with paintings, and Glasgow. Put those two elements together and come straight to me. That's all from me now. Carry on Sergeant."

"Sir."

Shore left the room. He wiped his hand across his face and thought how he deserved another big break. He was on a roll and had become something of an expert in the activities of criminals using the internet. He had his niece to thank for that introduction. He wondered how he could ever have lived without using this wonderful technology. He was shaking his head and smiling as he sat down in his office chair to think of his next move. Shore picked up his newspaper, and an article on page five grabbed his attention. He needed a cigarette, but he couldn't be bothered to walk outside the station and then to stand in the rain. The paper in front of him was far more important.

Spanish Masterpieces stolen from Barcelona resort

Catalan Police were shocked to rescue the elderly museum keepers, Mr and Mrs Montcada who were found handcuffed inside the Museu Cau Ferrat, Sitges, yesterday. Discovered by the morning cleaners who reported the incident to the Police, Mr and Mrs Montcada, both aged 68, were found reasonably well, despite being frightened, hungry, and dehydrated. The couple told the Police how an armed man of swarthy appearance, who spoke no words, had overwhelmed them. After careful examination of the scene, the staggering discovery was made that the man had escaped with three valuable paintings worth up to six million Euros. A reward has been offered by the Catalonian Government in Barcelona of 100,000 Euros for the safe return of the pictures. A spokesman from the Catalonian Police Federation said last night, "This has *been a terrible tragedy for Catalonia and for Spain. Those that have committed this crime have stolen our national heritage and must be punished with the full force of the law."* Full descriptions of the stolen paintings have not yet been released, but it is known that the Museu Cap Ferra collection includes works by Rusiñol, Picasso, El Greco, Utrillo, Zuloaga and Miro. Concern now preoccupies the Trustees of the museum that the artworks may have been taken out of Catalonia and perhaps may even have left Spain.*

Shore looked up from the paper. "I wonder. I bloody wonder."

*****

Guinness walked confidently down the echoing narrow Glasgow street. She was nervous but at the same time excited. She fiddled briefly with one of the buttons in her jacket pocket.

"Leave it a-bloody-lone." She heard in her almost invisible earpiece. It was her cameraman Brian. She quickly left alone the hidden buttonhole camera. Brian was safely inside the back of a white van which had 'Le Sable d'Or Patisserie' painted in flowery text on its side. He was about 30 yards away from the target address and he was watching the view from Guinness's hidden camera as she walked. He thought she seemed safe enough but considered the situation was nevertheless highly unpredictable with no certainly to its conclusion. Guinness had insisted that she entered the building alone. It was her big story and she was going to get it. It was as if she was recklessly exercising a desire to win a journalism prize by taking risks. She always said, "Move over war journalists, its time for the investigatives now."

Guinness had now reached the front door. Fortunately the street was well lit at this point and the doorway was perfectly framed within the shot of the tiny camera. Brian was pleased about that.

Guinness knocked on the door with her fist. There was no doorknocker and the bell didn't seem to work. There was no response. She knocked again, as hard as she could without making the blows seem too desperate. This time she noticed a response as the landing light was turned on, and footsteps came towards her down the stairs. This was a first floor flat and she hoped to find here the killer of her reporter Richie Brakes. Whilst she had rehearsed this moment a hundred times, nothing could prepare her for coming face to face with her friend's killer.

" Mr Hussein Nizar Al-Jamil?"

"Yes. What is it you want?"

"My name is Geraldine Smith, I work for the Tax office, specialising in National Insurance," her voice rose as if she was reciting lines from within a telephone call centre, "I'm sorry to call on you during the evening, but we find this is the best time to reach clients. We're investigating the impact on the increases in national insurance and tax on workers across the country and your name is on our random list of people to speak with. I'm sorry but it is the law to take part in these questionnaires."

"I'm sorry I don't understand."

Guinness showed him a fake identity card.

"It's just a routine series of questions that will only take a few minutes. Do you mind if I come in?"

"Wait a moment please."

Yousef closed the door and banged his fingers over his mouth. He did not fully understand the customs of this country but at the same time was pleased that it was not a Police officer visiting his flat. He ran upstairs and moved the pictures from his sofa to the bedroom, closed the door and ran back downstairs.

Guinness was shaking. Her legs were quaking and she could sense her right stiletto heel was vibrating on the paving stone through St Vitus dance. She knew she had come face to face with Richie's killer and realised that it was essential she continued with her charade, for fear of her life.

Yousef re-opened the door.

"Come in Miss Smith. I hope this won't take long."

"Thank you."

Guinness followed Yousef up the stairs and was beckoned to sit on the old sofa. The room was dark and she hoped that the picture Brian was getting was sufficiently clear. Guinness pulled a clipboard from a briefcase.

"Thank you Mr Al-Jamil for your co-operation. As I said, this won't take long. I just have a series of questions that I need to ask you and then I'll be on my way to bother one of your neighbours."

Yousef half-smiled, trying to be friendly. This was the first time a woman had entered his flat. He wondered if she would have sex with him. She reminded him of the women back in his own country. She was short and slightly overweight. But she was dressed so differently to the women back home. She was dressed so provocatively.

"First of all, can I confirm your place of work…"

"No I left. I mean I was working in a restaurant but unfortunately I was sacked."

"So you're no longer in employment."

"That is correct."

Guinness made a note on the clipboard every time Yousef spoke. She held the board on her right knee and wrote with her right hand so that there was a clear line of view from the camera hidden in her jacket towards Yousef.

"I need to ask you some questions now about your lifestyle and general activities. In the last three months, have you taken any holidays or trips out of the city?"

Yousef thought this was a strange question. He had to be careful. Anyone in authority could make the appropriate checks and know whether he had lied or not.

"Yes…I visited some friends in Spain recently. I was depressed after I lost my job and I thought a short break would be good."

Guinness didn't expect this response, but she continued.

"Do you feel in the last year that the amount you pay in tax has increased or decreased?"

"I don't know."

"Do you feel the amount of tax you pay has helped or hindered your ability to take holidays or trips away."

"I don't know."

"Do you feel that short breaks within Scotland are inexpensively priced and within most people's budget including your own?"

"I don't know. I suppose so."

"Have you in the last year taken any trips to other parts of Scotland or within the United Kingdom?"

"No," he lied.

"Do you feel the impact of tax affects how often you can take breaks away from home or how often you can engage in other leisure activities?"

"I don't know."

"Do you plan to move home in the next 12 months or thereabouts?"

"No."

"Do you feel satisfied, very satisfied, not very satisfied or do you not have an opinion about the level of taxation on wages in this country?"

"Er…I do not have an opinion." Yousef was starting to get bored.

"Do you feel satisfied, very satisfied, not very satisfied or do you not have an opinion about the level of National Insurance in the UK?"

"I don't have an opinion."

"You'll be pleased to know those are all the questions I need to ask you today so thank you for your time."

Guinness closed the cover of her clipboard. Her heart was

still racing and she wondered if the resonance of its beat was being picked up on the camera's microphone.

"Would you like a cup of tea?"

Guinness knew that if she stayed any longer he might suspect something. Against the wishes of her journalist's heart, her sensible head told her to leave. She had achieved in one night more than she could have imagined. She had spent time sitting opposite the Aberdeen killer.

"No thank you all the same. I've thirteen more houses to visit tonight and I can't be too late. Thank you again for your time Mr. Al-Jamil."

Guinness stood up and Yousef held his arm out to beckon her towards the staircase so she could leave. She took a deep breath and made her way carefully down the stairs. As she reached the front door, she turned and smiled, giving him a small wave by flicking the end of her fingertips. Then the door slammed behind her.

She walked towards the van parked along the street, running her fingers through her hair and breathing loudly. When she got to the van, she banged on the back door and Brian swung the door open so she could climb in.

"Did you get all of that Brian?"

"Oh yes. You were outstanding."

"I nearly cracked though. I just wanted to ask him, 'What the hell were you doing in Aberdeen and why did you kill my friend?', but I couldn't of course."

"Er no. I think that would have been suicide don't you think?"

"Of course. I know I know. Run the tape will you?"

Brian rewound the tape and played it back on the monitor.

"Did you hear how he denied even taking any trips to other parts of Scotland?"

"What did you expect? That he was going to fall at your feet and admit being in Aberdeen at the time the murders took place? I don't think so."

"What about that stuff about Spain?"

"Maybe he took a trip to Spain, I don't know. Do we care?"

"Brian, I'm saying that I wonder if the trip to Spain needs some checking. That's all."

"Guinness, millions of people in this country take trips to Spain every year. What possible significance can it be? Maybe he was visiting a friend there. Or maybe he knew that it could be checked that he passed through the airport and rather than saying he went to Aberdeen, he said he made a trip to Spain. Either way there's not going to be a stamp in his passport."

"True. I really don't know. I'm going to have to sleep on this one. Anyway, I think it's time to get us out of here? AND I've got no choice but to take this to the Police."

Brian switched off the monitor and climbed over to the driver's seat, then started the engine and pulled away. Brian's phone rang and he switched to hands free.

"Oh hi mate. Yeh it's OK to talk. Really? Really? Thanks very much mate, I owe you one."

"WHAT?" Guinness shrieked.

"You're not going to believe this?"

"WHAT for crying out loud?"

"That was my friend calling from the airport. It seems there is no such person as Mr Hussein Nizar Al-Jamil."

Guinness leaned over the front passenger seat from her place in of the rear seats. "What do you mean no such person as Mr Hussein Nizar Al-Jamil?"

"What I mean is, the passport that Al-Jamil is using is a false one."

Guinness dropped back into her seat. "Bloody hell. What have we got ourselves into Brian?"

"I don't know, but it's looking like quite a story isn't it?"

"You can say that again."

CHAPTER EIGHTEEN

Matisse surreptitiously followed Klarkey into the basement of the hotel. Neither of them had explored this area before but they were aware that a small gym with a sauna was secreted somewhere into the foundations of the building. When she approached the gym entrance, Matisse was surprised to find a brightly lit, well-equipped weights room. She had never been in a gym before in her life.

"Can I help you?" The receptionist purred, flashing the longest red fingernails Matisse had ever seen.

"I'm looking for my friend; he came in just a few moments ago."

"There was a gentleman who just arrived. He went into the men's changing room darling. Would you like to wait here?" She beckoned towards a small group of empty chairs next to tables with newspapers and magazines strewn across them. A television turned to an all-day news channel was fixed to a wall above head height.

"Thank you."

Matisse sat patiently and chose a fashion supplement from one of the Sunday papers. Klarkey swung open the door to the men's changing room and stood in the main room. Matisse looked over her magazine and blew him a kiss.

"Matisse! What are you doing here?"

"No, what are YOU doing here? In all the time I've known you I don't ever remember you using a gym."

"So I haven't used a gym in a couple of years. It's like riding a bicycle – you never forget what to do. It just hurts a bit the first few times you start back. Now is as good a time as any."

"I suppose so."

"Matisse will you get out of my way I want to use the equipment."

"Shouldn't you stretch a bit first?"

"I know that." Klarkey started to swing from side to side with his hands on hips. Matisse sat down on one of the benches.

Slightly out of breath, Klarkey barked to Matisse, "Haven't you got somewhere you should be right now?"

"No, I'm quite happy here with you thank you."

Klarkey sat on the floor and leaned forward towards his feet with his hands extended; therefore stretching both his body and legs. He grunted as he stretched.

"Klarkey…you've been acting a bit strangely of late. Is everything alright?"

"Of course everything's alright," Klarkey lied. He was planning his most daunting operation to date and had spent a lot of time on his own, considering his plans over multiple cups of strong coffee in various cafés.

"You haven't been spending much time with me and I've been getting lonely."

Klarkey stood up and made his way to the exercise machines.

"This is going to hurt in the morning." He ignored Matisse's comment and changed the weight on the shoulder press machine to 20 kilos. He sat down in the Weider seat, flicked his fingers in preparation to grip the machine's handle, and then started pressing up from the shoulders into the air.

"Breathe out Klarkey."

Klarkey dropped the weights down. "I AM BREATHING OUT. Do you have to sit here watching me?"

"I want to know what you're up to. You used to take me out all the time and in the last few days we've hardly done anything."

Klarkey continued to press up the weights. After ten repetitions he lowered the bar down slowly. "Now you're behaving like a spoilt brat. No I'm not up to anything. Besides, do we have to do EVERYTHING together?"

"Are you Christmas shopping? Secretly buying me lots of presents."

"Don't push it Matisse, I just spent a fortune on you with that teaset."

"I know you did and I'm grateful…but I'm trying to find out what you've been doing."

Matisse shook her fists like a child that had not got its way. Klarkey pushed for another ten repetitions.

"Read…my…lips Matisse. NOTHING. Besides, it's four weeks to Christmas and I'm a man. Do you really think I'd be organised enough to think about Christmas in November?"

"I suppose you're right."

"Of course I'm right. Now will you leave me alone?"

Matisse stood up to leave. "Nice shoulder muscles by the way." She winked at him with a smile.

"I'll see you upstairs in an hour."

Matisse left, and Klarkey reflected that he had thought of nothing else but Christmas, but gifts to Matisse were the last things on his mind.

*****

DI Rey-Smith was surprised to see Guinness again. After their last meeting it seemed to him that all she wanted was a story and he was in no mood to help. Guinness was happy to pursue her own lines of enquiry, but all she truly sought from the Police was justice for Richie's murder. Liaising with the Police would be the only real way she could achieve this. She also considered that helping the Police could mean they would owe her a favour, and that could be useful in the future.

"Come in Miss McWerter, it's a pleasure to see you again," Rey-Smith lied.

"I'll come straight to the point. Hussein Nizar Al-Jamil as he is known, is the man who appears on the video. He's the murderer of the three men. I have no idea if this is his real name, but what I can tell you is that he lives at 3A Doughty Place, Glasgow."

"And I suppose Miss McWerter you've visited him there and he's admitted to you his crime in a reveal-all type confession, filmed in bloody widescreen?"

"DI Re-Smith, of course he hasn't revealed all to me. I'm just a reporter doing my job. I thought you'd be pleased."

"Oh trust me, I am pleased. If this man is who you say he is then you'll have given valuable information to an inquiry and naturally I'm grateful."

"OK. Richie Brakes was a fine journalist and a friend of mine. I want to do whatever it takes to ensure his killer is brought to justice. I also want to know why he did it."

"We'll find him Miss McWerter don't worry. Is there anything else you'd like to share with us?"

"That's all for now I think."

"I'll see you out."

"Will you keep me informed about your progress?" They stood up to leave the room.

"Yes, I believe I will."

Guinness turned her head back to face the DI.

"I'm not your enemy you know. Just because I'm a journalist. I really do want to help."

Guinness noticed DI Rey-Smith smile for the first time. Perhaps he was warming to her side at last.

*****

Yousef had been on the train for nearly four hours and the countryside had turned into views of north London suburbs. He was carrying his precious cargo of pictures and a small sports bag with personal possessions. He sensed perhaps that he was never to return to Scotland, believing a new turn to his nomadic life was about to start.

After four hours and a minute, Yousef's train pulled into Kings Cross. He walked off the train and into the busy street. The bright cold early December day hit him sharply in the face, and he noticed the disruption on the streets that were being adapted to accommodate the new line of the Channel Tunnel Rail Link. As he stood staring at the road, his mind drifted back to the time when he had arrived in the UK at the Waterloo terminal of the Eurostar, not knowing what was to face him in another unfamiliar land.

"Yousef my man, how yah doin'?"

Yousef pulled himself together with a start. It was Prakash. His hair was longer and he had grown a goatee beard, but his voice was as distinctive as ever.

"Sorry Prakash, I didn't recognise you for a second."

"Long hair and beards were off the menu when we came over here weren't they. I think I've found myself now man. It's the look that suits me."

Yousef nodded. "Yes, you do look well."

"Is this the cargo man?" Prakash pointed at the wooden container. "Let's go. I live just around the corner in my own flat. You can stay with me until the deal's done. Then we'll have to part company and go our separate ways man."

"I'm glad you said that. I think that will be for the best."

Prakash carried Yousef's bag and Yousef hung the container of pictures over his shoulder as they walked around the block to Prakash's small modern flat overlooking the canal.

*****

DI Rey-Smith was sitting in an unmarked Police car with his opposite number from Strathclyde Police in Glasgow. He was given control of the operation despite it being outside of Aberdeen. Rey-Smith had been given clearance for this from the highest level and he intended to make sure that nothing went wrong.

He held the transmitter to his mouth until he was sure everyone was in place. It was 6am.

"GO GO GO."

Thirty-eight Policemen were assembled for this operation. The front guard wore stab vests and the largest of the officers forced a hand-held Police battering ram at the street door that led to Yousef's flat. Armed Police led the way up the stairs and into the flat. They cautiously made their way into each of the three rooms in the dark, using the light at the end of their weapons as a guide.

"Clear!"

"Clear!"

"Clear!"

The flat was empty.

The Glaswegian Police inspector looked at Rey-Smith in the car as they heard confirmation of the flat being empty.

"Shit." Rey-Smith had lost his man.

"It looks like the lights were on a timer guv."

Rey-Smith spoke into his radio for the last time that morning. "OK men stand down. Stand down."

It was time to go over the flat with a fine toothcomb in the search for clues for the man who he believed was the Aberdeen triple murderer.

*****

In London, Detective Superintendent was tapping a pencil on his desk, reaffirming his belief that there was no such thing as coincidences. He had checked with his friends at Scotland Yard in Arts and Antiques, and there had been nothing reported stolen of any significant value in weeks. He knew that criminals taking possession of anything extremely valuable would be keen to pass them on as soon as possible. His Police intuition convinced him that Johnny Brakes was trying to fence the stolen Spanish paintings. Through Operation Philistine he had to achieve three objectives. He needed to retrieve the paintings; he had to apprehend the fence taking receipt of them; then bring into custody the criminals selling them. It would also be a bonus if cash was also found. Large sums of money would no doubt be exchanged for the paintings and this was certain to be the proceeds from other illegal activities. Shore felt he was poised for another spectacular success.

Sergeant Morris knocked on Shore's door and entered.

"Sir we've got our first lead on Prakash for Operation Philistine."

Shore remained seated with his hands interlocked, resting on his elbows. He didn't invite Morris to sit down.

"What have you got sergeant?"

"We've tracked the computer used by Prakash to an internet café at the bottom of York Way right by Kings Cross Station."

"Well done Morris. Any preliminary information about the identity of this Prakash character?"

"Not yet Sir, we need to get you to authorise surveillance on the café before he makes the next contact with Brakes inside Enfield nick."

"That's fine, get straight onto it. Don't ask any questions of the café owner yet. We don't know if there's any association with Prakash and the internet café. We certainly don't want to risk scaring him off. Good work Morris."

"Sir." Morris closed the door behind him. It was now a race against time to trace Prakash, who would hopefully lead Shore to the missing paintings and further glory.

*****

Guinness was now working entirely alone. She didn't want to involve Brian or anyone else at this stage. She was prepared to put herself at risk, but wasn't going to allow anyone else to be put in the firing line or to be accused of impeding the Police enquiry. It was also because she knew in her heart that anyone who cared about her would attempt to dissuade her from the actions she was about to employ. She was compelled to act alone despite the danger.

After Guinness's frightening visit to Yousef in Glasgow, she decided to employ a private investigator for a few days to track him. She needed to assemble some background information on the man who was due to feature in her new documentary story. She hoped she would find some answers to why he did what he did.

The private investigator had provided Guinness with more information than she was prepared for. She hurriedly read the e-mail from him again.

The target known as Hussein Nizar Al-Jamil left his flat in Glasgow with a large rectangular package and a sports bag at 9am. He boarded the train at Glasgow Central railway station at 10am and arrived at London's Kings Cross at 4.01pm. The train had arrived on time and nothing unusual occurred during the journey. Soon after making his way onto the north-eastern corner of Euston Road, a man of Indian Sub-continental extraction met him; known in Police-speak as an IC4 male. The IC4 was of medium height, with long dark hair and wearing a goatee beard. They clearly knew each other as they embraced when they met. The IC4 then led the target to a flat at 11 Kings Cross Court, York Way, by the side of the Regents Canal. Both men have not yet left the flat.

This was the lead Guinness had been waiting for. She grabbed her handbag, picked up a couple of chocolate bars, a Dictaphone and a couple of spare batteries and called a cab to take her to the airport. She knew that if she was quick she would be able to make the last flight to Heathrow. She succeeded with minutes to spare.

*****

Yousef had been sitting in Prakash's flat for what seemed like hours. He was bored and wanted to get on with the job. He desperately needed to get cash for the paintings and to move on. Prakash had viewed the paintings already and did not express any opinion except that he couldn't understand how they were so valuable. Nevertheless, he took digital pictures of the artworks to show Johnny Brakes's man. Prakash was such an idiot in Yousef's opinion, but he needed him to turn the paintings into liquid assets.

"Come on man, let's go now." Prakash led Yousef to the internet café. He had to be there at a specific time in order that it would coincide with Johnny Brakes' use of the internet-connected computer inside Enfield Prison. They couldn't afford to be late.

Guinness came out of Kings Cross tube and started to walk towards her target's new address. Coming in the opposite direction on the other side of the road were two men. She recognised one immediately as the man she had been following. She was delighted - it was time she had some luck. From a discreet distance she followed them. She saw them go into an internet café where they remained for about fifteen minutes.

Shore's officers had been watching the internet café and saw their targets utilising the café computers. Surveillance at Enfield's IMR detailed the conversation with Johnny Brakes. The pair would meet Brakes's representative in 20 minutes in the burger bar inside Kings Cross Station. There they would confirm the details for the exchange, subject to confirmation that the artworks were what they were supposed to be.

Guinness watched the men come out of the café and make their way towards the station. She hoped they wouldn't be getting on a train; she really didn't want to travel any more this evening.

A woman with shoulder-length blonde hair complete with dark roots, wearing a light raincoat, approached Yousef and Prakash.

"I'm Jenny Brakes, Mrs. Which one of you jokers is Prakash?" She had a strong, loud Essex accent.

"Oh…er…it's me man. I didn't expect a woman."

"No one expects a woman. Johnny couldn't trust anyone else but me. Now where the hell are the paintings?"

"Mrs. Brakes, you didn't expect me to bring them out on the street with me did you?"

"Actually I did. And who's this?"

"This is my good friend Yousef, he obtained the paintings from Spain."

Jenny Brakes turned to Yousef and beamed. "Oh you're responsible for the paintings are you?"

"Yes Mrs." Yousef said shyly. He wasn't used to speaking with women.

Prakash interrupted. "How about looking at my camera man?" He pulled the digital camera from his pocket and pointed the rear-viewer to Brakes. He then moved the pictures on frame by frame so she could see the art in greater detail."

"Wow, you have come up trumps haven't you?"

"We have a deal then?"

"Oh we have a deal alright. Let me have a look a that camera. I'm going to need to take it with me"

"But it's valuable man!"

Brakes laughed, "Not as valuable as those pictures you want fenced. Give me the camera for crying out loud. I need to download the images onto a disc and show them to Johnny." She opened her large handbag putting the camera inside, pulling out a mobile phone."

"Take this phone. I'll call you on it when I'm ready to do the deal. I don't suppose you celebrate Christmas but I can tell you it's going to be a good one."

She walked away, moving deeper into the station leaving the two friends standing on the concourse.

Shore's undercover officers were continuing to observe the men. They hadn't got cash or the paintings with them, but they recognised Jenny Brakes. Shore knew he was close.

Guinness was also observing the men. She had purchased a bag of groceries while they had been in the internet café. She had a plan that didn't account for the fact that there might be two men, but nevertheless she had only one option, which was to proceed nevertheless. She walked slowly in their direction, watching as they came towards her. As she was about to pass them, she knocked into them and her groceries fell out of the large brown paper bag and onto the pavement.

"Here let me help you lady."

"Oh thank you so much," she said in response to Prakash's offer of assistance.

As they helped her place the goods into the bag, she seized her moment. She looked up at Yousef and spoke softly to him.

"Don't I know you?"

"I don't think so."

"No I'm sure I do. I live in Glasgow, I'm visiting my sister down here and I was just getting some shopping."

"No I don't think so."

"I remember. I met you through work. I must have come into your home to ask some questions for a survey."

"Oh yes, I remember," Yousef grudgingly agreed. Prakash was slightly taken aback but elbowed his friend as if to encourage him to engage in conversation with the woman.

"I'm Geraldine," Guinness offered her hand.

"Oh, I'm er Nizar. This is my friend Prakash."

Guinness could now make her move. "Look I don't mean to sound weird or anything, but my sister is out with her husband tonight and I wonder if you'd like to go for a drink. We Glaswegians should stick together you know. And we all like a drink, no?"

"Well I don't know about that…I don't really drink." Yousef looked at Prakash.

"Go on man. I don't mind." Prakash urged.

"How about in 20 minutes at The Kings Cross Tavern? It's a late night pub so we don't have to worry about closing time. I'll just drop off these things to the flat."

"OK, see you in a wee bit."

"Aye, see you."

"Well my friend," Prakash said, "It looks like sunny London is going to shine on you."

*****

"Who's the bloody hell's the other woman?" Shore barked to the sergeant.

"I don't know sir. We've another team following her but we think it might be someone he already knew."

"Make sure you DO follow her. We can't take any chances that they'll change their game plan. This woman might even work for Johnny and Jenny Brakes. What are the odds of that? Let's not screw this one up."

"No sir."

Guinness dumped the shopping and made her way across to the pub. She needed to stake her position in an unobtrusive corner. Fortunately for her, the venue wasn't busy and she bought two vodka and cokes and sat down on a bench within a discreet booth. She opened her handbag and pulled out a pill. It was rohypnol, commonly known as the 'date rape drug'. She had pre-crushed it and poured the powdered pill into a gel capsule. Now she opened the capsule and poured the contents into one of the drinks. She pushed this drink to the other side of the table and started drinking from the other. She thought to herself how easy it was to buy drugs on the streets of Aberdeen. Even so, she resolved that last night was the first and last time she would do it.

A few office workers on a late pub-crawl made their way into the bar area, laughing and joking with each other. Guinness fixed her eyes on the door. Then Yousef walked inside the public room and looked around. Guinness waved gently and he came over to her. She could smell strong cheap after-shave on him. He repulsed her but she had to continue with her plan. Her handbag was on the table and the Dictaphone was switched on. She had 60 minutes of talk time before she needed to turn the tape over.

"Sit down. I've already bought you a drink. I hope you like Vodka and coke."

"I don't really drink."

"Oh come on. You can't call yourself a Scotsman unless you drink."

"OK."

The next thirty minutes was taken up by small talk relating to the geography of London and Glasgow. It was fortunate that Guinness had studied in Glasgow so she was not thrown by any questions Yousef asked of her.

Then everything changed. Guinness had been waiting for this moment. Yousef's head fell heavily on his hands and he looked up at her with wide, lost eyes.

"Are you OK?"

"Yes I'm OK." He lied, not wanting to seem like a fool who couldn't cope with an alcoholic drink.

"Where do you come from, before Scotland I mean?"

Guinness thought she would start with simple, unobtrusive questions.

"I am from Iraq. My family were marsh Arabs. I left Iraq for a better life."

"Did you find a better life in Scotland?"

"I think so."

"It's much colder in Scotland than Iraq isn't it?"

"Winter in Iraq can be cold too."

"Is your name Hussein Nizar Al-Jamil?"

"No. My name is Yousef Al-Rashid."

"Why call yourself Hussein Nizar Al-Jamil?"

"That is the name on my passport. My new passport."

"Why did you need a new passport?"

"Because it is a British Passport. I needed it to travel to the UK"

"Who gave you this passport?"

"Nobody gave me the passport. I bought it as part of my studies in France?"

"Studies?"

"Yes English studies. At the Grosvenor School in Paris."

There was so much information to absorb, but Guinness had to ensure there was a flow of questions in order not to send Yousef to sleep, or allow him time to question and then think about what he was saying.

"Have you ever been to Aberdeen?"

"Oh yes, I was there a few weeks ago."

"Did you like it?"

"I don't know. I wasn't there for very long. I was doing a job."

A job? What kind of job?"

"I had to make a delivery to some people in the street. I don't know what it was for."

"Did someone ask you to make this delivery?"

"Yes."

"Who was it?"

"It was my friend"

"What's your friend's name?"

"It was Klarkey."

"Klarkey?"

"Who is Klarkey?"

"Klarkey is a very nice man. He helped me leave France. I owed him a favour and he paid me to make this delivery."

"Let me get this straight. A man called Klarkey gave you a package to deliver to some people on the streets of Aberdeen. You delivered it and got paid. Is that it?"

"That's it."

Guinness started to shake but somehow managed to keep calm.

"How did you know you were delivering to the right people?"

"I didn't. Klarkey said it didn't matter, just to give the package to some street people. That is what I did and I got paid for it."

Guinness was suddenly speechless. She simply couldn't comprehend what she was hearing. In the silence, Yousef's head fell onto his hands and his empty glass fell to the floor. Guinness couldn't wake him up and she reluctantly left the pub. As soon as she was outside, her squinting eyes that were now blinded by car headlights, started to pour with tears. She came to London to find answers to so many questions and had walked away from Yousef with even more questions reverberating inside her head.

As Guinness left the pub she felt a hand on her shoulder. She thought it was Yousef, but it was a plain-clothed Policeman who instructed her to accompany her to the station.

CHAPTER NINETEEN

"I ache in muscles I didn't even know I had," Klarkey moaned to Matisse.

"You've only been using the gym for a couple of days. Klarkey I'm proud of you. But don't expect me to start using it too." Matisse put her hand into a box of dark chocolates and carefully selected her next choice.

The film they had been watching had finished and Klarkey turned off the DVD player and the television. He breathed in deeply, inhaling the sweet smell of lilies that had been placed in the room a couple of days before, and now the petals were fully open.

"Matisse, I need to talk with you about something."

"Am I going to find out what you've been up to after all?"

"Well kind of."

"So?" She spluttered with her mouth filled with a strawberry cream.

"This isn't easy for me. Ever since I was young you know I've always needed to fight injustice."

"Like the caped crusader?"

"Maybe. But without the cape." They laughed.

"What I'm trying to say is that I've done some bad things recently, but mostly it's because of the need to revenge bad things others have done."

"An eye for an eye and a tooth for a tooth?"

"Sort of."

"I want to tell you about two things. Are you sure you want to hear them?"

"I'm as ready as I'll ever be Klarkey."

Klarkey proceeded to tell Matisse about his attack on the muggers in Portsmouth in revenge for the attack on Roberta. Then he described the killing of an illegal mini-cab driver in South London. This was his response to a vicious attack by the man on two of Klarkey's London friends following an evening of nightclubbing. He spoke passionately about his desire to avenge the wrongdoings of others and also about his opinion of the ineffectiveness of the Police.

Matisse was stunned. She was genuinely shocked and couldn't hide the emotion in her face. Klarkey considered it prudent not to tell her about the attacks in Aberdeen and he would certainly not give any clues about what was going to happen over the forthcoming Christmas holiday.

"I cannot believe that my friend Klarkey is a murderer. I feel sick and shocked." Matisse went into her room and slammed the door behind her. Klarkey stood up and spoke into her door.

"Matisse, I don't expect you to be jumping for joy about it. All I'm asking is that you try to see things from my point of view. I felt the need to react to other people's actions and to help the people I care about. That's all."

Matisse opened the door slightly. "That's all? I suppose I could try to forgive you Klarkey, but you have given me quite a shock." Matisse screwed her eyes up and clenched her fists. "I know how your mind works and I accept that you take personally all wrongdoings to people around you. You will have to give me time to get used to the madness of what you've done"

Matisse came back into the sitting room and they sat down again together.

"Of course." Klarkey leaned forward in his chair and took Matisse's hand in his.

"Matisse, you are my closest dearest friend. There's nothing I wouldn't do for you. There's nothing in my life I want to keep a secret from you."

Matisse withdrew her hand. "In other words I should accept the...there's a good English phrase, yes: the rough with the smooth?"

"That's about it, yes."

"OK, ok, I'll think about forgiving you. But please don't frighten me with any more bad surprises."

"I'll try not to. But I can't guarantee it."

*****

Guinness was not having a good day. It was the middle of the night and she was sitting in an interview room in a strange Police station, wondering why she had been kept there for hours. Wiping crusted mucus from her eyes, she sipped on the weak sweet tea she had been given by a friendly WPC and wondered whether she may have been followed all the way from Aberdeen. She considered it was possible that her desire to assist with the Police enquiry into Richie Brakes's death had ultimately led to her becoming the key lead in their enquiry. She was tired of speculating and wanted some answers.

The door of the interview room opened and Detective Superintendent Shore and a PC identified themselves to Guinness. They had spent the last couple of hours attempting to verify the identity of this woman and whether she could be connected to Brakes. They had so far failed to make any connection.

"Where's Inspector Rey-Smith? I thought I'd been kept waiting so long so that he could interview me."

"Inspector Rey-Smith? How do you know him?" Shore inquired completely ignorantly.

"I have been working closely with the Inspector on a case in Aberdeen. Don't tell me you don't know what this is about Mr. Shore."

"Miss McWerter, I'm going to level with you. I don't know who you are or why you are here in London. Perhaps you'd like to give me your account of events leading up to now and I will try to fill in the gaps."

"My full name is Harriet McWerter and I'm a television journalist. I was working on a programme with my reporter Richie Brakes in Aberdeen. He was living as a homeless person on the streets with another two men. The story was a human-interest documentary on the effects of homelessness. Except something went terribly wrong."

Guinness started to cry and the PC gave her a tissue box. She was tired and emotional and hated reliving the story.

"Thank you. We were recording Richie and the other two men asleep in the doorway one night. When we checked the tape in the morning, we realised that the three men had been killed. Well we didn't realise straight away, but we talked to the Police and reviewed the tape and came to discover that a mystery man had given the three men a lethal drink that had killed them. To cut a long story short, it turns out that the man who killed them called himself Hussein Nizar Al-Jamil. I found out tonight that his real name is Yousef Al-Rashid. Unfortunately I didn't find out why he killed them because I left the pub."

"You mean you drugged Al-Rashid and he didn't give you all the information you wanted."

"I mean he didn't give me the information that I wanted. I couldn't comment on anything else."

"What do you know about art Miss McWerter?"

"Art? Not a lot. Except what I've seen in the museums of Scotland. Sorry…what's this got to do with anything?"

"Have you heard of the artist El Greco?"

"No, I don't think so."

"Or Picasso?"

"Oh come on…everyone's heard of Picasso. What kind of question is that?"

The PC and Shore looked at each other.

Shore continued. "Do you have any connections with Spain?"

"No."

"Do you know a man called Prakash?"

"No I don't"

"Have you been offered any antique paintings for sale by the man you called Al-Rashid?"

"Of course not. I'm a journalist not an art dealer."

"OK Miss McWerter, I don't think there's any point in continuing this discussion for now. We'll see you out of the station, if you could leave your contact details with the Constable on your way out, we'll be in touch."

Guinness stood up and banged her fists onto the table.

"I'm sorry sir, but that's just not good enough. I've been here all night, waiting and hoping that I'd find some answers and all I get is a couple of minutes with you asking me about art." She shook her head and frowned deeply.

"I'm sorry too Ms McWerter, but it's our duty to fully investigate a serious offence. We believe the man you came into contact with is handling very expensive stolen goods. Any other criminal actions that are under current investigation by Scottish Police should be directed to them."

"And that's it?"

"I'm sorry madam, that is all for now."

Guinness was furious and was led out into the front office where she gave the Police Constable her business card.

Outside the station the morning light was already in evidence, despite being winter. She looked at her watch and it was 7.30am. She pulled her mobile from her handbag and called Detective Inspector Rey-Smith. The call went straight to voicemail.

"DI Rey-Smith, this is Harriet McWerter calling about the Richie Brakes murder. I'm in London at the moment. Don't ask me how, but I've found the man who was on the tape. It turns out he was already being watched by the Met, but they've been keeping an eye on him for a completely different enquiry: something about art. Anyway, call me when you get this message because I'm sure you would want to arrest our man for murder before the Met gets hold of him for handling stolen goods. I know I would prefer if you got there first. Thanks."

Unlike the character she had invented, Guinness had no sister in London and no friends to stay with. She contemplated taking the train back to Scotland and sleeping through the journey, but she quickly dismissed the idea, thinking that Rey-Smith may get her message and want to come straight to London. Despite feeling terribly tired and indecisive, she eventually chose to check into a cheap hotel near to the station and wait for the call. It was only a few days until Christmas and she hoped the holiday wouldn't stop the Police from continuing their investigations. Within half an hour she was naked, in bed, with her mobile switched to speaker on the cheap plastic bedside table next to her.

*****

Klarkey opted to leave Matisse in the hotel. He didn't think it was worth offering any further explanations about his behaviour. He was sure it was better to give her space and let her come to terms with the news.

Klarkey looked up at the Christmas decorations above the shopping streets. He hadn't given them much thought until now. Christmas Eve was going to be one of the most frightening, important, eventful and revengeful days of his life and he had to prepare.

His first stop was the supermarket Tesco. He found the alcohol aisle and perused the spirits. He needed to buy vodka. After taking three 20cl bottles of Russia's finest from the shelf, he made his way to the checkout. Klarkey's face started to flush with blood. He was behaving like someone guilty of a crime, which was premature. He considered this was the same feeling he had experienced when passing through the 'Nothing to Declare' channel at airport customs, despite really having nothing to declare.

After buying the three bottles and putting the carrier bag into his backpack, he glanced at the page he had printed out earlier: a list of local shops retrieved from the internet. He spent the remaining day calling into 54 off-licences, including independents, small stores and supermarkets. He needed to make two return trips to the hotel to drop off his shopping when the backpack became too heavy to carry. In each store he purchased three similarly sized bottles of vodka and finally returned to the hotel late in the evening, completely exhausted. Matisse remained in her room and that suited him. He thought about how much he missed Roberta. She was visiting her family on the Isle of Wight until just after Christmas. He longed to have her in his arms and in so many ways, he could barely wait for the Christmas period to be completely over. There was a knock on his door. Klarkey quickly hid the backpack full of bottles under his bed.

"Come in." He knew it was Matisse.

"Bonjour you," she said sheepishly.

Klarkey held out his arms, "Bonjour you."

Matisse hugged him and whispered into his ear.

"This doesn't mean you are forgiven, it's only that I don't want us to argue any more."

"I know, I know." Behind Matisse's back, Klarkey stretched out the corners of his mouth with a smile and thought to himself, 'If only she knew what was to come next. Perhaps she would never forgive me.'

*****

"How the bloody hell did you get hold of Al Rashid and more importantly, what the hell did you think you were doing following him?" DI Rey-Smith was not happy with Guinness, who had drowsily responded to the ring on her mobile having been asleep only for a couple of hours. It took her a few seconds to realise where she was and exactly what the officer was talking about.

"Oh…Detective Inspector…just a second." Guinness put the phone down by the side of the bed and stumbled into

the en-suite bathroom. She ran the cold water and threw
handfuls into her face, gasping. Taking a ripped white
towel from the metal rail, she wiped her face and returned to
the Scottish detective who was waiting patiently.

"Sorry, you woke me up. Do you know I was sitting in
a Police station for the most of the night."

"...and if I had my way you'd be sitting in my nick for
another night. What possessed you to take such a risk as to
follow this man to London? Let's just assume this is the
right man for a moment, and we don't know for sure, but
just assuming it is, do you have ANY idea what kind of
danger you've put yourself in? Not to mention the potential
obstruction to my investigation."

Guinness was a little taken aback by Rey-Smith's
attitude towards her. She had hoped that he would be
grateful to her for the assistance she had freely given to the
investigation. Instead, he was aggressive and unfriendly.
She considered for a moment that he might even be jealous
of her success.

"I don't know why you're being so tough on me. After
all, I have just located the man responsible for a triple
murder in Aberdeen...which is more than I can say you've
achieved."

"Listen lady, unless you want to be banged up the
second you cross the border, you'd better tell me everything
you know and give me the details of the officers that
questioned you last night."

*****

It was a tough decision for Shore to make, but this was
the kind of judgment that distinguished a mediocre detective
from a great one, and as he grew older and more successful,
he knew in which category he hoped to be remembered
following his retirement. Shore had really wanted to bring
in Yousef for questioning. He didn't know how he was
involved in the case, but Operation Philistine at this moment
had another suspect to watch. He didn't believe the

journalist from Scotland was involved. She had behaved too much like a journalist. Clearly Yousef, like so many criminals was involved in certain other crimes, but as far as Shore was concerned Operation Philistine was his number one priority. He needed to work out exactly what the relationship was between Yousef, his friend Prakash, and Mrs Jenny Brakes, wife of one of the UK's leading handlers of high quality stolen goods. Yousef had been left with his head in a drink in a bar in Kings Cross. An officer on Shore's team who had previously been a nurse, was sure he had been drugged. Shore decided it was better to leave him to sober up than to arrest him or take him in for questioning. He needed Yousef to lead him to the art and bringing him in could potentially scare him off. Then Shore could be left with nothing except a large overtime bill to explain to the Commander.

*****

Klarkey woke with a start. He'd been reliving a bad dream that hadn't bothered him since childhood. It was one of those guilt-laden dreams that leave a person's neck stinging with sweat and a racing mind preventing deep sleep. He knew why his brain was torturing him. He had thought about the way dreams come into the mind a thousand times before. He knew this was a premonition of events due to happen on Christmas Eve. He was thinking more about his sister. He saw her walking away from him on a distant beach, all in slow motion. The sound of the sea was deep and the light was blinding. The sand distracted him and waves of fear passed down his body, as he helplessly watched his sister disappear; never to be seen again.

Normally he would have a cool shower after a disturbed night, but this time he chose to turn the water to the setting that piped out extremely hot water. He could feel his skin scalding under the heat and he felt his body release sweat, despite being covered in fresh hot water. He needed to remove the smell of guilt from his body and he needed to feel pain. Then he turned the water to ice cold and his skin tightened and shivered. 'Am I going mad?', he thought to himself.

Klarkey dried himself hastily, then dressed in tracksuit bottoms, training shoes, a loose T-shirt and a green American flight jacket. He picked up the printed document he had produced the previous night and left the hotel for another morning of shopping. This time he visited fifteen hardware stores and plumbers merchants. He made a return trip to the hotel just once, halfway through his day to make one drop off before continuing his shopping expedition.

*****

DI Rey-Smith had to choose his words carefully. He was desperate to get hold of Yousef Al-Rashid, to question him over the murders, but he was well aware that if the Metropolitan Police were making their own enquiries, he could be pushed aside. The Met was always given priority over other forces and if there was any suggestion that terrorism could be involved; he may never get the chance to question his suspect. He called the number that Guinness had given to him and hoped for the best.

"Shore!"

"Good morning sir, this is DI Rey-Smith calling from Grampian Police in Aberdeen"

"Yes Rey-Smith, how can I help you?"

"Sir, I believe you may have been questioning someone assisting us with a current enquiry, Miss Harriet McWerter?"

"Don't beat around the bush with me Rey-Smith. Is it true this journalist has been muddying the waters you should have been dipping into yourselves?"

"It is true to say that Miss McWerter has been engaging in a journalistic investigation which could be associated with our own Police enquiry. I'll come straight to the point sir, we're interested in the man known as Yousef Al-Rashid. Can you tell me whether you have taken him into custody for any crime?"

"Al-Rashid? Actually no. However we do have him under surveillance."

"Sir, I think I should inform you that Al-Rashid is wanted for questioning by Grampian Police for three murders in Aberdeen. Would it be acceptable to you for me to send our officers to bring him in?"

"No it bloody well would not. It may be the case that you want him, and by God you can have him, when I'm finished with him…"

"…but sir…"

"Rey-Smith! What I'm saying is there are ways and means for us both to get exactly what we want?"

"Sir? What do you mean?"

"It's simple really. I'm not interested in Al-Rashid. At least I'm not interested in him personally, just in the company he keeps. We have an operation in place that should be over within the next few days. How about if we continue the observation of Al-Rashid until we conclude our operation, and then pass the man over to you? I don't think we're going to need him to conclude our investigations."

Well sir, that's an offer I reckon I can live with. If we can have Al-Rashid as soon as he's led you to where you need to go, that's fine by me."

"Good, I'm glad we can be of service to you. Call me in a couple of days and we should have him in custody ready for you to take him away."

Thank you very much sir…and Merry Christmas."

"Yes whatever."

Shore put the phone down. He had kept Rey-Smith from racing down to London and stopped him from impeding the progress of Operation Philistine. It had occurred to him that Yousef Al-Rashid may have been partly responsible for the theft of the paintings from Spain.

He couldn't provide any other reason why Al-Rashid had been brought into the meeting with Jenny Brakes. Even if it was so, he didn't feel it was his problem. He would hand the suspect over to Grampian Police when the time was right and they could have their own battle with the Spanish if Al-Rashid was a suspect in the theft.

CHAPTER TWENTY

It was Christmas Eve and Klarkey had enjoyed a light breakfast with Matisse. She planned to spend the rest of the day pampering herself in a luxury spa and health club, thanks to Klarkey's gift of a day pass to the Aphrodite Women's Gym & Spa.

"I'm looking forward to a very quiet day at home tomorrow. We'll have a traditional Christmas dinner brought in to us and we don't have to get dressed all day."

Klarkey agreed with Matisse. He too was really looking forward to Christmas Day, principally because it would mean that Christmas Eve would have passed.

Matisse kissed Klarkey on both cheeks and left for the spa.

"Don't wait up for me darling."

"Have a good time Matisse. I may be late myself, so don't worry if I'm not in when you get back. I'm going for a drink with a couple of mates from the old days."

"OK sweetie, ciao." Matisse closed the door behind her and there was silence in the sitting room. It was a cold grey day and Klarkey stared through the curtains. Now he was alone he had to make his own preparations.

He walked into his bedroom and crouched by the bed. He pulled out a large suitcase from under the bed in which he had hidden 160 small bottles of vodka and 30, one-litre bottles of sulphuric acid drain cleaner. He had rehearsed this day in his mind many times and now the enormity of the task ahead made Klarkey nervous. He rushed to the bathroom and released the contents of his bowels. His stomach was in pain and he took a couple of Imodium pills in an attempt to save him from another internal explosion. He added a couple of paracetamol to keep away the pain. Returning to the bedroom, he lifted the suitcase and wheeled it into the bathroom.

He opened the case and drew out a pair of large yellow rubber gloves, which he stretched onto his hands, making sure the air was removed from each of the fingers.

Then he took six of the small bottles of vodka, and removed most of the contents of each down the drain, leaving just a little vodka in each. He took a small wide topped funnel from the case and placed it in the first bottle, then lifted the first of the larger bottles of acid from the case and carefully poured the contents into each of the vodka bottles. He sniffed the bottles and was glad they still smelled of vodka. The clear liquids mixed well. He screwed the bottle tops back into place and stood the reconstituted bottles in a line on the tiled floor.

This exercise was repeated until all the little bottles were filled with a small amount of vodka and a larger proportion of sulphuric acid. Klarkey removed his gloves and proceeded to the next stage of his plan.

Wrapping each of the bottles tightly with bubble-wrap he placed each of them back into the large suitcase. It was lunchtime and he needed a break. He walked to a sandwich shop on the High Street and stood eating a chicken panini at the bar, washed down with an exotic fruit drink. By the time he returned to the hotel he couldn't even remember eating. He didn't know how he had found his way to the High Street and he didn't recall speaking with anyone. He was completely engrossed with the job in hand. He returned to the bathroom. The suitcase was positioned upright and closed. He opened it to check his earlier work. He saw the bubble-wrapped bottles and knew that he was ready to proceed and took a sharp intake of breath. It was 2pm and he still had several hours before the next phase of his plan. He was due to take a journey lasting about an hour. He would rest until five, before making his next move.

*****

Matisse was luxuriating in the bubbles of the jacuzzi. Three other women sat around her, all of their faces were caked in masks of various vegetable pastes. Matisse was wearing the skimpiest of bikinis. She adored the fact that when she climbed into the frothy water, the other women would notice her. She loved that she was completely accepted as one of them. At last she didn't feel like an outsider.

As she opened her arms to grip the side of the bath and closed her eyes, she thought how wonderful her life was. She contemplated how different life would be if she hadn't met Klarkey: Would she still be dancing in a sleazy bar in Paris?

After a few minutes, Matisse climbed out of the jacuzzi and returned to one of the cubicles, where her attendant was waiting to remove the cucumber mask from her face.

"Are you looking forward to Christmas madame?" The young girl had a friendly smile while she worked. Matisse liked that.

"Oh yes. I'm spending it quietly with my best friend"

"Not with your family?"

Matisse was a little taken aback with this question. It was hardly intrusive or over-inquisitive, but to Matisse, it was too personal.

"No my dear. My friends are my family now."

The girl remained silent for the rest of the treatment, blushing when she considered she might have caused offence.

*****

The pay-as-you-go phone had been resting on the side of the armchair all day in Prakash's flat. It was Christmas Eve afternoon and they were bored. They had already watched two feature films and were desperate to do something other than wait for the phone to ring.

Twelve minutes after the second film finished, the phone rang. For a few seconds both men hesitated to answer it.

This was what they had been waiting for, yet nerves prevented them from responding immediately. Finally Prakash grabbed at the handset and pressed the 'talk' button.

"Yeh man?"

"My dear it's Jenny Brakes."

"Yeh hi, Prakash here" Prakash covered the receiver and whispered to Yousef, "It's the ice queen."

"I want you to take the tube to Caledonian Road station. Turn left out of the station onto the industrial estate and into the Oversize Storage Depot. Go straight inside and on the first floor you'll find a lock up, number D12. Got it?"

"D12, yeh man."

"DON'T BE LATE. And don't forget to bring the paintings."

"No Mrs B. No probs. We'll be there in about 20 minutes."

*****

Klarkey awoke with a start. He'd set the alarm on the television and he'd woken up to Judge Judy handing out judgements to various small claimants from across America.

'If only justice could so easily be dispensed' Klarkey thought to himself as he climbed out of bed and into the bathroom. After washing he returned to the bedroom and pulled from the back of the wardrobe, twenty-four small Bibles that he had bought some time ago. He had already carefully cut out the majority of the centre pages, leaving a space in each sufficient to house a bubble-wrapped 20cl bottle of vodka. He wheeled the suitcase back from the bathroom into the bedroom and took out the top layer of twenty-four bottles arranged in 5 levels of six by four. He placed each one inside the hollowed Bibles and returned them into the tightly packed case. It was six o'clock.

Klarkey was ready now to transform himself.

He started by spraying Barrier Spray onto the skin over his lip and chin. Then he painted a layer of spirit gum onto the skin and let it dry completely. Both solutions would act as a shield against perspiration. Sweat would loosen the hair that was about to be attached. After adding another later of spirit gum, Klarkey took the full beard and moustache, made from real hair, and pressed them firmly into place. He pressed the edges down with a velour powder puff. Finally he smiled widely into the mirror to ensure he hadn't glued over his smile line. His face was ready.

Leaning into the wardrobe in his bedroom, he took out a dark suit and a white shirt topped with a white vicar's dog collar. When he was dressed he looked into the full-length mirror in his bedroom and said to himself, "Father Randall is born".

It was seven o'clock.

*****

Prakash and Yousef turned the dark street corner in north London into the industrial estate. The half-missing neon sign indicated the storage warehouse where they hoped to meet Jenny Brakes.

Walking straight passed a security guard reading a newspaper in a small hut, they headed for the stairs to the first floor.

When they found room D12 they knocked.

The room was surprisingly spacious and was completely empty, except for Jenny Brakes sitting on a chair behind an old desk on the far side of the storage room. The light was dim and a fluorescent tube reflected poorly off the dark coloured walls and cement floor.

She stood up.

"Come on you two I haven't got all day."

Yousef and Prakash shuffled forwards like two mischievous schoolboys in front of the headmistress.

"Let's see the goods in the flesh," she barked at them, tossing her long hair to the side of her head and rubbing her hands together.

Yousef opened the side of the wooden container and drew out the three paintings.

"Oh yes...let's have a look at these beauties." Jenny Brakes pulled an eyeglass from her blazer pocket and examined various areas of the oil pictures. She knew exactly what she was studying and was in no doubt the pieces were genuine. She had also made an effort to obtain every Spanish and Catalan newspaper article about the stolen paintings so she could be absolutely sure what she would find. After five minutes, she allowed the eyeglass to fall out into her hands and from the side of the desk pulled out a silver briefcase.

"Listen lads, there's been a slight change of plan. These pictures are the hottest, most searched for bits of art in the whole of Europe right now. Quite honestly I don't really want to touch them. There aren't many places we can offload them. That's for sure. But because I like you, and I promised I would do a deal with you, the best I can offer you is 250,000."

"250,000?" Yousef spoke for the first time.

"Come on man, you said for sure four fifty. You can't treat us like that man."

"I'm sorry boys," Brakes said with confidence, "but this is a take-it or leave-it situation. These pictures are hotter than the bloody desert. It's not your fault, or mine; it's just the situation.

Yousef and Prakash looked at each other. Yousef spoke first.

"You told me I'd get 250,000. You were going to take 200,000?"

"Finders fee man, it's normal. Don't beat yourself up over it."

Brakes was growing bored, "When you two love-birds are finished I've got work to do."

Yousef fixed his gaze on his friend and pointed aggressively at his chin, "You can have 50,000 and I'm keeping 200. That's final."

"Ok man, ok, let's do it." Prakash was in a corner and readily accepted.

Brakes handed the case to Yousef and the two men quickly counted a hundred bundles of £50 notes. In the meantime, Jenny Brakes had replaced the artworks into the wooden box knowing that she should make at least £250,000 profit within twenty-four hours.

"Pleasure doing business with you," Brakes said as she extended her hand to the men.

As they started to make their way towards the exit, the heavy metal door collapsed with an ear-drum piercing bang and six armed Police entered, pointing automatic rifles with bright lights attached, shining into their faces."

"ARMED POLICE! GET DOWN ON THE FLOOR. ALL OF YOU! NOW!"

All three of them were terrified and followed the Police demands. Yousef was suddenly transported mentally back to Iraq. He saw his whole life flash before him and started to cry. All he could think was that everything he had done since leaving Iraq had been a complete waste of time.

Prakash was unable to think of anything. He only repeated to himself, "No man, no man, I can't believe this man."

Jenny Brakes was stunned. In all the years of marriage to Johnny Brakes she hadn't come close to being arrested. Now it seemed that she would be joining her husband in jail. She felt sick, but also briefly thought how she was glad her children were now grown up. If this had happened ten years earlier they would have certainly been taken into foster care.

DS Shore entered the room when the three suspects had been securely handcuffed. A young officer videotaping the scene followed him.

"Hello Jenny."

Jenny Brakes attempted to spit in his face, but as she was lying on the floor, her phlegm managed only to reach his shoes.

"We have been a naughty girl. And there was me thinking husband Johnny was the black sheep of the family."

"Who the fuck are you?"

"I'm Detective Superintendent Shore. And I'm your number one fan. I've been following you for months and finally you've come up trumps." He lied about the surveillance in order to protect the truth – the Internet Monitoring Room had led to the successful conclusion of another case and he wasn't about to give away its secrets now.

*****

Klarkey arrived at Enfield Prison at 8pm. He left the hire car at the top of the street and wheeled his heavy suitcase down the slip road and into the prison entrance. He pushed through the double door and found the reception area deserted and quiet except for the low hum from a brightly lit angel on top of a Christmas tree. He rang the bell. This was Christmas Eve and outside of normal visiting hours. He didn't expect to be received by a welcoming party of officers.

A tattooed guard came towards him through a further set of doors.

"Ah good evening padre, merry Christmas and all that."

"Merry Christmas," Klarkey started cheerfully, staring at the large breasted women adorning the officer's forearms. "I'm Father Randall. You should have a letter of authority explaining my visit."

"Yes Father we knew you were coming." The officer put his hand under the desk and ruffled some papers, bringing out a letter from the Home Office which he read out:

"Blah blah blah....*all officers should be aware of the visit by Father Randall of the Holy Sepulchre Church to D Wing at Enfield Prison on Christmas Eve. This wing, occupied by especially difficult prisoners has experienced the highest level of overcrowding over the last year and it is the Home Office's wish to allow the prisoners some comfort through the spiritual visit of Father Randall on Christmas Eve. Father Randall will be permitted to present Bibles to the inmates for their quiet consideration of the Christmas festival.*"

"Would you like to have one of my Bibles officer?" Klarkey offered.

"No thanks Father. I'll stick to reading Arthur C. Clarke, another fantasy storyteller. No offence mind!"

"No offence taken. You're entitled to your opinion and not everyone is a believer. Would you like to see inside my case now? I think it's too big to sit on your X-ray machine."

"No that's alright Father."

"No I insist you at least look inside. We wouldn't want to get you into trouble now would we?"

"OK Father, I'll just have a little look."

Klarkey laid the case flat and undid the zip around the edge. Lifting the flap, the officer peered inside and clearly saw a layer of Bibles.

"OK Father, you can do the case up now. How would you like to proceed with this visit sir?"

Klarkey had given a lot of thought to every part of this process and whilst he spoke to the officer as if it was spontaneous, he had in fact rehearsed his words time and time again.

"Oh, well, I think you will agree that the inmates would probably not take too kindly if an officer was present in the cell with me. That's especially so if some of them wish to speak privately and perhaps even to confess some of their sins. How many cells do you have in the wing?" Klarkey knew exactly how many cells and prisoners were kept on D Wing.

"We've got about 160 prisoners crammed into 55 cells at the moment. There are between two and four prisoners in each cell. They might be a bit smelly I'm afraid."

"Don't worry about me officer," Klarkey stroked his beard with a black-gloved hand, as he spoke, "I'm not afraid of the prisoners or their smell. The Lord will guide me through."

"We'd better get started because it'll be time for lights out as soon as you're finished up here."

The officer led Klarkey through various corridors and across a cold cobbled quadrangle. They then passed through another locked door which had 'D Wing' painted in white emulsion on one of its reinforced glass panels. Fortunately there were no stairs to climb and the suitcase quietly followed behind Klarkey.

"In your own time Father, I'll open up each of the cells for you and then lock them behind you after you come out."

"That would be perfect. God bless you."

Klarkey entered the first cell and his heart was pounding. He closed the door behind him, squeezing his case inside the small area between the two pairs of bunk beds on each side.

The prisoners were amazed to see a priest.

"Father, what the fuck? How the fuck?"

"Don't talk now. I don't have much time. Firstly I'm here to wish you a merry Christmas."

"Merry Christmas to you too," they chorused.

"I have a gift for each of you."

The four men stared down at him. He felt like he was looking into the sleeping quarters on a submarine, the cell was so cramped. He also considered the officer was right –

it did smell horribly inside the cell. Klarkey thought to himself that these men were not the good men you would find on a submarine, but were in fact murderers and rapists; armed robbers and paedophiles and he had no empathy with them.

Klarkey took four Bibles from his case and opened out the contents. The men were shocked. There was a lot of noise coming from the other cells, which was normal, and their startled whoops couldn't be heard above the general noise of the Wing.

"I've got a bottle of vodka for each of you lads, but you can't save it because the officers will put you on report. Not to mention how much trouble I'd be in…and you wouldn't want that would you? You've got to drink it now. Raise your bottles and wish me a merry Christmas!"

"Jesus Joseph Mary mother of God," said one inmate. "Thank you Father."

The men took the bottles, ripping off the bubble wrapping and opened the screw caps. In a toast they raised the bottles in the air and glugged the contents. Klarkey screwed up his eyes as he watched the men writhe in pain, then fall to their beds with their hands gripping their foaming, burning, melting throats. He took a deep breath but he was shaking. He closed the suitcase, knocked on the door and returned to the landing, where the guard was waiting for him. He rushed behind Klarkey to lock the door behind him and prepared to open the next cell.

"A nice religious lot you've got here officer."

"Really? You'd never have known it Father."

Klarkey entered the next cell and repeated his deadly routine. He was sorry for the death of the men in Aberdeen, but he'd needed to prove that his murder method would work. Once proven, he knew he could put his plan into action at Enfield Prison. Tonight was Christmas Eve and his plan was well and truly engaged.

There were 55 cells to visit and he had passed through 39 like the angel of death. Cell number 40 had two prisoners. One of them was Matthew Groucher. This was the man who had killed Klarkey's sister 28 years earlier. This was the fundamental reason for his trip to Enfield Prison this Christmas Eve. Klarkey started to sweat and was worried that his beard or moustache would come loose, but he knew that he had applied the correct adhesives to prevent this. Now that he was with Groucher, he felt the need to find some answers to long-standing questions, but couldn't risk blowing his cover. He would have to be very careful.

"My name's Father Randall and I've brought you a Christmas drink."

"What, from the governor is it?" Groucher's cellmate spoke out dismissively.

"No, it's from the Church, and if you must know it's vodka, and the governor and the officers know nothing about it."

"Oh...nice one Father." The prisoner softened.

"Yeh nice one." Groucher spoke for the first time blowing smoke from a rolled up cigarette into Klarkey's face.

Klarkey continued. "Before I give you your gift, I need to ask you if you repent for your past sins? Do you feel bad about what you did in your past lives before coming to prison."

"I didn't ask for a bloody psychiatric visit Father," Groucher blurted.

"Hold up Grouch," the cellmate interceded, "You don't wanna go upsetting the vicar or we won't get our drink."

"Well you can stuff your drink, I didn't ask for it in the first place."

Klarkey needed to take control.

"Listen lads, it's alright, you can both have your drink. I'm not going to force out repentance from you if you don't want to."

"That's more like it Father, now where's that drink?" Groucher ungratefully grunted.

At this point Klarkey knew that he would never get an answer from Groucher. He would never learn why he killed his darling sister Charlotte. He determined that even if he wasn't doing God's work through his actions on this Christmas Eve night, he was without doubt fulfilling the dreams of millions of people who would consider his deeds as just and right. He hoped he would feel better for this considered vote of confidence.

Klarkey passed the bottles to the two men and insisted they drink the lot in a toast for Christmas. As the men drank, they followed the pattern of gripping their throats and falling back in extreme pain onto their beds. This time, Klarkey spoke to Groucher as he lay dying on the bed. Klarkey put his face just a few centimetres from Groucher's and he could smell the stench of burning flesh. He watched Groucher's eyes, bulging and bloodshot.

"Help…me," Groucher whispered as the deadly fluid took its toll on his tongue, throat and stomach.

"You…killed…my…sister." Klarkey spoke clearly and carefully clenching his teeth.

Groucher's eyes widened, even more bloodshot and frightened. He tried to reach out to Klarkey but he didn't have the strength to lift his arms away from his neck, and his fingers were now burning as they had become covered in the acid.

Klarkey spoke clearly and slowly. "You are here because of her and I am here because of you. Take that to your death."

Klarkey zipped up his case and rushed outside the cell, slightly breathless.

"The lads giving you a bit of a hard time now are they Father?" The officer said cheerily.

"No it's alright, some of them are just a bit upset about being away from their families at this time of year. They'll be OK I'm sure."

"Fair enough, onto the next one then."

Klarkey's heart was racing. He felt elation but also disgust. He felt revenged but also horror at his actions.

Klarkey completed his mission with the remaining fifteen cells and as he left the Wing passing back through the quadrangle, the bell rang for lights out. The men in D Wing wouldn't be discovered until Christmas morning, unable to benefit from an extra hour in bed thanks to the holiday. Groucher and his poisonous partners in crime would be long dead by then.

Klarkey drove home, tearing the false hair from his face and the dog collar from his neck. He pulled over behind a row of High Street stores about half way back to the hotel, somewhere in north London, and tossed his disguise in a black bin liner into the bins, already full with the Christmas Eve detritus. When he finally made it back to the hotel, he left the empty suitcase in the boot of the car and ran into his room, noticing that Matisse had still not returned from the health club. He ripped off his clothes and jumped into the shower. Barely drying himself properly he collapsed onto the bed and cried himself to sleep. He had imagined that he would feel a sense of euphoria at this point in the day. Instead he felt wretched.

*****

It was Christmas Day morning and Matisse bounded into Klarkey's room holding a book-shaped gift with coloured ribbons flowing from the wrapping.

"Merry Christmas Klarkey my darling. Wake up, wake up it's Christmas!"

Klarkey stirred but wasn't cheerful.

"Did you see the news yet today? Hundreds of people have been killed at a prison. It's shocking!"

"No I haven't seen it yet."

"They were horrible people the reporter said: murderers and rapists. I'm sure they deserved it."

"Matisse can we talk about something else?"

"Of course. Here's your gift Klarkey. Thank you so much for being a wonderful friend."

Klarkey said nothing. He opened the wrapping and saw the volume inside.

Matisse sat down on the bedside and read the front cover out loud.

"Price List and Catalogue; British Colonial and Foreign, by E Stanley Gibbons. It's a first edition darling and look…it's even signed by the man himself."

"Thanks Matisse. This must have cost you a fortune. Where did you get it?"

"Oh…I've been searching for ages. Now. What did you get me?"

"I'm sorry Matisse, I haven't got any presents for anyone. I've been too… preoccupied."

"Oh…no presents. OK. I'm just a little surprised that's all. You're normally so good with presents."

Klarkey did not want to enter into any discussion. "Matisse, will you just leave it. I'm not in the mood for anything right now. Why don't you get dressed and we'll order some breakfast. You had your spa day yesterday, what more do you want?"

Matisse went to the door. "Fine." She slammed the door closed and Klarkey fell back onto the bed. He really didn't know what was supposed to happen next. His plan had only extended to Christmas Eve. He considered that for most of his life he had been planning revenge against Groucher and now it was over, he had no real idea how to structure his future life. He switched on the television.

We bring you further breaking news of the tragedy that has befallen inmates at one of our oldest and most secure Prisons: Enfield Prison in north London. This morning, 160 men, all believed to have been held in one wing of the jail, were found dead. The Prison Service has provided no further information but as soon as we have more news for you, we will bring you an immediate update. Now over to Chayenne for a Christmas weather update.

Klarkey turned off the television and thought to himself, 'Looks like the shit's really hit the fan'.

CHAPTER TWENTY-ONE

Christmas Day was solemn and quiet across the UK. The news channels were filled with the mass murder at Enfield Prison and Matisse and Klarkey occupied themselves with a regular stream of old films from the wide selection of television channels available. They avoided chatting to each other with anything more than small talk and both decided on an early night.

After a dream-filled night's sleep, Klarkey crawled out of bed before sunrise and walked to the nearby newsstand where only two newspapers were for sale because of the Boxing Day holiday: *The Protector*, a left-wing broadsheet, and *The Daily Post,* a right-wing tabloid. Klarkey bought both papers and returned to find coffee and orange juice waiting for him in his room.

THE PROTECTOR

DEATH BEHIND THE GATES OF HELL

"In a tragedy not seen before in the UK, 160 lives were tragically snuffed out by a cunning killer last night at Enfield Prison in north London.

Initial reports suggest that a man, posing as a priest, entered the jail and systematically made his way through the cells, maiming and killing everyone resident in D Wing at the top security Prison.

Whilst no one will suggest these men were angels, indeed, they were mostly killers themselves, it is surely inhumane for society to passively accept the fate that has been dealt to these men.

The Prison Governor was unavailable for comment. The Prison's Minister is currently holidaying in Mauritius and is not expected to return until next week. A representative from the Prison Officer's Union has issued the following short statement: 'The officers in charge were clearly duped by a cold, calculating killer whose motive for murder remains unknown. Resources in the prison have been reduced since privatisation and the officers have been forced to work in conditions that have become totally unacceptable.'

Such carnage by the hands of one man has not been seen since the former doctor and serial killer, Harold Shipman. The murdered men were sent to Enfield Prison to protect of society, but also with the hope that they would find rehabilitation through incarceration. No possibility exists now for them to change their criminal ways and it remains the duty of the Police to catch the criminal who has perpetrated such a heinous crime, and bring him to justice.

So far, Enfield Prison has released no information about how the prisoners were murdered. A Police spokesman told The Protector, 'This is the earliest stage of our investigations and we are still gathering evidence. I can confirm that some time between 7pm and midnight last evening, 160 men, all inmates of D Wing at Enfield Prison, died. Until autopsies have been carried out to absolutely confirm time and cause of death, no further information will be supplied to the Press.'"

THE DAILY POST
160 DOING BIRD GET CHRISTMAS STUFFING
"Last night on Christmas Eve, Enfield Prison saw carnage on a scale never witnessed before. 160 of the country's worst and most evil criminals were murdered in their beds by what's thought to be a vigilante killer. Post insiders tell us the dead include, 44 murderers, 20 rapists, 13 armed robbers, 41 violent assaulters, 16 drug traffickers, 4 terrorists and 22 paedophiles. Are we sad? We don't think so. These prisoners were the lowest of the low, and any red-blooded man wanting justice would take his hat off to the person who left this trail of blood in one of Queen Victoria's starkest 19th century prisons.

Estimates so far suggest the deaths of these men has saved the taxpayer at least £5 million per year, and perhaps as much as ten times that figure due to the delay in the need to build a new prison because of the extra capacity created by these deaths.

Emily Mathers, whose husband was killed by one of the murdered inmates, told the Post, 'I'm damn glad they're dead. Hanging was too good for them and life don't ever mean life. They deserved what they got and I'm not ashamed to say I'm glad.'

Perhaps these are the normally unspoken sentiments of the nation?

What is certain is that the man who caused the deaths of these prisoners will, rightly or wrongly, have his health toasted across the land for what he has done on this day."

*****

Shore told his wife that he hated coming into work over the Christmas period. The truth was that one full day at home was quite enough for him. He was ready to sit at his desk, or to interview a suspect on Boxing Day, despite his right to take more of a holiday.

Yousef had been brought from his cell and was waiting patiently with a uniformed officer standing against the wall. Shore entered, with the authority of a king.

"Hello Yousef". Yousef stood up.

"Hello Sir"

Shore sat down.

"Sit down please. You've been read your rights and at this stage you are under caution, but not under arrest. Do you understand?"

"Yes sir. I think so." Yousef felt beaten and wanted to die. He felt there was nothing to live for and had no fight left in him.

"Would you like someone with you? Do you have a solicitor? We could organise someone for you if you like."

"No I don't care. Do what you like with me."

Shore leaned forward and stared into Yousef's face.

"You're in a lot of trouble. Do you know that?"

"I know."

"But you may be able to help me. Would you like to help me and therefore help yourself?"

"How can I help myself? You caught me didn't you?"

"Oh yes. We caught you. But you know, it could be possible that if you were prepared to assist us in our investigation, we might consider letting you go."

Shore raised an eyebrow and smiled. He was offering Yousef an opportunity to be free, or so Yousef was led to believe. Strictly speaking, Shore was telling the truth.

"You mean I could go?"

"I mean we would be prepared to release you from this station if you would consider telling us everything about the deal with Jenny Brakes. Tell us everything about Prakash and his arrangement with Brakes."

Shore didn't particularly care whether Prakash or Yousef was responsible for the theft of the paintings. That would be for the Catalan Police to worry about. He cared about getting a secure conviction against one of them for handling stolen goods and needed to obtain convincing written statements to put Jenny Brakes away too.

Yousef considered his choices.

"I want you to say on a tape that you will not charge me with anything if I give you my evidence."

"I didn't say I won't charge you. What I will promise is that I will bail you, so you can leave the station freely. If you give us the information we require about Prakash and Brakes, we will be able to keep them inside and we can bail you and let you go. What do you think Yousef? You don't want to be kept here in the station do you? You want to be able to walk free don't you? To smell the crisp fresh London air, or perhaps return to Glasgow? Or maybe start afresh somewhere else when this is all over?"

Yousef put his face in his hands for a few seconds continuing to consider his options. He realised that he

didn't have many. He wasn't happy about giving
information about Prakash, but clearly someone had messed
things up, and he knew he had behaved perfectly. It was
Prakash and Brakes that had caused his dream of freedom
and financial security to die in a secure storage unit in north
London.

"OK." Yousef looked up. "I'll do it."

"Good lad. Let's get you a cup of tea and put
everything down on tape shall we?"

*****

Guinness was bored in London. She had no friends, no
family and everything was closed for the holiday. It was
Christmastime and she wanted to be back in Aberdeen.
London was grey and miserable. Despite the Christmas
decorations in every shop window and the gaudily sprayed
greetings on residential windows, nothing matched the
beauty of a snow-covered Christmas in northeast Scotland.
She resolved to wait just two more days to see whether
Grampian Police would take Yousef Al-Rashid into
custody. She owed Richie that.

Whilst taking a quiet stroll through frosty Regents Park,
her phone rang. "What's happening Brian?"

"Alright Guinness. How's the big smoke?"

"Not smokey. Boring and unfriendly."

"Otherwise you're fine eh?"

"Yes, yes I suppose so. It's all a waiting game now.
You know how these things are."

"Aye. Listen, I've got some news for you that might be
of interest."

"Go on."

"Okay. You know you told me to get on to telecoms
about Yousef's phone bill."

"What of it?"

"Well I think I might have found something. Amongst
all the take-aways, calls to work and local numbers, there's

one mobile number that comes up twice in the weeks before the murders. It's a French phone, but I still found out who it's registered to."

"Well?"

"Someone called Francis Klarke based in Paris, but the calls were rerouted to London. It's just a hunch, but can you think of any other reason why he'd be calling someone in London apart from his friend Prakash?"

"And we know what he was up to with Prakash."

"Aye."

"It's a long shot, but it's worth a try. Give me the number and I'll call it."

"Maybe it's a travel agent..."

"Or a massage parlour."

Guinness grabbed a piece of paper and a pencil from her handbag and took down the number wishing Brian a merry Christmas.

Coughing with the cold, Guinness took a tissue from her bag and wiped the seat of a moist park bench. She called the number.

Holding a towel wrapped around her wet hair, Matisse walked into the sitting room where she heard Klarkey's mobile phone ringing. He'd gone out for breakfast leaving the phone behind and she considered washing her hair more significant than eating. She decided to answer it in case the call was important.

"Hello?"

"Hi", Guinness said cheerfully. "I'm sorry to bother you but I was wondering if you could help me. I'm friends with Yousef Al-Rashid and he's in a spot of bother at the moment and needs some help. You're friends with him are you not?"

Matisse thought this was a wrong number, but out of courtesy continued the conversation.

"I'm sorry, this is my friend's mobile. He left it behind and I thought I should answer it. I'm sure he doesn't know anyone by that name."

"Are you sure? My friend spoke to your friend on this number a few weeks ago, before he went to Aberdeen? Your friend is Francis Klarke?" Guinness made these statements in the form of questions.

Matisse went white, dropping the phone and the towel from over her head. Her hand became slippery with cold sweat. She knew this call must be about the deaths in Aberdeen and she panicked.

"I'm sorry I know nothing." Matisse barked into the phone.

Guinness knew she was on to something. She believed the person at the end of this call knew about the history of the Aberdeen deaths and she was determined to find out. She called Brian immediately.

"Brian…that number."

"What is it?"

"The number you gave me," Guinness could barely get the words out. "The person at the other end definitely knew something. I'm sure of it."

"Do you want me to come down?"

"Yes please. If you don't mind leaving your family."

"Nae you're alright. It's our first real lead to who's behind this business. I don't mind at all. I'll be knocking on your door tonight; aeroplanes permitting."

*****

Yousef gave a full statement that took two hours to handwrite. He omitted details about his trip to southern Spain. He omitted his crime of theft at the Museu Cau Ferrat in Sitges.

Shore continued to read back Yousef's statement out loud,

"After discovering the box of paintings outside my flat in Glasgow, I telephoned my friend Prakash, who lives in London. Prakash was known to have connections with art dealers and I supposed he could organise the sale of the pictures to our mutual financial benefit.

"Prakash invited me to London where I would meet his contact who would purchase the paintings. Prakash agreed to organise the sale of the paintings to a woman I came to know as Jenny Brakes and Prakash would be responsible for negotiating the value of the sale and would take a share of the money from the sale…"

The statement continued for several more pages. Yousef implicated himself, and gave sufficient evidence in his statement to charge Prakash and Jenny Brakes who were both waiting to be interviewed.

"Well done Yousef," Shore spoke appreciatively to his prisoner, "you've done the right thing. We're going to charge you for handling stolen goods, and as I promised, you will be released on bail from this Police station."

Yousef grabbed Shore's hand. "Thank you sir."

For a brief second, Shore felt a pang of guilt. This man was not argumentative, abusive or unpleasant. In fact, he had done exactly what Shore had wanted and he was almost sorry for him.

Yousef was taken to the custody sergeant and charged, then bailed to appear in Court at a later date.

Yousef was led to the front desk of the Police station and passed through the door that was buzzed open. On the other side, two Policemen, both in plain clothes identified themselves to Yousef.

"Good evening Yousef. I'm DI Rey-Smith and this is Sergeant Willis. I'm arresting you on suspicion of the murder of Richard Brakes, Jimmy McLovely and Calum Dermott in Aberdeen. You do not have to say anything. But it may harm your defence if you do not mention when questioned something, which you later rely on in court.

Anything you do say may be given in evidence. Do you understand?"

Yousef collapsed to the ground. This was not what he had expected.

Rey-Smith was sure they had the man responsible for the crimes. He knew he had Guinness to thank for the lead, but planned to take as much credit for the arrest as he could. He stared down at Yousef, raising his voice.

"I said, Do you understand what I have just said."

"Yes." Yousef said limply.

"Pick him up sergeant. We've got a long journey ahead of us."

Shore leaned over the reception counter at the station.

"Goodbye Yousef. I don't suppose we'll be needing to ask you for your address for the next few months eh?"

*****

Matisse was in a predicament that had been festering for twenty-four hours. She knew she should tell Klarkey about the call, but she didn't know how. She wanted to feel included in his life and in most ways she felt she was. At this time, however, she felt like she hardly knew her best friend and that was upsetting. She picked up Klarkey's phone and pressed the green button. The phone bleeped into action. She scrolled along to the Calls Received button and noted the number down, putting it into her pocket. It was a mobile, so the call could have been made from anywhere. She was certain the woman had a Scottish accent. It was one of the few distinct British accents Matisse could recognise.

She went into her room and pulled the piece of paper back out from her dressing gown and stared at the mobile number. Even if she called, she wasn't exactly sure what to say. Matisse was certain that both she and Klarkey could be at risk from this woman and she needed to discover precisely what she knew and what exactly the problem was with Yousef Al-Rashid.

Matisse took her new pay-as-you-go mobile from her handbag and dialled the number. It rang four times until it was answered by the same Scottish voice she had previously heard.

"Hallo?"

"Er, hello, you called my friend yesterday about a man called Yousef."

"Oh, HI!" Guinness was a little taken aback but very pleased to receive this call. She had not really considered what her next move would be and intended to fully discuss it with Brian before she took action. Events had forced her hand and she had to think quickly.

"I'm sorry, what is your name?" Guinness knew she had to ask despite not expecting a straight answer.

"Matisse. What's yours?" Matisse hadn't expected to be asked her name and couldn't lie fast enough.

"My name's Harriet, but everyone calls me Guinness." Guinness had no reason to lie and wanted to befriend Matisse to discover more about her friend and why he had been in contact with Yousef.

Matisse was unsure about talking on the telephone and felt more comfortable speaking face to face. She also wanted to personally assess this stranger by considering her body language and also to make sure she was alone.

"Guinness, I wonder if you would like to meet somewhere? Perhaps somewhere public so that we can talk freely with each other."

"That's fine by me," Guinness was thinking that this scoop could be the biggest journalistic Christmas present she had ever received. She also considered that she might finally get to the bottom of Richie Brakes' death.

"Do you know London well Guinness?"

"Not really. I know all the main sights but I'm no tour guide."

Matisse was building her confidence now. She had considered a location to meet and was ready to make her suggestion.

"Do you know the Millennium Bridge?"

"The walkway Bridge?

"Yes, the one that connects the St Paul's side of the City to the Tate Modern. Meet me in the middle of the bridge tomorrow evening at 7pm. Approach the bridge from the Tate side."

"How will I recognise you?"

"I'm tall, slim with long dark wavy hair." Matisse said.

Guinness hated her already. "I'm short, slightly chubby with a light brown bob hair style."

"I look forward to meeting you. Please come alone."

"Of course," Guinness agreed. She could hardly contain her excitement.

Matisse put the phone down and wondered if she had just orchestrated the most stupid action of her life. Klarkey banged the door of the suite returning from breakfast. Matisse made the first move into the communal sitting room.

"Bonjour you."

Klarkey smiled. "Bonjour you."

"I'm sorry Klarkey for being so ungrateful. You have been so good to me and I just went crazy on Christmas Day. It was completely stupid of me to be demanding for more presents. I mean, you give me so much. What was I thinking?"

Klarkey held out his hands to embrace his friend.

"No I'm sorry. I really am sorry. I'm not the person you thought I was you know?"

"What do you mean?"

"I don't really want to talk about it right now, but I want to say I'm sorry too. I know I haven't been the easiest person to live with over the last few days. I've had a lot on my mind."

"Were you thinking about your family?"

"Yes, partly. I've been thinking about many things. Don't worry though, I'll be fine."

Matisse was going to tell Klarkey about the call from Guinness, but decided he clearly had enough on his mind at present. She didn't know what was troubling her friend, but whatever it was he was clearly burdened. Matisse considered that if she could resolve the problem with Yousef and the woman named Guinness, she would succeed in helping Klarkey remove a difficulty he didn't even know he had.

CHAPTER TWENTY-TWO

Yousef was driven to Heathrow Airport in a Police car, handcuffed to the Sergeant. DI Rey-Smith sat in the front passenger seat. Three seats on the British Airways flight to Aberdeen had been hastily arranged and Rey-Smith was keen to interview Yousef as soon as possible back at the station.

Most of the journey was spent in silence. The officers could not be seen to be discussing anything relevant to the case with a suspect. Rey-Smith knew it was considered prudent to say nothing, rather than to state something that could be misconstrued or not recorded as taped evidence.

Rey-Smith decided to phone Guinness.

"It's me, DI Rey-Smith"

"Detective Inspector, I thought you'd never phone."

"Well I have. I told you I would didn't I?"

"Aye you did. I presume you're phoning to tell me our man's back in Aberdeen for questioning?"

"Let's just say he's on his way."

"And would there be any chance of an interview?"

"With him? No bloody way. I might consider giving one myself for your programme."

"Oh great. I do the work and you take the credit."

"Listen lady, you gave us some help as part of your civic duty, and the Force is happy and grateful for that. Anything more than that and you're getting yourself into very dodgy territory."

Guinness didn't like his change in tone and snapped, "I've got a hunch there was a conspiracy involved in these murders."

She bit her tongue when she had uttered these words. She didn't want to give Rey-Smith any more information until she had checked things out for herself.

"What do you mean by that?" Rey-Smith didn't want to use the word 'conspiracy' with Yousef listening in the back of the car.

"Oh it's nothing. Just a feeling. Ignore me. Call it woman's intuition or something."

"OK. Whatever. If your hunch decides to turn itself into fact, let me know."

"Oh I will DI Rey-Smith. I will. Thank you for telling me about Al-Rashid. I'm really grateful for that."

"No bother." Rey-Smith hung up and turned around to the sergeant who raised an eyebrow.

Yousef may have been listening but it seemed at this time he was oblivious to everything, staring blankly through the window. He was unable to think about what lay ahead. He knew he was to take a flight to Aberdeen and from there would be taken to the local Police station. Beyond that, he was unable to consider what the future held for him. When the plane took off, the three men sat in the front row seats. Yousef remained handcuffed, this time with one arm to the seat.

*****

Klarkey turned off the television and looked sombrely at Matisse.

"I don't like that look Klarkey. The last time I saw it you told me some very bad things."

"I'm afraid I've some very bad things to tell you now."

"What have you done this time?"

"You know me too well Matisse. I don't know where to start."

"Please try. You've been acting very strangely since before Christmas and I don't know what to do or how to help you."

"I'm not sure you can help me Matisse. Do you remember I told you about my sister Charlotte?"

"Of course."

"And I didn't know what I was going to do about her killer?"

"Yes but I thought that was all talk…"

"Not all talk Matisse. It was ME. Don't you see?"

"What was you?"

"It was ME that killed all those men in the prison?"

"It was you? The Prison? I don't believe it." Matisse flicked her hand sharply at the wrist, then stood up from the chair and smoothed out the creases in her skirt.

"I'm sorry Matisse. It WAS me. I've been planning it for ages. You know I had to kill Groucher. I had no choice but to kill all the other bastards as well, to cover my tracks. Otherwise the trail would have led straight back to me."

Matisse had a coughing fit and rushed to drink from a bottle of Evian she'd taken from the mini bar earlier.

"Klarkey I really don't know what to say? Have you got a taste for killing now? What is going on?"

"I'm sorry Matisse. I suppose you'll want to leave me now? I would understand if you did. But you did say you thought these men almost certainly deserved what they got."

"I did? When?" Matisse became defensive, clutching her jade necklace.

"On Christmas morning. You specifically said that."

"Don't throw this back onto me. You're the person who killed all these men. They probably did deserve it. It's just…it comes as something of a surprise when you know your best friend's turned into a mass murderer!"

"I'm sorry."

"You shouldn't be apologising to me. Maybe you should think about the families of the people who died."

"FAMILIES?!" By now Klarkey was shouting with emotion.

"What about the families of those killed by these men. Who will spare a thought for them? FOR US." Klarkey cried for the first time in a long time.

"My God. What are we going to do?" Matisse took Klarkey in her arms as he wept onto her shoulder uncontrollably.

*****

Since Christmas Day, South Enfield Police Station had been a hive of activity. All officers' leave had been cancelled; Superintendent Byward had been attempting to keep control over the officers, the Press and was also trying to avoid a possible riot at Enfield Prison.

Another day passed and Detective Superintendent Shore had called a press conference where he had planned to enjoy basking in the success of Operation Philistine. The room was packed with journalists and cameramen.

Shore entered the room, flanked by an Inspector and two sergeants.

"Ladies and Gentlemen, quieten down please. Let's have some quiet. Thank you."

The room was silent for a second, until a journalist shouted at Shore,

"Mr Shore. How close are you to catching the Enfield mass murderer?"

Then another spoke up,

"Where's Superintendent Byward? Shouldn't he be briefing us about the Prison Murders?"

"Gentlemen please!" Shore had to take control.

"I'm not here today to discuss the progress of Police investigations into the deaths at Enfield Prison."

A communal groan went up throughout the room.

"What I am here to talk to you about is the successful recovery of valuable paintings stolen in Spain, and the successful destruction of a major art and antiques criminal gang which stretches across the country and throughout Europe." Shore loved to embellish his reports to the press. The room fell silent.

"Some weeks ago, paintings by El Greco and Picasso were stolen from a museum near Barcelona in Spain.

Dedicated officers in South Enfield happened upon the discovery of the paintings in London. The pictures were tracked in order to identify members of the gang involved, and these criminals were arrested following days of intense surveillance and good old-fashioned policing. The value of the paintings is thought to be in excess of £5 million."

The first grumbles of interest came from the journalists.

"On Christmas Eve, officers led by me and in conjunction with SO19, specialist armed officers, stormed a unit on an industrial estate in north London. Here, arrests were made and I can tell you now that one female, who is a significant handler of stolen goods; and one male, are currently being held for questioning. They were charged on Boxing Day.

I am delighted to tell you that the three paintings were successfully recovered along with £250,000 in cash."

Shore knew from experience that the Press loved a good picture. He remembered revelling in his success in Operation Tricorne. He had made the front pages with the image of him holding the tricorne hat belonging to Mozart. That was one of the proudest days of his life and he felt the need to repeat such an event. Despite being concerned that the furore of the Prison deaths would overshadow his latest success, he nevertheless chose to repeat his tried and tested winning formula.

Leaning behind the desk, he pulled out a long wooden box.

"Ladies and gentlemen, these are the paintings that were recovered."

One by one he held up the three paintings and the mighty camera flashes burst into action.

Then he lifted a briefcase onto the desk.

"And here ladies and gentlemen, is £250,000 in crisp £50 notes."

Shore held the wide-open suitcase for everyone to see. Keeping it close to his chest he smiled. He knew the papers loved pictures of money. The flashbulbs flooded the room with light once again and Shore was blinded for a few delirious seconds.

"That's all I can give you today. We will of course be updating you at the appropriate time with news of our enquiry into the deaths at Enfield Prison. Thank you very much."

A barrage of questions hit the backs of the officers as they left the room. All questions related to the current enquiry and none of the journalists wanted to ask about Operation Philistine. Shore was furious with the perpetrator of the murders for stealing his moment, but he thought he'd made the best of the time. He'd still make some of the front pages.

The station's Superintendent was waiting for Shore when he returned to the corridor, with a wide smile on his face.

"Shore?"

"Byward?"

"A moment in my office…please?"

"Of course." Shore looked forward to being congratulated by his uniformed colleague.

Both men walked swiftly to the Superintendent's office.

Byward sat down in his chair leaving DS Shore standing.

"Bob, you've got to get a grip. I'm getting flack from the borough Commander for not prioritising the hell that is this mass murder."

"What's that got to do with me?"

"Can't you see what's going on? I've got the national press baying at my feet, smelling blood, desperate for a story on the Prison murders and you're calling bloody Press Conferences in my nick to talk about stolen paintings. Just what do you think you're doing."

"With respect …"

"With respect my arse. You're showing no respect. I saw how you were after the Tricorne op and you've got the taste for press coverage. The bug. It's addictive, like a drug. Normally we try to keep ourselves out of the press but you seem to be developing a taste for newsprint. Don't you think it's just a touch inappropriate to call a press conference now? So soon after the troubles at the prison."

"I'm sorry, but I thought it might be a good idea to give the press a positive news story. After all, we did recover millions of pounds worth of art and two hundred and fifty grand in cash. Not bad work don't you think? Look, if the prison murders hadn't happened, Operation Philistine would have been all over the front pages and you know it."

"Shore that's totally irrelevant. What is important is assessing what the priorities of this station are at any one time. My pleasure at seeing the successful conclusion of Operation Philistine is unquestionable, but calling a press conference now about it? I'm sorry Bob, it's just not on."

"I'm sorry you see it like that."

"Yes I do. And I'm making it an order that from now on, NO press conferences in this station will be called without my specific authorisation. Do I make myself clear."

"Crystal"

*****

Brian, Guinness's trusted cameraman had slept well in the hotel overnight. They met at the breakfast table in the dining room.

"Are you sure you should be eating that?" Brian pointed to the bacon and eggs on Guinness's plate.

"Ha bloody ha. Let's recap on exactly where we are, okay? DI Rey-Smith has taken Al-Rashid into custody. We know he killed Richie and the others and the Police will hopefully go to whatever extent is necessary to build the case against him. I'll make sure of that. We've also found a connection with the friend of this person called Matisse, who has some kind of European accent and I'm due to meet her tonight because she clearly knows something about what happened that night. Is that about the size of it?"

"Aye, I'd say so."

"So we're faced with our old dilemma. Do we tell the cops about a possible conspiracy and let them deal with it, or do we put ourselves in the firing line, possibly in danger as journalists to try to get the scoop of the century?"

"Let me think about that one for one millisecond. Uhh, we don't tell the cops as usual until we've got our story."

"How did I know you were going to say that?"

"So what's the plan?"

"The hard bit is that this Matisse wants to meet me in the middle of the Millennium Bridge tonight at 7. She also made a big deal about coming alone."

"There's no way you're going into this alone. What the hell do you think I came down here for?"

"I'm sorry Brian. It's the only way. I'll tell you what I want us to do. I want you to wire me up with a miniature camera in one of my blouse buttonholes. I'll wear a pack with the battery on my waistband and carry a bag if necessary. Let's do whatever we can to record the conversation and we'll review it afterwards. You can stay back by Tate Britain and watch with binoculars. She told me to approach from that side so you can be pretty sure she'll be coming from the St Paul's side."

"Fair enough. We'd better get going after breakfast and start sorting you out with some equipment and testing it. I reckon we'll only get one shot at this."

*****

Klarkey had recomposed himself. He was relieved to tell Matisse, his closest friend about his Christmas Eve activities, but he had one more person to enlighten. He hoped she would be as understanding.

He made his way by cab to Waterloo to pick up Roberta. He had spoken with her every day and she was one of the few reasons he considered his future was worth living. He knew that the next few hours would be very difficult, but he hoped that if Roberta sympathised with the circumstances leading to his actions, she may find herself able to forgive him.

"Wait here please," Klarkey said to the cab.

"Sorry pal, I can't stop here, you'll have to pay me and get another cab when you're ready."

Klarkey paid the driver and raced into the station to the platform where the train from Portsmouth was just pulling in. He was a bundle of nerves. He felt like a teenager, meeting his girlfriend for the second time. His stomach was tense and his head was sweating, despite the cold of the day.

When he saw Roberta he thought how amazing she looked. He couldn't wait to get her back to the suite. He couldn't wait to feel her flesh against his and to briefly forget about the events of the last few days.

When they arrived at the hotel Klarkey led Roberta by the hand to his room. Matisse was out. She preferred to be away from the suite when Klarkey and Roberta were together so they could enjoy complete privacy.

Roberta was overwhelmed by Klarkey's passion. She had never experienced anything like this before. All the time they made love, he kept telling her he loved her and she considered herself the luckiest woman on the planet.

Klarkey led Roberta into the shower and they lathered each other's bodies washing away the sweat and smells of lovemaking. Klarkey held Roberta's face in his hands.

"You are so beautiful. I love you so much."

"I love you so much too."

"Roberta I want to marry you!"

Roberta pulled away. "You're moving a bit fast don't you think? Surely we should get to know about each other a little more? Or at least live together for a while first."

"Oh…ok. We certainly should talk anyway."

Klarkey turned off the water of the shower and stretched out his hand for a large bath sheet towel.

He wiped and dabbed her pale soft skin gently as he spoke.

"We shouldn't have any secrets you know."

Roberta turned around and he pressed the towel against her breasts.

"I know that. I don't think I have any secrets. Why? Have you got something you want to tell me?"

"I think I do. Let's get dressed and have a drink."

"I'm not going to like this am I?"

"No Roberta, I don't think you are, but if you're going to love me, you need to know everything."

They silently got dressed. Roberta was intrigued. She was imagining all sorts of things: Had he fiddled his taxes? Was he already married? Were he and Matisse really lovers?

"Please sit down darling."

"I'm sitting, what is it?" Roberta was now growing impatient.

"This isn't easy for me."

"You're already married aren't you?"

"Er…NO. I'm not. Just listen sweetheart, really. I'm not going to beat around the bush. I've killed people. Lots of people."

"What?!"

" I said I'm responsible for the deaths of a lot of people."

"What does that mean? Are you saying you're some kind of mercenary, or were you a negligent surgeon? What do you mean? I don't understand."

"The prison deaths this last Christmas Eve. It was me."

"What do you mean, 'It was me'?

"What I mean is, that I entered the prison and killed those men. Can I spell it out any clearer to you?"

Roberta was in shock. She stood up. She held her hands up to him showing her palms.

"I ….I …don't understand."

"Roberta, honey, I had my reasons."

"Reasons? What? To ease the overcrowding? What reasons?"

"One of the men molested my sister and killed her when we were young. That's my reason."

"That's awful. I'm not going to take that away from you. But kill all those men? In cold blood?"

Roberta ran to the toilet and wretched, unable to vomit. She wiped her mouth and blew her nose.

"You can't go around playing God." Her eyes were now sore and red.

"I'm sorry Roberta. I did what I thought was right at the time."

"I…I…I can't be with you. I've got to get out."

"Please love, don't go. Let me explain some more. Please."

Roberta grabbed her coat from the sofa and ran out of the suite.

Klarkey ran after her but she ran with the speed of an athlete. When he reached the entrance to the building he could see her turning the corner into Kensington High Street. He banged his fist into the open Georgian door, grazing his knuckles.

Klarkey returned to the suite. "Shit. Shit. Shit."

CHAPTER TWENTY-THREE

Klarkey was in a rage. He was furious with himself. He was angry with the way things had ended with Roberta. He knew from the way she reacted there was no chance of them being reconciled. He would have to consider life without her. As he washed his fist under the tap, he stopped the bleeding with a flannel and put plasters on the small wounds most likely to open. He was forced into a corner and he had to act. He grabbed a navy blazer from the wardrobe, a pair of dark shoes and black trousers. After changing his clothes, taking care not to knock his delicate hand, he walked with purpose to Kensington High Street. It was towards the end of the lunchtime, and whilst many people were still off work enjoying their Christmas holidays, the streets were busy with traffic, everyone seemingly rushing to, or from the sales. It was impossible for Klarkey to get a cab. He decided to take the tube for a change. He knew it would most certainly be quicker.

Klarkey was breathing heavily. He was acting impulsively but he didn't know what other action to take. After a two-minute wait, the District and Circle line train arrived and a flotilla of women armed with shopping bags climbed aboard. He slowly counted off the stations: Gloucester Road; South Kensington; Sloane Square; Victoria; St James' Park; Westminster: his final stop. When he climbed out into the street, he gasped for breath. The air wasn't clean below or above ground, but the biting wind created a false sense of air purity. He faced Portcullis House, a building that he thought was magnificent, but this building wasn't his destination. He turned and faced the mighty Big Ben, crossing the road towards it. The view of this building never ceased to impress him.

He walked along the side of the building and made his way towards the visitors' entrance of the House of Commons. As he approached security he prepared to be frisked. He opened his blazer and lifted his shoes as a security officer searched him. Klarkey was familiar with the routine. He had been here several times before.

Once inside the security officer spoke to Klarkey.

"Who are you here to see sir?"

"Mr Newton-Banner. If you could tell him that Francis Klarke is here to see him.

"Very good sir. Please stand to one side."

Klarkey waited patiently as a stream of visitors and workers passed through the entrance.

Roderick Newton-Banner was a short, mop-haired, forty-something junior minister responsible for prisons. He arrived to meet Klarkey, red-faced. He handed him a visitor's pass to wear and took him by the arm, whispering into his ear.

"I told you not to come here again. What the hell are you doing?"

"I had to see you and talk with you. I'm desperate. We have to talk."

"I don't have any time now. I'm going to take you into the chamber and I'll collect you in about an hour."

Newton-Banner led Klarkey through a succession of corridors and stairs, past a shop selling all kinds of chocolates and mementos adorned with the House of Commons seal and logo; past various doors and offices and on through a door that led to the visitors' gallery overlooking the chamber of the House. It was already nearly 3pm and he had missed the exciting Prime Minister's Question Time session at noon. The chamber, along with the visitor's gallery had emptied out significantly since that intense half an hour. Klarkey quietly watched what seemed to him a rather dull debate about the effect of wind turbines on the landscape of the Welsh hills.

After an hour and ten minutes, Newton-Banner tapped Klarkey on the shoulder.

"Come on. I'm free now."

In silence Klarkey followed Newton-Banner into a lift. They were alone. After travelling to the top floor, the lift opened and Newton-Banner walked towards a window overlooking the central roofs of the Houses of Parliament.

"You see my dear Klarke, the gargoyles?"

"Yes...what of them?"

"They're beautiful aren't they? Very few people get to see the gargoyles as they're obscured from view to the public."

Suddenly, and completely without warning, Newton-Banner grabbed Klarkey by the upper arm and tried to kiss him. His attempt was somewhat hopeless as he was several inches shorter than Klarkey. Notwithstanding this, Klarkey pushed him away very forcibly.

"What the bloody hell are you doing Rod?"

"I'm sorry. I'm really terribly sorry old chap. I thought that was what you wanted. Did I get it completely wrong?"

"Yes you bloody well did. Is this why you've been so friendly to me for the past few months? You haven't given a toss about me or my feelings about Groucher in prison. You just wanted to get a piece of me!"

"No no no. You've got me all wrong. It's very difficult for me you know. Being a junior minister and...having feelings like this as well."

"You're a married man. This is your life. You chose it Rod. No one put you into this position. I know people who are gay and they didn't feel the need to get married."

"But you're not gay yourself?"

"No I'm not. Are you?"

"I wouldn't call myself gay. I just...well...I just like to participate. Or at least I would like to. But it's very hard for me; in my position."

"You make me sick. I thought you really cared about how I felt."

"Didn't I help you get into Enfield Prison?" Newton-Banner squinted at Klarkey.

"Yes you did. But I thought you did it because you wanted to help me and also because you felt the need to undermine the Secretary of State. I know how ambitious you are."

"And I didn't think you were going to kill off a whole bloody wing!"

"Don't you read the Post? Haven't I saved you a fortune in taxpayers money?"

"Listen Klarke. I'll say this now just once. Get into that lift, make your way to the exit and never EVER contact me again. Is that clear?"

"Oh yes. Don't worry. Now I know your real agenda I won't ever be contacting you again. Goodbye Rod. I hope you're going to be able to live with yourself."

The lift opened and Klarkey climbed in.

"I hope you can live with yourself too Klarke."

The lift closed and Klarkey made his way to the exit, handing his pass to the security officer as he left. As he made his way out in front of the Houses of Parliament, he realised he was truly on his own and there was no one he could turn to for help. He was probably in grave danger and would have to act soon to save himself.

*****

Shore stood at the front of the briefing room. Twenty Police officers, both uniformed and plain-clothed CID staff were present. This was the first briefing of the day and as far as Shore was concerned, time was passing too quickly without results. He had expected the investigation to provide the name of a credible suspect by now and he felt it was time to put pressure on officers of all ranks.

"I'm not going to take too much of your time, because I'd much rather you were out looking for this killer than spending precious overtime listening to me. I am in no doubt that our man must have visited the prison sometime within a few weeks before his crime. Obviously on

Christmas Eve he was in disguise. Sergeant Morris will pass you video captured images of the suspect from the Enfield Jail CCTV system. Sergeant."

Sergeant Morris jumped to attention and passed around A4 pages of the image of the killer. Shore continued.

"I want you to divide yourselves into two teams. You will NOT leave this nick until you get what I want. Team one, led by Sergeant Morris, will scan the IMR logs for any reference to a visitor who was not known to any prisoners at Enfield. And I don't just mean visitors of those who died. Check EVERY visitor to the prison whether it was to someone in D Wing or elsewhere. Report to me with every lead and we'll check them out. The second team is going to watch TV for the rest of the day. Yes, you are going to watch the CCTV for every visiting session to Enfield Prison in the last two months. Match the picture to our man and we're in business."

Everyone nodded, keen to proceed.

"I'm glad I make myself clear at last. Let's catch ourselves a killer. Sergeant Morris, sort out the groups now will you?"

Shore returned to his office and poured himself a whiskey. He was sure that he would catch the killer.

*****

In Aberdeen, DI Rey-Smith led Yousef immediately to an interview room.

"Coffee Yousef?"

"Yes please sir."

"Get some coffees please Sergeant."

A few minutes later, the DI was questioning Yousef. Legal representation had been provided for Yousef and a pinstriped solicitor sat beside him.

Rey-Smith pressed the start and record button on the tape.

The lawyer had advised Yousef to deny everything and to say very little. Yousef complied willingly.

Rey-Smith was not amused. "I didn't fly you hundreds of miles back to Aberdeen to get nothing from you. We can place you in Aberdeen at the time of the murders. We can place you coming through the airport just before the murders took place. We can place you at the scene of the crime."

Yousef looked up. He was sure that he had not left any fingerprints on the beer cans and he was sure that he had left no evidence of his visit to Aberdeen. He was sure the Policeman was bluffing.

"Yousef, why did you come to London just before visiting Aberdeen?"

Yousef was thrown by this question, but his lawyer encouraged him to answer.

"I was...visiting a friend. We had lunch in Oxford Street. I forget where."

"And what was this friend's name?"

"My friend Klarkey. He used to run the school where I studied English in France."

Rey-Smith had no reason to accept Yousef was not telling the truth and moved on.

"Why did you come to Aberdeen? You travelled to Aberdeen using a different name? Why did you do this?"

"I don't know. I thought it would be easier to travel with a British passport. I wanted to see other parts of Scotland besides Glasgow. Is that a crime?"

"It is a crime to travel on a false passport."

"Then charge me with that crime if you must. I am not a murderer. I just want to live in peace."

"Interview terminated at 18.30." Rey-Smith flicked the switch of the tape recorder to 'off'. "I think we'll take a break until the morning don't you?"

Rey-Smith left the room and spoke to his sergeant.

"Do a cross-reference check for this Klarkey and see if anything comes up will you?"

"Sir." The sergeant nodded.

*****

It had been dark for over three hours and it was only 7pm. Guinness walked from the Tate Modern waterfront onto the sleek Millennium Bridge. The air was biting-cold and the bridge was deserted. Brian was hidden out of view close to the edge of the Tate with a flask of coffee and a pair of binoculars to accompany him. Guinness was certain he would see nothing in this light, and the streetlamps and bridge lighting was unhelpful on this slightly foggy evening. Guinness was very nervous, but at the same time filled with excitement. She knew the tiny camera placed in her blouse was likely to provide the only recording of the conversation with this stranger known as Matisse, and she considered that it would form a pivotal part of her documentary on the deaths in Aberdeen.

Matisse climbed out of the taxi, which had parked as close to the northern edge of the bridge as possible. She was wearing black heels and a smart wool Chanel suit and pillbox hat. She imagined herself as Joan Collins, during her momentous entrance into the Hollywood television series Dynasty. Joan Collins entered the courtroom with her first appearance in the show and everyone recognised how she could make her presence felt. Matisse felt wonderful and wanted everyone to know it.

As she clipperty-clicked her heels along the bridge, she carefully eyed her way ahead, looking for a short, dumpy, bob-haired woman. Guinness was waiting for her at the centre of the bridge and they stopped in front of each other like cowboys about to draw their guns in a Western movie.

"I'm Guinness. You must be Matisse?"

"Yes. What do you want exactly?"

"Does your friend Francis Klarke know you're here?"

"What does he have to do with you?"

"He's a friend of Yousef Al-Rashid is he not?"

"So? I don't know."

"Oh come on, you wouldn't be here if he wasn't a friend of Yousef's."

"So what if he is? What has that to do with you?"

"Yousef Al-Rashid killed three innocent men in Aberdeen where I live. One of them was my friend. I wondered if your friend, Francis Klarke…"

"Call him Klarkey…"

"…your friend KLARKEY, knew why he might have killed them."

"Are you a Policewoman?"

"No, I'm a friend of one of the dead men."

"And Yousef?"

"He's in custody in the Police station in Aberdeen. I helped to put him there and I want to know why he did it."

"You HELPED to put Yousef in jail?" Matisse was losing her composure.

"I played a small part. If you're friend was murdered wouldn't you do what you could to help?"

"Where did you get Klarkey's phone number from?"

Guinness thought for a moment.

"I found out that Yousef and your friend Klarkey were talking on the phone before the murders happened. I wondered if your friend knew about Yousef and what he was going to do in Aberdeen."

"Are you suggesting that Klarkey knew about these murders?"

"I don't know. Are you?"

"Don't be ridiculous. Why would I suggest such a thing?"

Matisse was becoming more annoyed with this woman. She knew that Guinness had helped the Police already with Yousef. If she suspected Klarkey was involved in her friend's death it could only be a matter of time before she led the Police to Klarkey.

Matisse stepped forward towards Guinness and grabbed the back of her hair.

"What are doing you mad woman?" Guinness shouted.

No one was on the bridge and she was acutely aware of this fact. She only hoped the camera was recording every second of the incident, or that Brian might help; but he could see nothing. She grabbed the air and caught Matisse's necklace, then pushed her back with all her strength. Matisse fell backwards breaking one of her heels, and the large jade beads of her necklace fell in a shower onto the floor of the bridge. Matisse was angry. As far as she was concerned, Guinness had defiled her. She had taken away her womanhood just like the bullies had when she was a young boy. She ripped off the other heel of her good shoe and let out a war cry pushing Guinness back against the railings of the bridge. Guinness lost her balance falling awkwardly and tumbled over the side of the bridge, splashing into the cold Thames below. Matisse gasped. Then she hyperventilated uncontrollably. Suddenly she realised the enormity of the events of the last few minutes and looked around her. There was still no one on the bridge and no sound coming from the fast flowing river below. The precious jade beads were also lost over the side. She knew Guinness must have died. Matisse staggered in her broken shoes back to the north side of the bridge and hailed a taxi back to the hotel. Now she was as bad as Klarkey and she felt wretched.

*****

Roberta had been sitting in her small terraced house for 24 hours, unable to sleep or to speak with anyone else. Klarkey had left messages on her machine begging her for another chance, but she was clear their relationship was over. There was no way in the world she would continue an affair with a murderer. She was reminded of the serial killer

Harold Shipman and his wife, Primrose. She had stood by him, unfailing, as the evidence had become more and more damning. There was no way Roberta would become involved with Klarkey in the same way.

Roberta was in no doubt about her decision to end the relationship with Klarkey, but she was less sure how to morally respond to her former lover's admission. Finally, she decided to make a call.

"Hello Crimestoppers can I help you?"

"Yes," Roberta started nervously. "I'd like to report a crime but I don't want to say my name."

"That's fine madam. We offer a confidential service here so every call will be treated in the strictest of confidence."

"It's about the murders at the prison in London at Christmas,"

"Yes, go on,"

"The man responsible is called Klarkey. That's all I can tell you but he lives in London and his name's Klarkey."

"Do you have an address for this person, Klarkey?"

"All I can tell you is his name's Klarkey and he lives in London. You'll find him in Kensington."

Roberta started to blush, aware that in the criminal world she would be known as a 'grass'. But she wasn't a criminal, and she felt this call was the right course of action to take.

"That's all I can tell you now. Goodbye." Roberta put the phone down hoping this call would bring her some kind of closure to the events that had taken place. Unfortunately for her, she felt no better after the phone call than she had before.

*****

Matisse rushed into the suite and pulled off her broken shoes. She had run up the stairs and was out of breath. Klarkey was reading a Ben Elton novel and looked up at her.

"Bloody hell you look a mess. What happened? By the way, Roberta won't return my calls so I think I've messed up that relationship. What can I do eh? At least I was honest." Klarkey realised Matisse looked very distressed. He put down his book and took her shoulders in his hands.

"What's happened Matisse?"

"Something terrible. I didn't mean it. Everything went wrong. Mon Dieu I'm in so much trouble. Help me Klarkey!"

Klarkey poured her a cognac from a decanter and she drank it down, holding the glass with both hands. They sat down and Matisse proceeded to tell him the whole course of events. She finished by saying, "I'm only sorry I every answered your phone in the first place."

"Matisse, it was an accident. You said so yourself."

"Yes it was. Kind of. I was angry. Does that count as an accident?"

"I don't know. I think it's time we took some action before we get into an even bigger mess than we're already in. Agreed?"

"Agreed."

Klarkey led Matisse into her room, clasping his right hand around her wrist. The forefinger on his left hand pressed into his mouth and he started biting his nails. He kicked that habit when he was twenty-one years old and became aware of a heightened level of nervousness he hadn't experienced for many years.

The dire extent of their situation suddenly registered with Klarkey.

"Sit down."

Matisse obediently sat.

"Let's look at the facts. Not so long ago, I entered a prison and killed a whole load of people. A few weeks before, I paid three people to kill in three provincial areas around the country. Today you're telling me that you've accidentally killed someone who found out about Yousef and the Aberdeen murders."

Matisse looked at Klarkey and laughed. "It doesn't look good does it?"

"No it bloody doesn't look good Matisse. I want you to pack your two suitcases as full as you can." Klarkey pulled his mobile phone from his pocket and took it into Matisse's bathroom. He stamped on it hard and the plastic split into several fragments. He took the sim-card from the rubbish and put it in his pocket, putting the debris into the bin.

"I'm going to drop this in a bin somewhere far from here. When you've packed your bags I'm going to take you to the airport and we'll get you a flight to Paris. You can get the fast train to Tours from there. You have to go to see your parents. You have to stay there until I contact you."

"But I haven't spoken to them for such a long time. I'm not sure that's the right thing to do. I want to be with you."

"I don't know what the hell to do with myself yet. While you're packing, I'm going to go down to the High Street and buy a couple of pay-as-you-go phones. I'll have to find ones that work in Europe. We can stay in touch that way. It's vital that we get out of here though. I don't know how much time we have. You have to trust me on this."

"I do trust you. I'm so scared. I could handle anything that you have done, but for me. I don't know if I can look at myself. I feel so dirty."

"Don't worry about anything right now. Pack your bags. Don't leave anything behind and I'll be back soon."

Klarkey stroked Matisse's face as he stood up and put his thumbnail into his mouth. The cuticle was almost at bleeding-point on his index finger. He had to get a grip on reality and work out a plan for them both.

*****

Sergeant Morris rushed to Shore's office. Out of breath he banged and entered straight away. Shore was holding his mouth and hands out of the window, with a cigarette passing between them. Coughing violently, Shore tossed the cigarette out of the window and waved the smoke away from his face.

"I thought you'd given all of that up after Tricorne sir." Morris spoke with a smile on his face. Shore respected Morris and saw him as an equal despite the differences in rank."

"Piss off Morris. It's for medicinal reasons. What do you want anyway?"

"The lads might have found a lead from the IMR logs of conversations with some of the prisoners."

Shore moved towards the door rubbing his hands.

"Come on then Sergeant, SHOW ME THESE LOGS!"

The two men walked down a flight of stairs and into the open plan office where a team of officers were working.

Morris walked towards a young female constable. "Tell Mr Shore what you told us earlier."

"Yes Sarge. Sir, I was checking the logs in the Internet Monitoring Room, cross referencing prisoners who had used the IMR in the last two months before Christmas and those who had talked to strangers, at least non-family members."

"Good. How many individuals came up?"

"471"

"Oh God."

"Then I extrapolated the 471 with the number of visitors orders issued and used. The murderer had to have had first hand knowledge of the Prison before coming inside to do the job."

"OK, how did that affect the numbers?"

"We got down to 36."

"I suppose that's manageable."

"Just a moment sir. We knew we were looking for a man, so that reduced it down to 23."

"Even better."

"That was first thing this morning. We printed out the transcripts and obtained ISP references for each of the computers and the telephone lines from where they were used."

"So you know exactly where the computers are that were used for those conversations."

"Yes sir. Some of them were internet cafés, some were private addresses and a couple were hotels. Two of the names used in the conversations didn't match the ISP registration which suggests they were lying about their names."

"And why should someone befriend an inmate and lie about their name unless they were up to no good?"

"Exactly sir."

"OK Morris, check out those two addresses discreetly and find out who could have made those calls. I want some surveillance on the properties and I want the neighbours to be shown the mug shot of our man to see if we can identify him. We've got to move fast on this."

"Sir, I'm already onto it."

"Good work constable." Shore beamed at the young female Policewoman and returned to his office. He felt he was close to finding the person responsible for the murders but he was sure the perpetrator wouldn't be too foolish to leave clues along the way.

CHAPTER TWENTY-FOUR

Matisse took her first tentative steps for years along the road towards the family bakery in the French city of Tours. Leaving her two large cases checked into the lockers at the railway station, she felt most comfortable carrying only her Gucci sports bag. She had no idea what or who she would find. It had been so long since she had seen her family and they would be sure to get a shock to see her as the finally fully-female: Matisse Espère.

She decided to sit for a while on the window ledge of a clothes store opposite the family boulangerie. It was early and the fashion shop was not yet open, but she knew the bakery would have been serving to the public for hours already and her mind drifted back to her youth; the strong smells of baking bread and fingers dipped in chocolate or almonds or icing sugar. Her heart missed a beat as she saw one of her brothers inside the doorway. He had grown so much but she recognised his face immediately. It was Hervé. He was transferring croissants from an oven tray to the display area on the counter. Biting her top lip, she couldn't hold back any more and went inside.

"Hervé? …C'est moi. Matisse" Her body shuddered and her face went white with the fear of rejection.

"Matisse? Ma Soeur Matisse?" *My sister Matisse?* He shouted, screwing up the corner of his mouth and nose. Throwing the tray down, he continued,

"I had a brother Matisse. He is dead. You can't be my sister."

*"I **am** your sister. I **was** your brother."*

Matisse's mother walked into the shop front.

"Matisse? MATISSE? Is that you? Do I have a daughter? Can it really be you?"

"Yes Mother. I'm so sorry that I have not been in touch. It has been a terrible journey for me." Matisse

bowed her head demurely. She knew how to get her
mother's sympathy.

*"I blame myself. Your hair is so beautiful. I tried to
make you into something that you were not and I lost you
because of it."*

*"No mother. You were good to me really. You did
what you thought was right. I chose to become a
woman…and I am a woman. Really."*

"Oh Matisse!"

They embraced and cried. Even her brother wiped
away a tear. Then her father came from the back of the
bakery to find out what was happening in his shop front.
He said nothing. He solidly embraced Matisse. She was
completely relieved and sobbed in her father's giant arms.

*"I'm so happy. I never thought you would want to see
me again father."*

*"Matisse, we didn't know if you were alive or dead. We
blamed ourselves for you leaving. I know your mother
thinks of you every day. Do you really think we would reject
you now? We love you. We always have and we always
will. I suppose you live in Paris?"*

*"No papa, I live in London, but it's a long story. Can I
stay with you for a little while?"*

"Matisse…"

*****

Shore was positioned in an unmarked car in a small
turning off Kensington High Street. Other officers were
located near various entrances to the hotel and armed Police
were preparing to take their places on the top of buildings
surrounding the hotel.

Shore heard a crackle over his walky-talky.

"Everyone in position sir."

Shore needed to move quickly. Having obtained the
warrant to search the Kensington Boutique Hotel, he needed
to find the man who had called himself Sam Stevens: the
man who had obtained a visiting order to enter Enfield

Prison. The staff member responsible for Sam Steven's post office box in Holborn had recognised Klarkey from the prison CCTV pictures. Having identified their target, they had to find out his true identity. Then they had a stroke of luck. Crimestoppers had passed them information given anonymously, about someone called 'Klarkey', based in Kensington, who was allegedly responsible for the murders. They had received several crank calls but this particular caller seemed genuine because the information linked neatly to their own enquiry. After cross-referencing the name in the national database, they found Aberdeen CID investigating three murders that may have been instigated by someone also called Klarkey. They knew they had to act fast. The internet connection joining the chatroom with one of the prisoners was traced to the southwest London address that Matisse and Klarkey had made their home for some time. The hotel management had been co-operative, and despite making a small fortune from Klarkey's residency, recognised their loyalties should lie towards the Police, rather than in favour of a suspected criminal. They too had identified Klarkey from the pictures supplied.

"GO GO GO!!" Shore barked into the handset, as he rushed breathless out of the car to follow the group of officers entering the hotel, making their way towards the suite occupied by their target.

The armed men of the elite SO19 squad led the CID officers through the rooms of the suite.

"Clear."

"Clear."

"Clear."

Each of the rooms was checked for evidence, but no one was home.

Shore wasn't used to failure. He spoke into the walky-talky for the last time that day. "It looks like we just missed him. Stand down everyone. Stand down."

*****

During the night before, when Klarkey knew that Matisse was safely in France, he packed his bags and made his escape. The hotel had been paid monthly in advance so there was no outstanding bill. There was no need to alert any of the staff about his plan and the concierge chose to remain conveniently discreet after two crisp £50 notes were tucked into his open palm. He also hired a forensic cleaner to ensure no prints were left behind. For the time being, Klarkey was resigned to a life on the run. But he had one last job to do in the UK.

He jumped out of the minicab and asked the driver to wait. Leaving his cases in the boot, he took his briefcase under his arm. As Klarkey entered the school without being challenged, he followed the line of the long corridor where he could see into every class through the windows. The smell of bleached parquet flooring took him briefly back to his childhood. When he found the door he was looking for, he knocked lightly on one of the small glass panes and entered. Roberta was addressing a group of 15 year olds.

"So to summarise: alliteration occurs when a consonant is repeated, such as 'people pulling-power'".

Roberta grew red in the face and the class started to giggle, sensing that it wasn't another teacher who had interrupted their English lesson. She continued nevertheless.

"Whereas assonance is when the sound of a vowel is repeated in a phrase, such as 'Bad, glad, sad and mad'. Mr Klarke, could I see you outside please? The giggles grew louder.

Roberta spoke in a hushed shout, "What the hell are doing here? I told you it's over and it is."

"I know I know. I needed to see you one last time. To tell you what I'm doing. I'm leaving."

"What do you mean, you're leaving?"

"Exactly that. I'm going overseas."

"Well goodbye then." Roberta started to turn but Klarkey took hold of her shoulder.

"Get off me!"

"Roberta...I love you. Doesn't that mean anything to you? I'm truly sorry for everything that's happened. Please come away with me. We could start afresh. You and me together."

Roberta was genuinely stunned. "You want ME to go away with you? After...what you've done? You have got to be kidding. To be forever running away? Forever looking over our shoulders? Never safe? That's no life. Goodbye Klarkey and don't come to find me again."

Roberta broke away from Klarkey's hold and pushed open the classroom door to cheers and applause from the students. Dejected, Klarkey made his way out of the building and back to the car.

*****

Mr and Mrs McWerter walked into St Thomas's Hospital accompanied by their daughter's friend and colleague Brian. Mrs McWerter was a large, smartly dressed woman. She couldn't contain her tears and a flaking tissue was permanently attached to the corner of her puffy eyes.

The morgue staff had removed the body from the sliding fridge, checking first the name in felt tip on the filing-cabinet-type drawer. They lifted the body from the shelf and carefully put it onto a trolley, moving it towards the chapel.

"Look dear, this is the home of the Florence Nightingale Museum. It's terribly interesting."

Her husband couldn't distract her and she continued to sob.

As they walked towards the morgue, a Police officer approached them.

"Mr & Mrs McWerter? I'm DC Hayland. I'll take you down to the chapel."

"The chapel?" Mr McWerter asked.

"Yes sir, the…body has been removed from the morgue and is waiting for you in the chapel."

"I see."

They followed the officer towards the chapel. The room was dimmed and a central table supported the body covered in a wide-striped duvet. A thin vase of silk roses decorated the bare room at either end of the cadaver.

The officer pulled back the top of the duvet to reveal a porcelain-white female face framed by a mop of hair. Her lips were blue and her head rested on a pillow.

"She looks so peaceful. She shouldn't be here. Oh my baby. My wee baby girl!"

Mrs McWerter sobbed uncontrollably."

The Police officer steeled himself to speak. "I'm sorry. I have to ask you this. Is this your daughter, Harriet McWerter?"

"Yes," Mr McWerter started, revealing emotion for the first time. He was a kidney surgeon and was convinced he was immune to the sight of blood, bodies and even death. He coughed, wriggling his nose and holding back tears, "aye, this is my daughter." He looked up, raising his eyebrows. "Death by suffocation from submersion is it? Drowning?"

"I'm not sure at this stage sir. We can't be certain until the post mortem. But I can tell you she was found in the river." The Police officer put his hand out towards the cotton duvet, to cover Guinness' head, but thought better of it. "I'll leave you alone for a minute."

While his wife wept, Mr McWerter stood ashen-faced. He was drawn and gaunt, unable to express the could-have-beens, the should-have-beens, the would-have-beens. If only he'd made time to give to his only daughter; made time to learn how meaningfully to communicate with her. And now he was unable even to express his guilt at the lack of interest he'd shown in his child over her life. This was guilt only manifested through her death; unreversible, so painfully final. It was too late.

Brian held his fist to his mouth, also trying not to cry. He'd been standing behind the McWerters and finally stepped forward. "Goodbye Guinness mate." He stroked her hair and left the chapel so the couple could be alone with their daughter. Out on the street he flared his nostrils and drank in the polluted air of Lambeth Palace Road, stamping the heel of his boot into the curb of the pavement in anger, muttering under his breath.

"Your memory won't ever be forgotten Guinness. Never forgotten."

*****

Klarkey was travelling on a French passport. Having lived for most of his adult life in France, he spoke French "sans accent". He knew that he was a man on the run in England, but he guessed the British Police would be looking for an Englishman. For the time being any personal references to England would be dropped. His progress through Europe was fast and determined. He took the train from London to Dover and then travelled on the ferry as a foot passenger. The journey to Calais was short and from there it was another train journey to Paris. He decided against the Eurostar: there was no need to let nostalgia into this journey by using his old smuggling routes.

From Paris, the overnight train took him to Madrid and as every kilometre passed, Klarkey felt more and more secure in his flight from the UK. He was sure there was little chance of finding him now but he had to travel much further to be sure to be safe.

Klarkey had been travelling for more than half a day and managed to snatch some sleep on the two-berth train hotel carriage, which he was fortunate not to have to share. He took a shower on the train during which he laughed out loud for the first time on his journey. He fell from side to side in the cubicle as the train sped towards Madrid, and he thought to himself that this kind of journey would be good practice for earthquake training. Klarkey was normally so full of life. In Madrid he spent a lethargic day eating paella and drinking strong coffee, watching the world of international tourism pass him by. He spoke broken Spanish with a French accent and made his way back to Madrid Chamartan station for his next overnight train to Algeciras on the south east coast of Spain. Another two-berth cabin; another night of broken sleep and another wobbly shower later, Klarkey arrived at the town across the bay from Gibraltar. As he waited the few hours by the ferry terminal, two Americans approached him.

"Hi, excuse me sir, we've just come from Tarifa and these guys wouldn't let us get on the boat to Tangier there. Said we had to come here. Do you know if we can go from here sir?"

Klarkey thought they looked rather sad, but chose not to break his cover. He was not English and spoke with an over-indulgent heavy French accent.

"Pardon Messieurs, I do not know about zis. You can get zee boat from ere to Tangier. Pas de problème." Klarkey punched his fist into the palm of his hand. "Do not forget to stamp your passport on zee boat."

This answer brought smiles to their faces and they left him in peace.

"Merci monsieur." A pretty girl with a face full of perfect white teeth beamed at him. He wished for a second that he had chosen to be English.

The 3 o'clock ferry took Klarkey towards Africa, starting with the most breathtaking view of the Rock of Gibraltar. He looked ahead at Africa, breathing deeply the fresh air, with the mountains rising majestically in the background and small white villages dotted within the foreground of his view.

Tangier, three hours away was dirty, shocking, stifling and the people were pushy and demanding. Klarkey loved the chaos, but he suspected his American co-travellers would hate every second of it.

After taking some mint tea impregnated with the local herbs, he left directly for the airport. From Tangier he flew to Entebbe airport at Kampala. Then from Kampala to Nairobi. His final flight from Nairobi took him to his eventual destination – Mahé Island in The Seychelles.

*****

The Daily Post broke their scoop of the year in a blaze of self-congratulation:

"THE DAILY POST - MURDER AND THE MINISTER"

"With the country still reeling from its worst mass murder since Shipman, The Daily Post can reveal exclusively that Prisons Minister, Roderick Newton-Banner PERSONALLY authorised the entry of the mystery murderer into Enfield Prison. Whilst this newspaper does not suggest that Mr Newton-Banner knew of the man's ultimate intention, the Minister must take full responsibility for his negligent actions that led to the deaths of so many men on Christmas Eve night."

Newton-Banner was pushed into a corner. He had received a call from the political editor of the Daily Post, only to be told the newspaper had possession of the letter to Enfield Prison, authorising "Father Randall" to visit the inmates. He had a simple choice: To remain in office and deal with any further revelations the Daily Post and other newspapers may uncover; or to resign and deny responsibility for his actions. He chose to write to Downing Street:

Prime Minister,

It is with sincere regret that I have to offer you my resignation as Prisons Minister. It is indeed true that I chose, perhaps foolishly, to accept a request by a Father

*Randall of the Holy Sepulchre Church, to visit inmates at
Enfield Prison on the night of Christmas Eve last.*

*Hindsight condemns me to a future of regret, during
which time I will be forever sorry that the credentials of the
applicant, "Father Randall" were not thoroughly checked;
nor did Prison staff adequately search him. For this I take
full responsibility and with deep regret I humbly apologise
to you, the Government, the People, and perhaps most of all
to the relatives of those who perished at the hands of Father
Randall.*

*I will do everything within my power to assist the Home
Office and Police with their enquiries in the search for truth
and justice. I hope it will be acknowledged that in my
desire to bring joy and Christmas cheer to those suffering in
prison at this difficult time, I agreed to the visit of Father
Randall in good faith.*

*Once again, I wish to express my sincere apologies to
you sir.*

Yours ever, Rod Newton-Banner.

Newton-Banner's resignation was hastily and publicly
accepted and the Prime Minister endured a difficult
Question Time in the House.

*****

The briefing room in Enfield was packed once again. A
large white board at one end of the room was covered in
photographs relating to the crimes at Enfield Prison.
Various red felt-tip lines joined pictures, locations and
times, indicating the connections between the events leading
up to the Christmas Eve murders. Detective Superintendent
Shore entered the room and the noise level reduced to a
revered hush.

"This investigation is probably going to be the most
expensive and the most extensive in your careers. It will be
the case that has the most bodies, and requires the most

professional and thorough Police work, which is expected from you, the elite of the Metropolitan Police.

"We have provisionally connected murders in Aberdeen and possibly another murder in London to a man who we believe to be known as Klarkey or Sam Stevens or Francis Klarke. Whilst we believe that he represents himself and is not part of any organisation, we DO know he had various foot soldiers working for him. However, we are certain that it was our man, using a disguise, who was personally responsible for the murders in Enfield Prison. We need to find him. Number one priority. We need to find out exactly why he killed and whether he could kill again. We need to resecure the confidence of the public by catching this man and we must leave no stone unturned. We need to ensure his actions are not the tip of the iceberg, and we need to stop his criminal activities as soon as possible. Ladies and gentlemen, many of you will have heard me stand here before and say how important it is that we catch this or that criminal. I can't emphasise enough how absolutely vital it is that we succeed in this case. Your sergeants will brief you on all areas that need urgent attention. Good luck and lets find this man before he kills again."

*****

Klarkey had taken a room at the Banyan Beach Resort on the south of the island. Mahé basked in a warm climate, but one that was protected from extremes. As he sat 20 metres in front of his hotel chalet, his legs rested on the warm white sand. His toes were lapped by the gently frothing Indian Ocean. Few people were around, and the beach was covered in more toppled coconut trees than tourists. He squinted through his nearly closed eyes and enjoyed the peace, where the outline of the beach was only broken in the distance by an elderly giant tortoise. He could relax at last; far away from the turmoil, noise and pain of

London. For the first time in a long time he simply didn't know what turn his life would take next; and he didn't care.

The Seychellois waiters were very attentive and every couple of hours they would approach him on the beach to provide a drink or a snack. Despite the currency of Seychelles Rupees, it was the law for tourists to pay in foreign currency and the staff liked Klarkey. He always tipped well in US Dollars. Klarkey heard the familiar flip-flopped steps approach him and he chose to lie still enjoying every second of the afternoon sun. Then he sat up with a start.

"Bonjour You."

It was Matisse.

"Well Bonjour YOU!" Klarkey jumped up and lifted Matisse off the beach and spun her round. He lost his footing in the loose sand and they fell over in a pile onto the splayed leaves of a toppled palm tree.

"I had no idea you'd be here so quickly. I thought you would be weeks."

"Klarkey darling, do you really think I could stand to spend any more time than I had to with my family? Don't worry, everything was wonderful when I saw them all. It's just…you know…sometimes you just want to see your family, say what you have to say and then leave after a couple of days."

"I guess so. And you followed my instructions carefully to get here?"

"Of course I did. Darling if I had flown directly from Paris I could have been here two days earlier."

"I know. But we have to be careful. You know…"

"Yes I know. How do you feel about…what happened?"

Matisse sat down in the sand next to Klarkey. He thought she looked very glamorous in a sarong, flip-flops and enormous sunglasses.

Klarkey rubbed his face with his hands and took off his Ray Bans.

"I feel numb. I keep saying to myself that I should feel good. That I should feel elated. Free. To have killed the man who killed my sister was my lifelong ambition. Is that sick?" Matisse shrugged. "All I feel is nothing. Not elated. Not depressed.

Just nothing. I know I'm not sorry for what I've done, but I can't help feeling for some of the families left behind. OK, so they were married or related to some of the most horrid criminals in the country, but it wasn't their fault. I do feel something for them."

"That shows you're not all bad. Why don't we have a drink?"

The waiter approached them with a broad smile and a silver tray.

*****

Yousef had been left in the interview room alone. He couldn't continue. He threw the near empty polystyrene cup of cold coffee on the floor and started to sob. He had betrayed his friends and there was little doubt he was due to spend the majority of the rest of his life in prison. He couldn't do it. He couldn't accept his fate.

Letting out a great roar he stood up and grabbed the wooden chair by its back support and smashed it against the wall of the interview room.

The chair was flimsy and fell apart, the legs falling in a pile of splintered sticks to the floor.

He took one of the legs with sharpest exposed wooden barbs, and pointed the rough surface to his inner wrist. Tossing his head back and shrieking "God forgive me" in Arabic, he pressed the wooden weapon into his skin and drew it down his arm towards the inside of his elbow. He fell down onto to floor. The blood gushed red torrents across his body, on the floor, and under the interview room door. This was not a cry for help, but a cry to die.

Two officers rushed into the room when they saw the blood creeping along the corridor from under the door.

"Bloody hell" one said, pressing the alarm. It was too late. Yousef was already dead.

*****

Brian sat alone in the editing suite. He drew heavily on a large Dutch cigar, pressed the play button and pushed his chair back, putting his feet up onto the desk. He had finished the 53-minute film and was silently watching it before sending the final edit to the television station that had commissioned it. The credits started to roll:

The Streets of Scotland
(Where you walk, they sleep)
A film dedicated to the memory of
Harriet "Guinness" McWerter
And
Richie Brakes
They gave their lives in the making of this film

At last Brian was a journalist and not just a cameraman. He hoped that Guinness and Richie would be looking at him from on high somewhere, happy that he had done a good job.

*****

Klarkey and Matisse had moved to a pair of toppled trees with hammocks stretched underneath them. They lay down with exotic juice drinks and watched a small boat arrive at the shore. The driver was a dark Seychellois man and a woman sat in the back. They carefully manoeuvred between the rocks and threw down the anchor. A Seychelles kestrel hovered magically overhead, trying to spy any fishy titbits.

They spoke in the Seychelles pigeon dialect, which Klarkey struggled to hear. Not only was he out of earshot, but also the combination of French, English and other languages was too much for his ears.

The woman was holding up what appeared to Klarkey to be fish netting and the man was now towering above her. The bird escaped the commotion, soaring across the rocks heading inland. She started crying into her hands and the man gripped her by the shoulders, dropping his bottle of rum. He was shouting at her and this woke Matisse. Klarkey quickly put his hand on Matisse's forehead indicating she should lie back down. The woman on the boat was now trying to disembark, but the man was stopping her. He was raising his hands to her face and she was sobbing. The lapping of the ocean against the rocks was masking the sound, but he was becoming more aggressive as he took up his bottle for another swig of alcohol.

Klarkey resigned himself to the truth that even in this paradise, bad things can happen. He felt a familiar tightening in his chest. When the man slapped the woman's face and she fell backwards into the boat, Klarkey knew what he had to do.

If you would like to be kept informed about the second novel in this series, please send your e-mail address to

mail@eastofcitypress.com

Your e-mail address will not be passed to any third parties